WHEN LIGHTNING BREAKS

THE SUPERHUMAN SERIES
BOOK ONE
BEEBE EVANS

BE BOOKS, LLC

THE SUPERHUMAN SERIES
PLAYLIST

Open Spotify to Scan

NIBERIA

PRISON ISLAND

MOIRSIDE

MONTICELL

NATIONAL CITY

CAPITAL CITY

ENOCH

SUMER

NATIONAL CITY

SUMER MILITARY CAMP

ANUNNAKI MILITARY CAMP

GRAND VIEW

ANUNNAKI

MIESVILLE

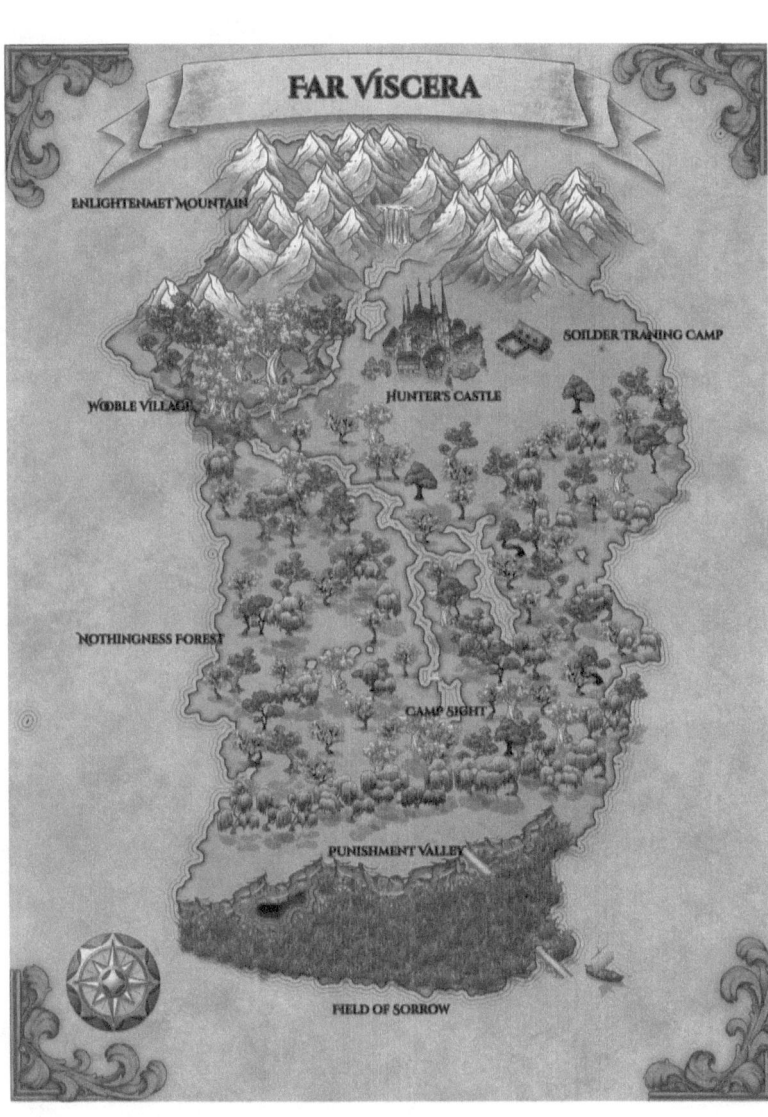

This book is dedicated to my sisters by choice, especially when all they want is a good set of horns to hold on to and aren't afraid to use them.

Content Warning

This novel is intended for an adult audience and may contain themes and element troubling or unsuitable for some readers, which includes graphic language, violence and sexual activities on page. For a full list of content warnings, please visit my website at beebeevans.com

THE PROPHECY

THE SIX LAWS

1. Thou shall not kill

2. Thou shall not steal

3. Thou shall not commit adultery

4. Thou shall not bear false witness

5. Thou shall not contempt thy parents

6. Thou shall keep the species pure

PROLOGUE

To prepare for the upcoming feast, King Hunter led his servants up the grand staircase. In appearance, he was as imposing as his name suggested, a tall and unyielding figure dominating the room with his broad shoulders encased in spiked armor. He dressed entirely in leather of the richest, darkest hue of black, reflecting his sense of power. His gloves were of the same make, meticulously handcrafted to fit him perfectly. His hair, black as the midnight sky, cascaded down to his shoulders in a waterfall of ebony silk. A stark contrast to his skin, it framed his face in a halo of darkness. His eyes matched his hair, so dark they seemed almost black, windows to a soul that held depths unseen. His boots were sturdy, reaching just below his knees, giving him an air of invincibility. No one knew the full extent of the prophecy and what it meant for their world. For now, all eyes fixated on the king, a ruler radiating strength and demanding respect with each step.

When he approached his judgment chambers, his younger brother's presence leaning against the red double doors, arms crossed, with a sly smile, surprised him. Lord Gorgon had always been a daunting figure, known by many as the Lord of Darkness. He matched his ominous nickname with his attire. He wore garments made of black leather. His trousers and jacket clung to his muscular frame, amplifying his formidable presence. His shirt was semi-open, revealing glimpses of a complex chest tattoo that told tales of battles fought and victories won in the Underworld. Thick, curly, brown hair crowned the lord's handsome face, flowing down his broad shoulders and framing his silvery eyes that were sharp and unyielding. His beard added an element of raw masculinity to his appearance, tracing the lines of his sharp jaw, intensifying his threatening aura.

"Gorgon, what brings you to my kingdom?" King Hunter asked incredulously.

"I don't believe I need a reason to escape from that dungeon of hell that I call a kingdom," Lord Gorgon replied sardonically. "As much pleasure as I receive from tormenting souls in the Underworld, even I must come up for some fresh air since our elder brother has exiled me from the Afterlife."

"You would be welcome in the Afterlife if you would stop trying to overthrow Anu," he pointed out, throwing open the doors.

"Well, how would you suggest I fill my days?" Gorgon mumbled with a sense of disgust as he sauntered past the reigning king, brashly claiming a seat on his older brother's throne.

Ignoring his brother's indignant tone, Hunter offered, "Since you are here, would you like to join us for the feast tonight?" The servants had rushed in around Hunter to open the wall panels, making them disappear behind the white marble columns, exposing the dining room. They had laid long, rectangular tables with white tablecloths, lined up silverware next to plates, and set wine glasses at intervals around the perimeter of the room. A small group of them had returned to get more chairs, creating rows of tall-backed wooden seats in alternating dark and light brown tones. Once the feast was complete, guests could have left their seats to move into the king's judgment chambers for the social hour of the celebration. The feast was a ritual to celebrate and give thanks by verbally pledging their loyalty to his kingdom. "You'll be my guest of honor tonight."

"I'll stay for the wine," he agreed.

"I would not get comfortable on my husband's throne," Queen Circe commanded, entering from their private chambers, her presence a force among the men in the room. Her body was an exquisite work of art, heightened by a red velvet dress that hugged her curves. The fabric swayed as she walked gracefully across the floor, mesmerizing everyone with each step. Her black, curly hair cascaded down her back and shoulders like soft waves of silk, nearly obscuring her cleavage. When she pulled her hair back with delicate fingers, the world seemed to stop for a moment. She leaned over Gorgon so he could drench himself in her perfume. "Hunter's going to need that for tonight."

"Don't worry, dollface," Gorgon said to her. "There are other places I'd rather get comfortable."

"You forget too easily that I'm married."

"So am I, but that never stopped me before." He chuckled.

"It should. You have a very jealous wife," Circe reminded him. She took a step back. "Will Anasazi be joining us this evening?"

Before Gorgon could answer the question, the pool of blood turned and parted like curtains on a stage. The cover with three inward-facing swirls had opened, revealing a crown made of silver thorns forcing its way through, filling Hunter's judgment chambers with an icy chill, announcing evil's arrival. The shape of a woman formed, hidden within the churning crimson pool that dissolved around her, trickling down to reveal Lady Anasazi. She stepped onto the stone ring that held the blood. Her eyes were dark green with jealousy, becoming even deeper when she looked at her husband. Lady Anasazi elegantly lifted her long black dress to step down. Her presence would have provoked more fear than her husband's. Her appearance and facial expressions were always cold, wearing a velvet dress that covered up everything to her neck. As she walked across the room, her back was straight, her hips swaying very little. She folded one hand in front of the other, clasping them together with her long, pale fingers.

"Yes, my beautiful wife will join us." He groaned as he slumped back on Hunter's throne.

"I will expect both of you to behave," Hunter warned, his eyes shifting from Gorgon to Anasazi. "I don't need another argument erupting in the middle of the celebration, like last time."

As the hours passed, Hunter sat on this throne watching the celebration grow more and more unruly. To his right, his brother was sulking, sitting by himself at the head table, cradling the goblet between his hands. To his left, Anasazi was ordering around his servants like they were hers to command. For now, they were at least ignoring each other.

"Your Majesty, someone has a request," Delphi, his ever so loyal servant, said as she approached.

As Hunter turned his head, he caught sight of his daughter peeking out from behind Delphi. A warm smile spread across his face as she stepped fully into view. Her cheeks were flushed with joy, and her eyes sparkled with excitement. A gush of love engulfed him as she sprinted toward him, arms wide open for a hug. He bent down and scooped the little girl up onto his lap.

"You should be in bed, little angel." He chuckled.

"Dance with me, Daddy."

"One dance, and Delphi is going to take you to bed." Hunter stood, cradling the little girl in his arms. "Let's go find Mommy on the dance floor."

When his daughter wrapped her arms around his neck, he knew what happiness was. With each step he took toward the dance floor, Circe seemed to come alive in motion, her body swaying gracefully as she danced with a soldier. Her glittering gown flowed and twirled around her, enhancing her beauty as she moved with grace and poise. Next to the little one he carried, Circe was his first love.

As he twirled around the dance floor with his daughter, he caught glimpses of his wife's stunning face out of the corner of his eye. Her smile lit up the entire room as she effortlessly charmed everyone around her. Above the beat of the music, he could hear her infectious laughter, filling him with a warmth and joy that only she could bring.

After a few more turns, he noticed her disappearing into the crowd. Concern crept into his chest, slowly replacing the joy he felt just moments before. It quickly rose to anger when his gaze fell on Circe and Gorgon across the room. His brother had her by the arm, pulling her behind a tall marble column in the corner. She looked as if she were resisting him, but Hunter couldn't be sure.

Before he could investigate Gorgon's questionable actions, Hunter broke his attention away with a sudden and unexpected appearance of a ball of light descending to him. The ball flashed to reveal Emperor Anu and Empress Ki standing in front of him.

Hunter's older brother, Emperor Anu, was a figure who exuded an air of wisdom and authority. His age reflected in his silvery white hair, a stark contrast to his rich, dark skin. Weathered yet radiant, his face bore the traces of time, and his eyes held an indomitable spirit that spoke volumes to the wisdom he had gathered over the years. He wore an immaculate white robe trimmed with intricate patterns of gold that hinted at his royal lineage.

The surrounding crowd felt his presence, but his wife drew the attention away. The Empress Ki, magnificent in her white dress adorned with gold trim, was the living embodiment of classic elegance, with gold leaf on her arms and hair. Her radiant golden skin seemed to glow against her snow-white hair, which shimmered like diamonds under any source of light. Her eyes were like full moons on a clear winter night.

"Something is wrong, brother," Anu explained to Hunter. "The balance of power is about to shift."

"I know," he said. "Our brother with his damn raging hormones is tempting my wife. I have to save her before Anasazi finds out."

"She's aware." Ki pointed.

Hunter turned his head to the other side of the judgment chambers; Anasazi was pushing her way through the crowd of drunken soldiers. With anger etched on her face, ice flames swirled around her feet, encompassing her legs, consuming Lady Anasazi's existence.

Forming an ice ball in her palm, Anasazi pushed her arms outward from her chest, releasing it from her bitter heart. Striking the column where Hunter had last seen his wife, icicles formed at the base, crawling upward. With the core of the structure beginning to cool, she summoned all of her magical strength to form another ice ball even colder and larger to hurl across the room.

The building material of the column exploded in all directions, showering the crowd with deadly fragments. The throng of people stumbled backward as they watched in terror while she launched a third icy sphere toward the weakened column. With an almighty crash, the column collapsed into pieces, showering marble shards on Circe. All music ceased, and pandemonium with screaming ensued. Hunter watched in horror as Circe and Gorgon collided with the wall, which was now scattered with column fragments.

Hunter knew his beloved wife was in mortal danger.

Handing his daughter to Delphi, Hunter pushed through the shocked crowd. His feet felt like heavy weights as he charged to reach his wife, screaming her name. He couldn't get to her fast enough. Panic and worry set in as the crowd parted to allow him through. Lying on the floor, buried in the rubble from the waist down, Circe was unconscious and unresponsive.

He rushed to his wife, falling to his knees, cradling her fragile body against his chest. "Circe," Hunter cried, brushing the dust from her face and pushing a piece of her black hair back. He held on to his wife's limp body, tears in his eyes, feeling her warmth draining away with each passing second. Blood trickled down the side of her face, her hair matted from the wound just above her ear. Turning his attention to Anasazi, he asked, "What have you done? Circe has done nothing to deserve this."

"You are a fool if you truly believe that," Anasazi insisted. "She cast a spell on my husband to tempt him. I hear him call her name in his sleep."

Hunter held his limp wife close to his chest. The room fell silent as his cries filled the hallways of the castle and echoed throughout the kingdom. The light dimmed to nothingness with the loss of their goddess queen. From the Field of Sorrow to the top of Enlightenment Mountain, everyone felt King Hunter's pain. When Anu tried to pull his brother away from his dead wife, he gripped her even harder.

He begged his brother, "Please, bring her back to me."

"I can't," Anu muttered, bowing his head helplessly.

"Yes, you can. You have the power, brother!" he yelled.

"My power has limits. It doesn't work on immortals," Anu explained. "I can't save her. Circe is gone."

Empress Ki abruptly spoke up. "She can be reborn. We can remove her spirit and soul and place them into an unborn child. It has been done with mortals."

"Will she remember who she is?" Hunter asked. "Will she remember me?"

"No, she will have no memory of this life, and she may be mortal," Ki warned. "She will have to be born into the living world."

"I will find her again," Hunter insisted.

"She won't be the same," Ki warned.

"I don't have any other choice," he said with a heavy heart, tears blocking his sight. He hugged his wife's body one last time, leaning over to kiss her on the forehead. He whispered, "I will find you again, my love."

In a grand display of sorrow and hope, Hunter gently laid his beloved wife's head down, creating a space for Anu and Ki to perform their sacred chant. They stood on each side of Queen Circe's lifeless body, their hands extended over her serene form.

Fingers spread wide to harness the queen's magic, they chanted, "From this body, extract the spirit and soul to bring our loved one back as a whole. Please guide them to the living side. Come now across the great divide." As they continued chanting with passion and devotion, a radiant brilliance enveloped Circe's body. The light emanating from her being grew steadily brighter and more intense until it seemed to consume her entirely. "Take this one to fulfill an unborn's eyes. Hear her voice in this child's cries. Three times greatness in her name. One, but not the same."

In response to their powerful invocation, a shimmering sphere of pure white light emerged from Circe, now giving her physical body to the empty void. A place of no existence, like a wasteland of the forgotten slain in the Far Viscera. Floating gracefully above the crowd, it seemed to hold all the love, strength, and essence that had once lived within her. Transcending the bounds of physicality, the ball of light began its journey toward the towering red double doors at the far end of the chamber.

With an otherworldly gust of wind from across dimensions, the majestic doors swung open, creating a portal through which the white ball of light would pass. The force of this divine wind propelled the ethereal essence with unparalleled swiftness and pur- pose, carrying it across realms and weaving it into the tapestry of existence.

Hunter watched in awe and anguish as the visible remnants of his wife wove their way toward the threshold of birth. His heart ached for what he had lost, yet he clung to the hope that lay within this extraordinary ritual. The room stood in reverent silence, witnessing the transcendence of Circe's spirit and soul as they embarked on their journey to be reborn.

Circe was his everything, but now he had nothing. He grabbed his chest, feeling the tightness of his loss. Rubbing his shirt, he tried to soothe his pain, but it only made the emptiness linger. It seemed like someone had stolen his breath.

She was his life.

Among the rubble, one small piece of his wife flickered to catch his attention. Upon retrieving the object, he realized it was Circe's wedding ring. He had forged the opal and white onyx band from gems found in the Earth debris that make up the rings of the planet Niberia. It was now all he had left of his love. "This was supposed to protect you."

Holding the ring, a wave of revenge unexpectedly consumed his thoughts. In his pain, he blinded himself to anger, searching for the one who had caused his grief. The taste of vengeance felt sweet upon his lips as he called, "Anasazi!" The crowd willingly parted to allow Hunter to look the accused in the eye. "I want your head as a trophy."

"Oh, please," Anasazi laughed, "your threats are meaningless to me."

Her words only fueled Hunter's rage and hunger for revenge. He opened his right hand to summon his staff. In a swirl of light smoke, his loyal and accurate weapon appeared. He had forged the staff from the magic of the Saqqara bird's claw, which rested on top of the staff, fueling the red sapphire gem it held. His battle cry reverberated through the chamber. The sharp hiss of smoke from his loyal staff created a thunderous boom as it surged across the room toward Lady Anasazi. The red sapphire gem pulsed with magical power, turning it into a deadly spear. Before the blade struck, Lady Anasazi's form dissipated into a swirling cloud of ice smoke, her laugh lingering in its wake.

King Hunter never recovered from Queen Circe's death. All the goodness died in him that night, making his heart cold. Now in complete isolation, he stood staring at the pool of blood, a shadow of his former existence.

He neglected his responsibilities as the judge of souls. The signs were subtle at first, disguised as grief as a widower. Once his grief turned into anger and obsession, it became harder to hide his fear of failure and loss of power.

Hunter surrounded himself with security guards, trying to make his world right again by building an army of souls. Even with the army, Hunter had doubts about finding his love again, so with the risk of becoming consumed with the dark evil, he turned to blood magic. He took the last piece he had of Circe and cursed it. Calling upon the spirits in the pool, the blood swirled around the ring, taking it to the living world as he chanted, "With this ring, I shall bind, for my love it will find. Soul to soul, believing in extremes. Spirit to spirit, invade her dreams."

CHAPTER ONE

TALIA

"This is my world, which I will defend until my last breath," the Niberians said collectively.

According to the known passages in the Book of the Dead, it was tradition every Niberian was required to take an oath the year of their twenty-first birthday. Each region swore allegiance to their god and their societies. This celebration took place across the planet of Niberia as a rite of passage into adulthood every mid-year on the summer solstice.

In 3021 A.H., thousands of young adults were gathering to take this oath. Within the massive crowds, four young Niberians came together to change their world, and this oath set in motion a series of events that made that fate possible. Twins from Anunnaki, a convict from Sumer, and a scientist from Enoch took their respective oaths on that day.

"As peacekeepers of our gods to the Far Viscera, King Hunter and Queen Circe, I take this oath to preserve the balance between good and bad, right and wrong, and pure and evil," Talia and Olivia promised, along with the other Anunnakians from Central Niberia.

"As soldiers of our gods to the Underworld, Lord Gorgon, and Lady Anasazi, I take this oath of loyalty and courage to maintain freedom and individuality of choice," Storm, a convict from Sumer, swore along with the other Sumerians from West Niberia.

"As messengers of our gods to the Afterlife, Emperor Anu, and Empress Ki, I take this oath of goodness to spread tranquility and enlightenment," Scooter, a scientist from Enoch, vowed along with the other Enochians from East Niberia.

"United as one, divided by one," the Niberians promised collectively.

After the oath, the Trismegist family invited their relatives and friends over to the house to celebrate the transition for the twins. Everyone was filled with excitement except for Talia. She fidgeted nervously at the thought of leaving her safe place to go off to college in a few months. Despite having control over her unique abilities for several years, she glanced back at the charred remains of her father's old workshop. She curled the corner of her lip and bit down hard. Only one wall remained standing, a reminder of the time when her anger had spiraled out of control during her childhood. She was grateful the fire hadn't spread to the nearby forest, avoiding a disaster for the whole town.

"Damnit, Talia. You could have at least dressed up for the occasion." Olivia criticized her sister's wardrobe choice with a turned-up nose as she joined Talia at the back of the yard. "We are celebrating our adulthood and giving thanks to our gods."

Olivia was the life of the party, shining as brightly as ever. She was floating around to socialize with everyone and having a good time, her laughter filling the yard. She had on her favorite shimmery pink dress with over-the-top shoulder accents, a low-cut neckline, and a metallic silver colored skirt. She completed her look with matching pink hair pulled up high on her head in a ponytail. It was a dress she had designed and made herself. Her designs were unique, and she had talent. Talia wondered how she could walk in the four-inch-high-heeled pink boots that went up to her knees.

"I did. I wore my black dress pants." Talia smirked. "Besides, I don't think King Hunter and Queen Circe are looking down from the Far Viscera and judging me for my wardrobe choice. They haven't stepped foot on Niberia in over three thousand years."

Talia found herself more comfortable standing in the background, watching the surrounding people. She dressed in her usual cargo pants, but in black for the special occasion. She wore a long sleeve shirt with open, flowing cuffs to show off the silver bracers on her wrists. Over the high collar shirt, she had accented her breasts with a center-laced front closure bodice. Her outfit was never complete without her warrior belt to hold her Chakram on her side. Normally, she would wear her signature leather jacket to cover her weapon, but on that day, it was much too warm.

"Do you have to carry that weapon so openly?" Olivia pointed to Talia's warrior belt.

"Do you have to wear boots that are such a death trap?" she shot back. "No, you don't, but you want to. It has been over ten years. Are you still jealous?"

She pulled the weapon from her belt, showing off the sliver Chakram with the center carved out in three inward-facing spirals. Dad had made the weapon with a sharp edge, but not too sharp to hold. The weapon, made of silver, conducted Talia's lightning power. It had a purple and blue coating of vanadium dioxide that kept it cool enough to hold. Only she could use this weapon because it was coded to her DNA, making it unique to her. It was a source of tension between the twins for years.

When Dad gave her the Chakram on her tenth birthday, he said it was a symbol of their gods. Each swirl represents the three realms of their dimension, and it balanced good and evil. She spent hours in the forest, channeling her lightning powers through the weapon. It was safer than burning up appliances and blowing up lightbulbs in the house. He told her it was the key to her destiny with their goddess, Queen Circe, and someday she would find her shield.

"I would not say I was ever jealous."

When Talia's attention turned to the other side of the yard, she asked, "Do you know who Dad is talking to?" A woman approached their father and stopped him as he was walking out the back door. At first, he looked confused, trying to place why her face was familiar. He appeared to know her but didn't recognize her.

She was a mature woman of indeterminate age. Her stature was on the lower end of average, yet her body was robust, enriched by the years she had lived. Her hair was an enchanting mix of silver and ash gray, chopped quite short in a fashion that highlighted her astute intelligence. It framed a wholesome face dominated by two deep-set brown eyes that expressed kindness more profoundly than any words could communicate. When the woman handed Bud two letters, he seemed to remember her.

"I don't know who she is. Let's go find out," Oliva insisted as she grabbed her sister's hand. Before she could object, Olivia was dragging her across the yard, weaving through the crowd.

"Let me introduce you to my daughters," Dad said as he waved the twins over. Their father, Bud, was a towering figure, standing head and shoulders above the crowd, his slender but sturdy frame giving him an air of calm strength. His short, dirty-blond hair complimented his striking blue eyes. Hidden behind the glasses that reflected the light in curious ways, those eyes held a depth of intelligence and knowledge that few could match. "This is Talia and Olivia. Girls, this is Delphi."

"Oh, my word. You two grew up to be such lovely young women," Delphi said as she put her hands over her heart.

"Thank you," the twins said in unison.

"Now that you've taken the oath, what big plans have you made for the future? Have you decided on a college yet?" Delphi asked.

"I've narrowed down my list to my top three choices," Talia said.

Delphi smiled. "Well, I hope Grand View University is on your list."

"I don't remember applying to that college," Olivia said, confused.

"Sure, you do," Dad said, dismissing the confused looks he received from his daughters. "Delphi delivered your acceptance letters." Dad handed each of them a letter with their names on it.

Talia looked over at Olivia and said to her telepathically, *I know I didn't apply to this college because it was too expensive.*

"I guess I will have to add Grand View University to my list." Olivia smiled, holding up the letter. She looked back at her sister. *We'll have to talk about this later.*

Talia nodded in agreement.

"This is an incredible opportunity. I will add this one to my list."

"Brutus is here," Olivia predicted.

Olivia could feel Brutus' presence before she even saw him, and sure enough, he soon rounded the corner of the house. Being an empath, she would tell her things before they were going to happen, and she always knew what everyone around her was feeling. Talia found that annoying because she couldn't hide anything from her sister.

Talia rolled her eyes as she dropped their conversation to run to Brutus, catching Dad's furrowed brow out of the corner of her eye. She watched her sister's ponytail sway, brushing against her Nibmarks on her back. Her dress was so low cut in the back, it showed all her markings from her neck to her waist. Talia felt a glint of jealousy at not being able to show off her own Nibmarks like her sister did.

Dad sighed. "She should've worn something to cover her Nibmarks. I hope that boy doesn't know where the right ones are."

Oh, Dad, he knows. That's why she designed the dress that way.

Olivia leaped into his powerful arms and clung to his neck, and they shared an intense kiss in a display of their excitement at being together. Brutus rubbed the back of her neck, dangerously close to her stimulant Nibmark.

Leaning over to Dad, Talia patted her Chakram at her hip and whispered, "If he gets any closer, Dad, I've got my weapon ready."

"My fierce warrior." He kissed her forehead. "As much as I dislike him, your sister will never forgive you if you cut her boyfriend's throat and fry him."

Talia rubbed the back of her neck where her Nibmarks would be, but hers were not real. They were given to her every birthday by her parents as tattoos to match her twin sister. Nibmarks were Niberian birthmarks that began at birth with a single, raised black dot at the back of the neck and grew each year. The direction of growth depended on which region you were born into. Anunnakians spread across their back, Enochians grow to their right shoulders, and Sumerians formed on their left shoulders. These Nibmarks could be used for identification because each Niberian family had a unique pattern, and certain ones were used for sexual arousal.

Since Talia had no interest in finding a mate, she was thankful hers were fake. It also meant she had to cover up her back. As the sun beat down, she wished she could pull her long black hair in a ponytail like her sister. At least, it was true until she saw Brutus wrap his hands around Olivia's and pull her head back to kiss her neck.

I don't think a ponytail would look good on me.

Talia never really liked Brutus; she thought he was simple-minded and foolish, and it was hard for her to converse with him. Despite his shortness of brain cells, she admired how devotedly he followed her sister around. Olivia had once confided in her that she enjoyed having Brutus beside her, as he was easy to manipulate, letting his views mirror hers. He looked perfect in his tight t-shirt, flaunting every muscle on his arms and chest, jeans clinging to his legs, and hair messily falling across his forehead.

"Hey, babe," Brutus said when they came up for air between kisses.

"I have something to show you," Olivia said as she jumped down from wrapping herself around him. She held up the letter addressed to her with the Grand View University shield on the opposite side. "This is my acceptance letter from Grand View University. This is huge news."

"Wow, babe. That is so..." Brutus found it difficult to find the words to express himself.

"I know. I'm so excited. I could study with the top designers in the world at Grand View." Her eyes lit up the more she talked about the opportunity. "This is an Ivy League college."

"Wow, babe. That is so far away." Brutus's voice lost its excitement.

"I know we talked about going to a local college, but this college isn't that far. It's only a six-hour car ride. You can come visit me on the weekends while you finish your senior year here. We could go to Capital City," Olivia said, trying to give him all the reasons he should be as excited as she was.

"I've always wanted to go to Capital City and see a game," he admitted.

"We could also eat at all the famous restaurants." Olivia redirected his attention. "This would make me happy."

"Then that makes me happy." He smiled before he kissed her to show his support for her decision.

Talia shook her head and chuckled at how easily her sister could convince Brutus it was a good idea. *He is such a doofus,* she thought. When she saw Olivia narrowing her eyes, she realized her sister had read her mind. *Well, he is.*

Keep your opinions to yourself. Olivia narrowed her eyes even more.

I was until you decided to go roaming around in my mind. I don't like him, and you know that.

Hunter, damnit!

Don't let Mom hear you swear like that. I am not fighting about this today. We can do that tomorrow.

Olivia childishly stuck her tongue out.

Shrugging off her sister's annoyance and immaturity, Talia effectively excused herself to go into the house. She wasn't so easy to convince. She had another plan in her head, which included staying close to home and going to a local college with her sister. It was where she was comfortable. She sat at the kitchen table by herself, staring at the unopened message from Grand View College.

It was always a secret dream to attend a major university, but she didn't think it was possible. Over the past thirteen years, she had learned to control her powers, hiding them from the world. With this opportunity staring back at her, she felt being that far away from home would put that at risk. She bowed her head for a moment to say an unspoken prayer to King Hunter for guidance.

What should I do?

"Is everything okay? What are you doing in here by yourself?" her mother, Carol, asked as she came into the kitchen to get more food for the party. Strands of her sun-bleached hair slipped out from a hastily fashioned bun, framing her fair features. Her normally serene blue eyes now burned with strength, marked with flashes of brighter cerulean. She wore exhaustion on her face from her all-night food preparation; still, her beauty shined through her tired eyes. Talia imagined her sister would look like that someday.

"I was just thinking. What does an Ivy League college want with two small-town girls from Miesville?" Talia asked, not expecting an answer.

"You two are smart and talented," Mom said as she sat down next to her daughter.

"You have to say that. You are my mom."

"I think it's time I tell you an important story." Mom sighed. "You and Olivia being accepted to this college was no accident. When I was pregnant, our gods gave your dad and me a gift. That gift was you. A second baby. The night that I went into a labor, the ground shook, and I heard the cries of King Hunter. It was a warning from our gods. I was struck with a blinding white light."

Straightening her posture, she asked, "Was it lightning?"

"Yes, it was, but it didn't hurt me. It filled me with a sense of warmth and purpose from Queen Circe." Mom placed her hands over her heart as she spoke. "We were so grateful to be chosen to be your parents, but we were also so scared. We knew we had to protect you because our people wouldn't accept you. They wouldn't understand your abilities. If the Council found out about you, they would take you away. We couldn't let that happen." Mom's eyes filled with tears and her lips quivered. Her face contorted with grief as she struggled to speak through the tears. She let out a heavy sigh, trying to contain her emotions.

"You and Dad did a great job protecting me. I'm still here. I would not exactly call my childhood normal, but I know you tried." Talia chuckled when flashes of memories flooded her mind of her parents trying to control her supernatural abilities. "I didn't make it easy."

"Nothing about you was ever easy." Mom smiled through her tears. "Your dad and I had no idea what we were doing. We needed help. Our prayers to King Hunter were answered when we met Delphi. She was my delivery nurse. She knew about you. I don't know how, but she helped us to keep you a secret."

Before she uttered a word, the rusty hinges of the back door creaked open, causing them to be startled. As she turned toward the sound, Talia's gaze landed on her father, standing in the doorway with a questioning expression on his face. His shoulders were tense, and his hands were buried deep in the pockets of his pants.

"Why the sad faces, ladies?" Dad asked. "We're having a party."

Mom nodded. "Bud, it's time to tell the twins the truth."

"Oh, we are having that conversation right now. I'll get Olivia," Dad offered.

"Dad, there no need to yell across the yard. I'll get her in here."

Olivia, Mom and Dad need to talk to us.

What did you do now?

Nothing. Untangle your lips from Brutus and whatever else you have wrapped around his body. Get your ass in the house. This is important.

She entered through the back door. Olivia's tone conveyed apparent frustration as she asked, "What's so important?"

"Your mom and I have something to tell you two," Dad said, gesturing for her to take a seat next to Talia and locking the back door.

"Ugh, story time in the middle of the party." She rolled her eyes as she slumped down in the chair.

Hunter, damnit! This is serious. Mom and Dad have a secret.

What? That you're weird? It's not a secret. I'm telling Mom you're swearing.

You said it first.

Dad moved behind Mom and placed a reassuring hand on her shoulder. "You're both about to enter the real world," he said seriously, his eyes shifting between the twins. "We won't always be there to protect you, but we will arm you with the truth so you can protect each other."

"Truth about what?" Olivia said, adjusting her posture.

"Talia," Dad said, with his gaze landing on her, "what your mom is trying to say is you were the first of your kind born on our planet in over three thousand years. You're a human like King Hunter and Queen Circe."

Talia sat in stunned silence, her mind reeling at the revelation her father had just shared. The weight of his words hung heavy in her mind, as if the entire world had shifted. She stared at her parents, searching their faces for any hint of deceit or uncertainty, but all she found was a profound sense of honesty and love.

As the truth settled in, a flood of memories rushed through her mind, moments of inexplicable power, of feeling out of place among her peers, of the strange occurrences that seemed to follow her wherever she went. Everything suddenly made sense, yet nothing felt familiar anymore. She had always known she was different, but to hear it spoken aloud, to be told she was a human, was more truth than she could reconcile.

Her father's words about being the first of her kind in over three thousand years echoed in her mind, stirring up a whirlwind of thoughts about her place in the world and the implications of her existence. Her heart beat a little faster as she tried to grasp the magnitude of what it meant to be a human in a world that may not fully understand or accept her true nature.

"Is that why you tattoo my Nibmarks on my back every year? I am not a Niberian?" she asked, allowing her back to fall against the chair, using it as an anchor against questions swirling in her mind.

"Yes, you are human." Mom touched her daughter's hand. "We believe you to be the reincarnation of our Queen Circe."

"Your mom and I decided not to tell you because we wanted you to have a normal childhood."

"We can't protect you within these walls for the rest of your life. Talia, you are a spirited warrior. You need to have adventures, and this town is getting too small for you." Mom squeezed her hand. "We trust Delphi. She kept our family secret."

"What does Delphi want from us now?" Olivia asked.

"She wants to look out for you now so you can go away to college. She knows how important you are, and she made this opportunity possible for both of you." Mom pointed to the letter.

"We can't afford this college," Talia said.

"If this is what you want, your dad and I will worry about that. Besides, Delphi said she has an apartment to rent only blocks from the college. We will make this work. One thing you will learn about Delphi is that she always seems to be there when you need her, and she always knows what to do." Mom smiled. "If she gave you this letter personally, there is a bigger reason that you need to be there. It's your decision, but at least you can open the letter first."

CHAPTER TWO

TALIA

It was only two months later when the Trismegist family drove into Grand View pulling a small trailer packed full of the twins' things. They drove past the large campus, which went on for several blocks of buildings, landscaping, and student housing.

Perched atop a hill was the main building, gray bricks that told tales, looking over its dominion. That was the town of Grand View. A colossal statue demanding attention stood proudly in the courtyard, paying homage to the humans' first touchdown on this alien terrain by casting an interstellar space shuttle in stone.

This wasn't just some decorative afterthought or misplaced artistic license. The six human explorers used this very hill as the landing site and built the university here. The belief ran deep. This fine thread spun deeply into everything around it as well. Grand View didn't just awake one day to find itself built. It emerged from a singular exuberant belief—Humans were the first to set foot here three thousand years ago.

As the family cruised the town roads, a sense of familiarity seeped into their veins. The whispers of history were loud in Talia's ears as the energy of the place nuzzled against her senses right from the moment they veered onto the main street. Being highly sensitive toward spirits, it puzzled her to notice some who hovered unattached.

A middle-aged man's spirit caught her eye, particularly at one such corner where Dad halted for a red light. He stood there looking utterly bemused about his whereabouts and destination, as an unmoored spirit just inches away from Talia's car window. When he looked back, her keen eyes locked on to him; he realized she could really see him.

Even though blessed with this unusual ability to perceive spirits, teenage angst made young Talia give up that path a while ago. In all honesty, it was easy in a town like Miesville, a sleepy hamlet housing fewer than three hundred people. Suffocating small-town gossip dubbed her as 'the weird kid' often found 'talking' to herself. Ditching that infamy meant she could no longer guide spirits to Far Viscera to make peace with their judgment.

In her newfound sanctuary and role as a student, showing normalcy was high on her list. Lost among class schedules on day one or pulling strenuous all-nighters muddled with major choices paralleled general freshman blues. That was how she envisioned fitting right in without raising any eyebrows, especially since she was struggling to accept the truth surrounding her birth. She had always felt different, but it never occurred to her how much of an outsider she truly was.

As the Trismegist family pulled up to Delphi's place, Talia noticed how distinct it looked compared to the surrounding buildings. In the heart of town, this unique structure stood proudly as a testament to the past. The oldest building in the area, it boasted a charming facade made entirely of weathered bricks that had witnessed the passing of time.

Among the landscape of modern developments, Delphi's antique shop stood as an island of nostalgia. Its exterior remained untouched, preserving its historical significance, while neighboring houses and businesses had succumbed to demolition or modern refurbishment. The shop occupied the ground level at the front of the building, showcasing an eclectic collection of vintage treasures that beckoned passersby to step inside and explore.

Behind the antique shop, tucked away from prying eyes, was Delphi's personal domain. A door at the back of the shop led to her residence on the main level. The warmth and coziness exuded from behind those walls was palpable, promising a home filled with cherished memories and comforting familiarity.

As the car came to a stop, Delphi emerged from her beloved shop to greet the Trismegist family. Her presence radiated an ageless wisdom and an air of mystery that seemed to dance in perfect harmony with the enchanting surroundings. "I am so glad you made it. How was the trip?"

"It was a long car ride," Olivia said as she got out of the car to stretch her legs.

"The apartment is upstairs. You guys have your own entrance at the back of the house. Here are the keys. I hope you like it." Delphi handed a key to Talia and one to Olivia. "I'll let you look around, and I'll come up later to check on you two."

"Thank you so much," Talia said, holding up her key.

"By the way, if you run into a young man in the back yard, that's just my nephew. He lives in the basement," Delphi announced over her shoulder as she walked back into the store.

Because the house was built on a slight hill, it looked so much bigger from the back. Under the stairwell to their apartment was a recessed patio with two small steps down to a sliding glass door leading to the basement. Talia found it odd the blinds were closed, showing no sign of life, in the middle of the afternoon.

She went up the stairs first. Before she put her key in the door, she said a little blessing, placing her hands on each side of the door. Believing this ritual would protect the building, she began with a whisper, and each time she repeated the blessing, her voice got louder.

"Please, I beg of thee, just let this home be, cloaked from evil forces and shielded from unseen sources," Talia chanted, repeating it three times.

Her palms tingled as she summoned her power, the invisible shield spreading around the house like a second skin. She let out her breath and felt a sense of security wash over her, easing the anxiety and pressure that had been building since leaving home.

"Are you going to unlock the door? This box isn't getting any lighter," Olivia said, sounding a little impatient as she stood on the landing, waiting to walk up the last few steps to the door. She shifted her weight to adjust her grip on the box while Talia unlocked the door.

The Trismegist twins stepped into their new apartment. The spaciousness and charm of the living room and kitchen area immediately captivated Talia. The vaulted ceilings created an airy, open atmosphere, allowing light to flood in through large windows adorned with delicate lace curtains. The walls, painted in a soft, warm shade of cream, stressed the natural beauty of the exposed brickwork that lined one side of the room.

A sofa in a deep shade of burgundy sat against one wall, accompanied by a pair of matching armchairs, inviting relaxation and conversation. A rustic coffee table adorned with carefully arranged trinkets and a vase of fresh flowers served as the centerpiece of the seating area. Talia inhaled the comforting smell coming from the plate of cookies on the edge of the table displayed as a welcome to them.

The kitchen was small but charming, excluding any updates in the last twenty years. It was functional. A farmhouse-style dining table stood in the center of the room, surrounded by mismatched chairs that conveyed character and personality. Above the table, a simple chandelier cast a soft, warm glow.

Leaving the living room behind, a short hallway beckoned the twins to explore further. Along this corridor were two bedrooms, each having its own unique ambiance. The first bedroom had a cozy aesthetic with walls painted in soothing shades of sky blue. A plush queen bed covered in crisp, white linens sat against one wall, flanked by weathered bedside tables displaying antique lamps.

The second bedroom was an oasis of tranquility and whimsy. Soft, lavender-colored walls harmonized with delicate floral wallpaper. A queen bed with an intricately carved wooden frame stood against the opposite wall, adorned with colorful quilts and cushions that added a touch of playfulness to the room. Sunlight filtered through gauzy curtains, casting a soft shimmer that created a serene atmosphere.

The bathroom between the two bedrooms featured vintage fixtures that harmonized with the overall theme of the apartment. A claw-foot bathtub beckoned for leisurely bubble baths, while an antique vanity with an ornate mirror and delicate porcelain sink offered a charming space for primping and pampering.

On the opposite side of the living room, next to the kitchen, a doorway caught their attention. As they stepped through it, a spiral staircase revealed itself, leading down into the enchanting realm of Delphi's antique store. The staircase was wrought iron with elegantly curved banisters, reminiscent of a bygone era. Soft ambient lighting illuminated each step, casting intriguing shadows on the walls.

"Is this it?" Olivia groaned.

"This is it," she said with more excitement in her voice, taking one cookie. The sweetness of warm chocolate filled her mouth and delighted her taste buds. "I like it. This feels like home."

Walking into one bedroom, Olivia announced over her shoulder, "There's only one closet in the bedrooms. How am I going to fit all my clothes? It's not motorized, so I will have to search for everything manually."

"Don't be so dramatic. It's all we can afford," she reminded her sister.

"Well, this place is cozy," Mom said as she and Dad walked in carrying boxes. "That was a nice touch with the cookies."

"That is a nice way of saying small." Olivia rolled her eyes, walking out of the bedroom.

"Olivia Trismegist, it's clean and close to campus. Be thankful," Dad said with a hint of disappointment in his daughter's attitude. "It's more than your mother and I had when we went to college."

"Girls, can you find some kitchen boxes in the trailer? I'm going to unpack these dishes," Mom said.

"I don't get why Dad is so upset." Olivia shrugged as the two of them walked down the steps to the trailer.

"Really?" she said sarcastically, since Olivia's selfish comments were always so obvious to everyone else. "You can at least pretend to be grateful."

Talia pushed her way past her sister when they reached the landing. She tried to shrug off her frustration with Olivia as she walked up the trailer ramp. With her hands on her hips, she scanned the trailer for a box with her name on it. Feeling even more frustrated, all she could find was that most of the boxes belonged to Olivia.

"Do you need some help?" a young man's voice asked, breaking her train of thought.

As Talia examined the contents of the trailer, she suddenly felt her heart race, a keen awareness coming over her. She turned around to be greeted by a god-like figure, a shirtless Sumerian man who was delicious on the eyes. His broad shoulders and muscular arms made her breath hitch in her throat.

His chest was a work of art, etched with muscle that flexed every time he moved. The sun highlighted his Nibmarks along his left shoulder with a predominate scar; it was ruggedly sexy. His neatly groomed facial hair barely hid his strong jawline and his shapely lips. His eyes met hers, intense as the cerulean sea in summer, causing a rush of heat to course through her.

He lounged casually against the staircase's support beam, his daunting frame rippling with strength. He had a tattoo on his inner forearm, a shield housing a familiar symbol that gave him an air of mystery and danger. His hair was a wild mane of wavy brown locks that just begged for her touch.

Am I having a stroke? What the hell is wrong with me?

Her eyes traced the perfectly chiseled valleys defining his abs under the afternoon sun. "Do you need some help?" he asked again, breaking into her thoughts.

His voice was rich, like the dark chocolate that lingered in her mouth, making her stomach do somersaults. Talia shifted her weight, forgetting what she was doing. Biting the corner of her lip, she lost herself in the moment with this stranger. She stuttered out something about boxes before taking in the full breadth of him once more.

Words, speak words. Open your damn mouth and make your voice say something that isn't weird.

A bolt of desire shot straight from her belly to between her thighs, heating her insides like molten lava as she dared herself to meet those vivid blue eyes once more. She could not form a single word with the knot in her throat.

The corners of his lips twitched in amusement, as if he knew exactly what effect he had on her. "Here, let me take that," he said smoothly, closing the distance between them while she handed over a box marked 'Talia.' Their fingers brushed when he accepted it, and an electrical current passed between them, making her gasp softly. The devilish smile that danced across his lips suggested he felt it, too.

The scent of his cologne filled her senses. It was an intoxicating mix of musk and cedar. She was struggling to keep herself from becoming consumed by his scent. His hot breath fanned against her skin as he whispered in a low baritone, "You must be the new roommates."

"You must be the nephew, and you're a Sumerian. I wasn't expecting that," Olivia said.

Talia tried to take a deep breath, hoping for a moment to gather her thoughts, but his stare held her captive. The intensity of his eyes made her squirm awkwardly. She shifted her weight from one foot to the other, trying to ignore the way he rattled all her senses.

"Yes, Storm Smoke." He held out his hand to Olivia but kept his eyes on Talia.

Olivia introduced herself, taking his firm handshake. "Olivia Trismegist." Storm pulled his gaze away from her to greet her sister, giving her enough time to adjust her posture and calm her nerves before Olivia spoke again. "This is my sister, Talia."

When Storm turned to extend his hand to Talia, she instead grabbed another box and dumped it in his arms. It was the only thing she could think of doing to make him stop looking at her. He adjusted easily to the weight of the second box. Peering over the top, he deepened his smile, showing off his dimples. "Pleasure to meet you, Talia Trismegist." He winked at her before running up the stairs, skipping every other one.

"Wow. I just found the first positive thing about this place. He is good-looking," Olivia said after Storm was out of hearing range.

"He's a show-off and a Sumerian pirate. I don't trust him," Talia said as she turned up her nose.

"But you like him!" Olivia sounded surprised. "I'm glad you found your voice."

"Get out of my head," she warned.

"I don't need to read your mind, sis. Your nipples are telling the story." Olivia pointed to her sister's chest.

Talia looked down in horror and saw her nipples standing erect, revealing her secrets. "Shit. Do you think he noticed?"

"He winked at you. Of course, he noticed. He almost gave you a stroke with his hormones."

CHAPTER THREE

TALIA

W hen Talia and Olivia stepped into the lively courtyard a week later for their first day of college, they found themselves thrust into an atmosphere bristling with energy. They were no longer in a world of isolation under their parents' watchful eye. The campus was buzzing with students congregating in small clusters, anticipation weaving an electric hum in the air. Every corner of the courtyard burst with vibrancy. Tenderly flowers and plants adorned its expanse, welcoming everyone back to school. A procession of freshly painted benches created a pathway that led straight to a cultural centerpiece, an imposing monument.

In this bustling epicenter stood an awe-inspiring statue marking humanity's extraterrestrial landing, some three millennia ago, on Niberia. At twenty-five feet tall, it dwarfed everything else in the courtyard, casting long afternoon shadows over groups of chattering students, making for a postcard-worthy picture. It was those six human explorers who were now worshiped as the Niberian gods.

Yet what Talia saw here was entirely unusual. Grand View was no ordinary town, being full of paranormal activity. Here in this courtyard, specifically, spirits found a home away from oblivion. They clung to objects or places like silent echoes living beyond time, while others curiously latched themselves on to unsuspecting passersby.

She intently observed one such spirit, a woman seemingly from another era who kept ambling behind a student. Her mannerisms were inexplicitly motherly as she called out reminders trailing after the oblivious pupil much like a doting parent would do so before sending off her child to school. It seemed painfully ironic because she clearly existed inaudible and unseen by anyone but special observers like Talia.

The moment this spectral woman happened upon Talia's observant gaze, she paused, appearing surprised by her own visibility. However, reality kicked back quickly as her attention returned to where it belonged, on the fleeing student having no inkling about his ghostly company, forcing her to drift back after him again. The ghost resumed her list.

"The women are getting younger and much better looking," Talia overheard an older man say as she and Olivia walked in front of a bench. She looked over and saw two elderly men's spirits sitting on the bench watching the young women walk by.

"Dirty old man," she whispered to them.

"We're in trouble. She can hear us." The other old man's spirit laughed, nudging his friend.

Talia looked right at them over her shoulder and said, "Stop looking." She pulled down her leather jacket in the back.

"Stop looking at what?" Olivia asked, assuming Talia was talking to her.

"Can you feel what is going on?" Talia asked, stopping her sister.

"I can feel the energy in the air. There is a lot of anxiety and intensity around us, but I could be picking up the emotions of the students," she admitted. "What are you seeing?"

"There are so many spirits around us. I've never seen so many in one place. There are almost as many spirits as there are people here," Talia explained. "If I talk to them, pretend you are talking to me."

"Can't you just ignore them?"

"There are too many of them, and they know I can see them." She leaned toward her sister with her eyebrows raised and whispered, "Please, I don't want to be the weird kid again."

"I know. We may not agree on a lot of things, but I'm the only one who gets to call you out on your weirdness, like that outfit."

"What is wrong with my outfit? This is what I wear all the time," she asked, looking down at her clothes.

"Why do you always dress like you're going into battle?" Olivia pointed to Talia's warrior belt, her Chakram, the silver bracers on her wrists, and her center laced bodice.

"Why do you always dress like you're going to a party?" She pointed to Olivia's outrageous purple dress, matching hair color, and high heel shoes. "If you trip in those shoes, I'm going to let you fall." She smiled, putting her hands up in the air. "Those shoes are a self-inflicted injury waiting to happen."

"I know my outfit is a bit much for the first day, but I need to stand out in all my classes."

Her clothes were cutting edge and a little risqué and not realistic for the average person. Olivia had worn a shimmery purple full-body suit that accented every curve of her body with a short, see-through skirt and a silver jacket that was blinding when it reflected the sun. She had changed her hair color to deep purple with shiny silver highlights. She changed her hair color daily to match her outfit. Dad had built her a cone-shaped hairdryer that temporarily changed the color. Talia made jokes about how strange she looked with the hairdryer on her head, which never got old to her.

"I think you are trying to blind your professors."

"Hey, Storm," Olivia greeted him before she even turned around, as if she just sensed he was near.

"How did you see me?" Storm asked, coming up behind the sisters.

"I didn't." She turned around. "I just knew you were there."

Talia heard Olivia's voice in her head. *I sensed the sexual arousal coming from him. Just so you know, he has no interest in me. He is looking at you, Talia. If I didn't know better, I would say he has a thing for you.*

You can tell him to keep his thing in his pants, Talia shot back. *Do not leave me alone with him.*

"Well, I should get to class," Olivia said out loud before rushing off.

Bitch. Talia stared at her sister crossing the courtyard.

You will thank me later when he makes a woman out of you. Olivia's laugh echoed in Talia's head. *He's hot and ready. Take advantage, sis!*

"Everything good?" he asked, breaking the mental conversation she was having with Olivia.

"Yes, my sister is just being my sister." She sighed. "I should also be on my way."

"Which direction are you headed?" He smiled. "Maybe I could help you navigate the campus easier."

"I'm perfectly capable of finding my own way."

It seemed his testosterone was radiating. Talia noticed his allure was drawing in the ladies. A few women had their eyes on him as they strolled by the couple. Her face flushed with embarrassment when she noticed some of them gawking at Storm. She looked away when she noticed all eyes in their direction. She felt disconcerted by the attention he was getting.

"I don't doubt that. I've seen the way you move."

"That doesn't surprise me. I've heard about you. I'm aware of your reputation, and your charm doesn't interest me."

She started to walk away, but he insisted on following her.

"That was fast. You've only been here a week." He smirked. "How about you experience it for yourself first and then decide?"

Storm's gaze was solely fixed on her. He ignored every other woman around them. Every step they took, she tried to put some distance between them. As other students rushed by, Storm seemingly took every opportunity to move in closer, brushing against her. Talia's heart raced as the warm pressure of his hand settled on her lower back. He guided her deftly through the crowd, with his fingers pressing against her clothes, making her more aware of the way she moved her body.

Please, don't trip right now. Focus on your movements with grace and agility and you should remain upright. You're a warrior, so act like one.

"I know enough about you. I don't need to know more. I am sure there are other women who would love to have your attention."

As the pair walked through the courtyard, Talia noticed the energy of the place. It seemed like it was humming with excitement and anxiety all at once, almost as if there were a pulse everyone could feel. Everywhere they looked, there were students hurrying to their classes, chatting with friends, or sitting under trees studying.

Storm seemed unaffected by the surrounding atmosphere. He walked casually beside Talia, his eyes occasionally drifting toward something behind her before snapping back into focus when she turned to face him again. He smiled reassuringly but said nothing. Talia thought he was content just being near, but by the third time, she caught him checking out her walk.

Before she could call him out, a voice called frantically from across the courtyard. "Storm!" A whirlwind of red hair and a white lab coat rushed over.

"A friend of yours?" she asked.

"That's Scooter. You will have to excuse him," Storm warned.

Scooter stepped between them, diving into the conversation with Storm as if they had been talking for an hour. He was gushing about the energy field in the air and pointing to a handheld device. His arms were flying wildly as he spoke. Talia took a step back to avoid a collision. He was enthusiastic about something.

"The energy readings this morning are going crazy." Scooter waved the device in Storm's face, his head twitching slightly to the left.

"Scooter, you are being rude to my friend," Storm pointed out. "Please, introduce yourself."

He looked over his shoulder to briefly state, "Hi, I'm Scooter."

"Talia," she responded.

"I don't think you understand the importance of what I am saying." He turned back to Storm to continue his rant. "These are the strongest readings I have ever had. I have to get to Middle Park and take readings at the Eternal Flame. They will be off the chart!"

Seizing the opportunity of Storm's preoccupation, Talia made her escape to class, claiming a seat in the epicenter of the vast, round, amphitheater-like lecture hall. She was a cocktail of nerves, excitement, and sweet anticipation. As she slid out her sleek tablet to load her textbook and fired up her digital notebook app, a familiar face flickered into her peripheral vision. It was too late for retreat or concealment.

Storm sauntered toward her, oozing confidence as he settled into his seat directly behind her. So close, she could feel his hot gaze searing into the back of her head like a damn branding iron. She was still trying to calm her breathing and her heartrate from their walk to class and now she would have to spend the next hour in front of him. He was too close for comfort. She messed around with her hair to cover her nape as if it would give her an ounce of protection.

She felt utterly exposed under his potent gaze, as if she were center stage with every twitch and shiver under scrutiny. Her heart pounded out a tribal beat while heat flushed through her veins like molten lava. She could feel the intensity of his gaze boring into her, lighting a match to her nerves.

What the fuck is wrong with me?

As she shifted uncomfortably in her seat, a seductive hint of his cologne reached her senses, causing a dizzying moment where she lost herself in his masculine essence.

Why does he have to smell so fucking good?

"Storm, I didn't know you were in this class," a tall, busty blonde with a high-pitched, immature voice greeted him. Talia turned her head in time to see her and her friend snuggled up on each side of Storm. They made themselves comfortable and tried to get as close to Storm as possible without sitting in his lap.

Talia bit her lip, a surge of annoyance washing over her. She turned back, still moving in her seat. She dreaded being forced to hear the conversation, she didn't want to witness it as well. She slumped against the back of her chair.

"I took the class to see you," Storm said to the blonde girl. Talia could hear the smirk painted all over his words, even without looking. With a soft rustle and the creak of his chair, she felt Storm's hot breath in her ear. His voice was low, smooth, and so damn assertive. "I can smell your jealousy."

Jealousy?

Talia's breath caught in her throat as she turned her head to meet Storm's piercing gaze. He was closer than she had anticipated, his strong presence overwhelming her. She fought to maintain her composure, trying to hide the fluttering of nerves in her stomach. "You should get your nose checked," she managed to say, keeping her voice steady. "It's actually annoyance that you're detecting." She held his gaze, determined not to let him see how much he affected her.

"Whatever you call it, it smells primal, almost intoxicating." He smiled as he retreated to his seat.

I hope you choke on it.

Talia sat with her arms tightly crossed, her posture slumped, head lowered, eyes looking at the ground. Her lips were pursed in a thin line, conveying her irritation toward Storm's words. She felt defeated and ready to retreat into herself. A prickling sensation brushed the back of her neck, a sign that he was getting under her skin. She wondered how he could cause her to melt in heat with the touch of his hand, but smolder in resentment with his words.

The professor walking into the lecture room abruptly recaptured her focus, trailed closely by the spirit of a young man. Despite her best efforts, Talia found it impossible to disregard the amusing specter.

As the professor prepared for his lecture, Talia's eyes locked on the spirit's movements around him. He danced with an irresistible beat that made her smile. His deliberate mockery of the professor entertained her, and she struggled not to let out a chuckle at each exaggerated facial gesture.

The professor was an unfortunate target with his short stature, outdated tweed jacket, and thick glasses, a stark contrast to the ghost's wild allure. As soon as the lecture began, the spectral man positioned himself behind the oblivious professor, skillfully mirroring his actions and words. His every move was fluid and amusing, making him utterly captivating.

"Sumerians have been known for their brutal and barbaric force and their distaste for their gods. Lord Gorgon, God of the Underworld, and Lady Anasazi, Goddess of Misery are not kind to the Sumerians who worship them," the professor explained.

"I disagree. Not all Sumerians are barbaric." Storm spoke up, which reminded Talia he was still there. "Take Commander Jitatma, for example. During his military career, he peacefully negotiated the border dispute between the Sumerians and the Anunnakians."

"For his peaceful actions during wartime, Sumerian officials threw him in prison." Talia turned to face him and continued her argument. "There were also rumors that Commander Jitatma brutally assaulted a fellow prisoner, almost fatally stabbing the victim to mangle his Nibmark. Because of that brawl, the Commander now holds the same rank among our gods in King Hunter's royal guard as a permanent member of the Far Viscera unable to tip the scale of judgment. That sounds barbaric to me."

"Commander Jitatma cannot tip the scale of judgment because he has not been judged. Our god, Lord Gorgon, has treated him unfairly and continues to challenge his ability to command an army of souls. Your god, King Hunter, refuses to do his job because he is grieving his wife. The Enochian god, Emperor Anu, is too busy being perfect to interfere." Storm leaned over his desk, closer to her. "I don't know how your gods treat you, but I do agree all Niberians are getting a raw deal being trapped in the middle of a battle of the egos. That's barbaric."

"Would you prefer the goddesses to step in, like Lady Anasazi or Empress Ki?"

"The only one who can clean up that mess is Queen Circe. That is the only goddess I can get behind." Talia caught her breath in her throat as the name of her goddess left his lips, his voice dancing as he said it. Smoke flashed a mischievous smile, winking at her. "She's dead, a victim of the void."

"Who said she's gone?" she said, narrowing her eyes.

Did he know her secret? Storm lowered his eyes at her like he could see right through her. Again, Talia felt utterly exposed under his gaze, but this time she was under the spotlight with every movement truly under scrutiny. She had captured Storm Smoke's full attention.

She wondered if he had seen the resemblance to Queen Circe in her eyes. In every text, Talia had seen her own reflection when she came across a picture of her goddess. She was staring at her own black hair, violet eyes, and the same shaped face, but she never dared say it out loud.

Her connection to her goddess went beyond similarities in their features. She wanted to be Circe. The queen was loved and admired by the Anunnakians for her might and bravery. She was a powerful goddess, wielding her magic with a grace Talia had yet to master. She was everything to Talia. Even with the knowledge she was human, still, the understanding that she was the reincarnation of someone so great was difficult for her to believe. Was Storm looking at Queen Circe's face at that moment? What was he seeing?

"Mr. Smoke, you just gave me an idea for your midterm paper. Find me a leader of a society who did not fit into their society's expectations and how they were treated."

As soon as class ended, Talia hurried out to create space between herself and Storm. He made a half-hearted attempt at blocking her path, but she quickly slipped past him when the blonde girl grabbed him by the arm.

Still shaking her head in frustration, Talia heard his footsteps gaining on her as he jogged behind her. They reached the courtyard just before the spacecraft statue, and Storm easily matched her pace. Deciding to make things difficult for him, Talia refused to slow down or give in.

Out of breath, Storm asked, "Since we have some of the same classes, I was wondering if you would like to study together."

"No," she said flatly.

"What do you mean, no?" he asked with a tone of slight shock as he grabbed her arm to stop the marathon she was running.

"I know you are not used to hearing that from a woman, so let me make myself very clear. I have no interest in you. I'm not interested in being your study partner. I'm not interested in getting to know you. I'm not interested in sleeping with you. I find you to be a narcissistic, skirt-chasing, self-centered pirate, and I have no room in my life to stroke your immature ego."

"That's every man, living or dead," the old man's spirit offered.

"Shut up!" Talia yelled at the empty bench before stomping off.

"That's fine with me. I wouldn't want a stubborn, tree-hugging, know-it-all maverick stroking anything of mine. Ego or otherwise!" Storm yelled at her back as she turned.

"Your new girlfriend?" Scooter asked Storm as he passed her.

"I do not like that girl, but I love watching her walk away," Storm said. "She is something."

For the love of all the gods, he is staring at my ass again. Fine. If he wants to play games, I will give him a show.

She moved with grace and precision, her hips swaying in perfect tempo as she made her way through the courtyard. Years of observing her sister manipulate men had finally paid off, and Talia was now using those skills to her advantage. It seemed only fair, considering how uncomfortable the man had made her feel in class. She wanted him to experience the same discomfort that he had caused her.

I hope you need a cold shower now. Your turn, Pirate.

CHAPTER FOUR

TALIA

The news of Talia's spirit-seeing abilities traveled fast in the spirit world, and by the time she made it back home, a throng of spirits were following her around. It was utter chaos as she tried to make it to her apartment door without getting waylaid. The blessing placed on the house ensured no ghost could enter without being invited, so when she finally reached the doorway, she waved goodbye to the dejected crowd before shutting them out. With her safe zone secured, she could finally have some peace.

In her childhood, spirits were her constant companions and source of comfort in lonely moments. Before she began attending school, she believed everyone could see and interact with them. However, as she grew older and started to explore beyond the boundaries of her home, she realized she differed from others. While other children couldn't see the spirits, she could, which led to teasing and bullying from her peers.

Olivia always came to her defense when the other children hurled their cruel words, but despite her sister's valiant efforts, the bullies still managed to find their mark. Talia retreated even further into her own world. A world where she was safe from the judgment and ridicule of those who couldn't see past her differences.

Deep in the forest, there was a spirit unlike any other. Her name was Princess Johara, and Talia had grown quite fond of her. Unlike the other spirits, she possessed magic and an air of tangible reality. While the others would appear at random, Johara could be summoned only by Talia's call.

In the heart of the woods, Talia would spend countless hours with Johara, honing her own magical abilities through training and practice under the guidance of the gracious princess. As each session unfolded, her understanding of herself and her abilities grew. Johara guided her through various meditative practices, allowing her to establish a profound connection with her inner self. They explored the depths of Talia's emotions and harnessed them for a greater purpose.

In those serene moments, she learned to recognize and disperse the negative energy that threatened to engulf her. With Johara's patient guidance, she discovered that by closing her eyes and focusing on her breath, she could envision a brilliant orb of white light surrounding her entire being. This protective shield of light acted as a barrier, warding off any darkness that sought to seep into her consciousness.

Through these sessions, she also honed the ability to differentiate between the light within her that was pure and radiant and the dark light that harbored negativity. Johara emphasized the importance of embracing love, compassion, and happiness as the driving forces behind her powers. By visualizing these positive emotions emanating from her heart, she could strengthen her connection to the divine light within.

As time passed, her once scattered energy gradually became more focused and controlled. The river acted as a conduit for her transformation, its glistening waters mirroring the shimmering essence of her growing power. Johara taught her how to tap into the raw energy present in the natural world and bend it to her will.

Six long years had passed since Talia had last lain eyes on her. She could still remember their final training session, the tension and worry etched into the princess's face as she shared news of an ongoing battle with an evil king in her own kingdom. Despite wanting to see each other, it wasn't safe for her to travel to Talia's home. The princess had made a promise that if she ever needed her, she would come. With Talia's need for tranquility and ease, she wondered if her dear friend would keep her word.

"Tough first day?" Olivia asked as she came out of her bedroom. She had wrapped several fabric samples over her shoulder, and she was wearing a pincushion on her wrist. It was her usual look when she was starting a new design. "I am sensing the entire spectrum of emotions from you."

"You have no idea." Talia sighed. "Storm was in my first class, and I was such a bitch to him. He had me on a rollercoaster of emotions all morning."

Olivia read her state of emotions. "Now I am sensing guilt mixed with a little regret."

"What I said was right, but the way I said it was wrong," she admitted. "I was honest. I think he's arrogant, and he expects women to do whatever he asks. Women fall at his feet. He was shocked when I told him no, as if he had never heard that before. It made me want to resist him even more. He tries so hard to pull me in."

"Why are you resisting?" she asked.

"He's a pirate," Talia said, dropping her bag as she sank into the couch.

"That's not a reason. It's an excuse." Olivia sat down next to her sister on the edge of the cushion. She untangled herself from the fabric she was draped in. "You have this weird connection to him. I felt it the moment we met him. You run from him because he scares you."

"Nothing scares me," she insisted.

"That is not true. There was a time when your powers scared you until you learned about them. Do you remember that huge fight we had when we were kids? It was the first time lightning shot out of your hands," Olivia reminded her sister, taking Talia back to that moment.

Hey, that's not fair.

In the heat of a board game battle, tensions rose between the twins. Players strategically positioned shapes on the board to obstruct each other while linking those of the same color. Olivia had cheated by placing two shapes in one turn, prompting Talia to accuse her sister of foul play.

That's cheating!

No, it's not. It was my turn. Olivia narrowed her eyes at her sister to justify her decision.

You used two pieces.

It was one turn.

"Cheater!" Talia yelled out loud, jumping to her feet, standing over her sister.

"Liar!" she yelled back.

The argument between the twins shot to a boiling point faster than a kettle on high heat. Their voices twisted in anger, fiercely confronting each other without backing down, and they became lost in a storm of their own making. Olivia, unable to hold herself back any longer, tipped over the board out of sheer frustration. Game pieces flew like unexpected hailstones, clattering against the wooden floorboards and skipping across the room.

Talia's fury seeped into every corner of her surroundings like an angry frostbite. Sensing her sister's guilt, Talia narrowed her eyes. Olivia refused to back down, crossing her arms and tensing her shoulders.

The lights flickered nervously in the house like a neon SOS. Talia heard Mom's footsteps echoing down the hallway. As she swung the door open, Mom stepped in the middle of an explosive stand-off. The twins faced each other down in an epic battle of sibling rivalry.

Tiny threads of sizzling lightning escaped from Talia's fingertips. They scurried up the cracks of the paint-peeled bedroom wall, weaving a snaking lattice of electricity that sizzled across the ceiling. An acrid scent of burned air and a faint tingle suffused the entire room, making her skin prickle.

Mom could only stand frozen. Talia was livid. Livid enough to raise her palm toward Olivia with electric energy whipping wildly around her fingertips like tiny, storm-hungry serpents ready to strike. Defiance echoed in every corner. "I'm not some damn liar!"

It was typical Talia, really, all fire and fury. A lightning bolt tore free from her left hand, rocketing toward Olivia, who had been two steps ahead this whole time. She effortlessly dove away, leaving behind nothing but air for the vicious lightning bolt to slam into. Instead, it impacted the wall, creating a gaping hole to view the outside.

A wave of understanding overcame Talia, and her simmering anger tipped over into an icy pool of fear and anguish, setting off a jittery spark of sapphire lightning from her trembling right hand. Mom, with all the love laden in her gaze, stepped forward to console her visibly distressed daughter.

As her gut coiled tighter with an uneasy dread, she spontaneously shot out her hand. Olivia grabbed Mom's arm, which stopped her from unwittingly walking straight into another rogue jolt of electricity that crackled fiercely. It smashed onto the hardwood floor near Mom's feet.

The scent of scorched wood filled the room. Mom clenched her chest with surprise in her eyes, but then her expression gave way to concern as her brow began to soften. They locked worried gazes, a mother scared for her supernaturally charged child, and the girl terrified by the magnitude of power pulsating from within. Tears clouded her eyes as she warned, "Please stay away. I don't want to hurt anyone."

"It's okay, Talia," Mom said carefully to calm the energy in the room.

"No, it's not okay," she cried, backing up. "I can't control the lightning." The sparks continued to surround them in the bedroom, weaving up the walls and across the ceiling. It hovered over them like a threatening cloud. The more upset Talia became, the more the electrical energy increased. In her grief, she put up her shields in her mind to push her sister out.

"Talia, I know you are mad, but don't shut me out," Olivia begged.

"I am so sorry," Talia cried, running out of the room and through the back door.

Her heart pounded in her chest as she sprinted through the dense woods, her fear intensifying with each crackling bolt of lightning that escaped from her fingertips. The once serene forest now trembled under the onslaught of her uncontrollable energy. The sparks danced dangerously, illuminating the darkness as they collided with the surrounding trees, setting off small bursts of flame and showering the area with smoldering embers.

Olivia leaned forward, fingers tapping on the wooden table in front of them. "This thing with Storm scares you because you can't fight your way out of this. No matter how many hours you have spent training, it never prepared you for that man." She continued with a gentle but firm voice. "Look, I'm not saying you have to be in a relationship with him, but you should at least allow him to be a friend."

"Do I have to?" she sighed.

"Maybe that's your problem. You hate all the attention he gets from other women. Are you jealous?"

"I just get annoyed by the way he reacts to the attention. It's a game for him. He is such a pirate." Talia sank deeper into the couch, thinking back to class. "He does this thing."

"That thing with his eyes? It's called admiring you," she said, a surprised giggle escaping her mouth.

"It makes me so uncomfortable. It feels like his eyes are burning holes in my skin. Do I really have to be nice to him?"

"He is our neighbor. We see him daily, and he's in several of your classes, so it would be weird if you didn't. I thought you didn't want to be the weird kid anymore."

"You're right. I should start with an apology. Then I will try to be nicer," she promised. There was a knock at the front door. Olivia and Talia exchanged confused glances. "Are you expecting someone?"

"No, you think I would have seen this coming?" Olivia swung open the door to be greeted by a familiar face. "Brutus!" Her voice hitched. In an instinctive reaction, she leaped onto him, wrapping her legs around his muscular waist. His hard body rippled under his shirt as he took a step back to adjust to her unexpected assault. "What are you doing here? It's only been a week."

Before he could answer, she assaulted him with her lips. His bag fell onto the floor with a thud at the entrance of their apartment. There was no room for distractions—only for them and the flame that danced between their bodies which were now locked in a passionate embrace. With a swift movement of his foot, the door slammed closed.

"It was a good week, too." Talia smirked mostly to herself. *Why is he here?*

Brutus' hands possessively roamed Olivia's body. His large fingers traced circles down her spine, making her arch against him in response while his lips trailed kisses down her neck, eliciting soft moans that echoed through the otherwise silent apartment. She arched her head back, inviting him in as he ravaged her neck with his kisses. He moved his lips down to suckle on her earlobe, nipping it lightly. He spun her around, his hard body pressing her against the wall.

He looks like he is going to devour her like an animal.

"Damn, girl, I missed you too," he managed to say. "My classes don't start until next week, and I wanted to see you this weekend."

"You drove six hours for a hot weekend, but it's the middle of the week. We better get started now." Olivia giggled.

Great, not only do I have to witness this, but I'll also be hearing it from her bedroom later.

"As much as I would love to watch this reunion," Talia drawled from the sidelines, "I am going to find Storm."

Talia felt envious as she watched her sister casually give and receive affection from men. She wished she could be more like her, with her easy charm and ability to attract attention. She had built walls around herself over the years, standing in the background while Olivia soaked up all the spotlight.

She wasn't going to let any Sumerian pirate break through those walls, especially not one who liked to play childish games. She wanted something more meaningful and authentic with a man who was kind, considerate, and protective. That was the kind of passion she longed for, and she wasn't going to find it in Storm Smoke.

CHAPTER FIVE

TALIA

T alia made her way down the cramped steel spiral staircase at the back of the store, only to hear a chorus of excited giggles as she came around the corner. Stopping in her tracks, she looked up to find Storm captivating an audience of three women at the store counter. With each passing second, they found new ways to touch him and flirt with him. Talia shook her head to herself and let out a heavy sigh before reaching the bottom of the steps. Like a car accident, she couldn't look away from this unfolding scene. She leaned against the stair railing, crossed her arms, and began critically observing.

"What do you mean, only one woman can wear this ring?" one of them asked, leaning in closer to Storm.

The woman pretended to be examining a ring, but Talia could tell she was giving Storm a better view of her cleavage. She had witnessed Olivia do the same move a hundred times, and she would tell Talia that even if a man preferred to stare at her ass, she could still at least get his attention with her cleavage.

Don't fall for the trap.

When Storm's gaze traced down the line of the girl's shirt, Talia felt a little disappointed.

Down the hole he goes. I was hoping he would be smarter than that.

"According to the legend, King Hunter forged this ring from the outer ring of the planet," he said, adjusting his stance slightly to look the women in the face.

Nice recovering. So, the hole wasn't that deep.

Storm held up the opal gem nestled in the white onyx band, and it shined in the light. Talia had seen that glow before, and she felt drawn to the ring. It was a connection she couldn't ignore, losing herself for a moment. Her lips parted in wonder as she held her breath, captivated by the mysterious gem.

"It was forged with magic so powerful only one woman can harness it."

"Let's see if I'm the one," the woman said, snatching the ring from Storm and slipping it on her left ring finger.

"I wouldn't do that," he warned.

"Why not? It seems fine." She shrugged, but as soon as she finished the statement, the ring burned her finger. The women quickly pulled the ring off and threw it back at Storm. Disgusted at the red burn around her left ring finger, she yelled, "What kind of parlor trick is that?"

"I warned you." He smirked, struggling to contain a laugh.

"You can keep your ring." The women turned and walked out of the store. He watched their hips sway back and forth, still smiling, leaning over the counter to get a better view.

Now he is back down the hole and has landed in the Underworld.

"Wow. You can stop drooling now," Talia said. She shook her head, allowing a mocking giggle to escape her mouth. He suddenly stood and composed himself, as if Talia had caught him doing something wrong.

"How long have you been standing there?" he asked, clearing his throat.

Talia pushed herself away from the staircase and walked toward him. "Long enough to witness you make a fool of yourself. Oh,

Storm, let me stroke your ego," she said in a sarcastic, high-pitched voice. "I can't believe you fell for the lean." Talia giggled. "Blah."

"Come on. It wasn't like that." He shrugged, his voice lighter. It was a tone she had not heard before, but he then quickly adjusted back to his deep tone when he said, "What lean? Why don't you show me?"

"I could get Olivia to demonstrate. She's an expert." She smiled, leaning against the counter, careful not to give him a view down her shirt. "My lean is different. It requires a punch to the gut first. While you're bent over staring at my chest, I would follow that with a knee to the face. Would you like me to demonstrate that?"

"That sounds like great foreplay."

"Of course, you would like that." She rolled her eyes. "What is it about you that women find so attractive? I don't see the appeal."

"If you haven't noticed, there aren't too many Sumerian men around here," he pointed out. "They want what they can't have. There are many rumors about Sumerian men as lovers."

"I suppose I can see why that would intrigue some," she agreed.

"But not you?"

"Not in that way," she said. "I would agree that you are a handsome man, until you open your mouth. It kills the attraction every time. I can't think of you in that way."

"Not yet, anyway." He smiled.

"I came down here to apologize for being so rude, but you make that difficult. You are so arrogant." She sighed.

"What did you call me again? I believe you said that I was a narcissistic, skirt-chasing, self-centered pirate, and you have no room in your life to stroke my immature ego. I would not use those words in my dating profile." He chuckled.

"Well, I would not call myself a stubborn, tree-hugging, know-it-all maverick. The closest thing I would get to hugging a tree would be when I am lying in wait for my prey."

"Maverick." His voice was smooth and low.

"Pirate."

As Storm pushed his sleeves up to his elbows, revealing the tattoo on his inner right forearm, her eyes were immediately drawn to the intricate design. The tattoo depicted a vibrant purple shield with a circle containing three inward-facing swirls. It was the same design as her Chakram, a symbol that held the ability to wield and control her powers. She knew the shield was the mark of a protector, but she didn't know what Storm was keeping safe.

"Where did you get your tattoo?" she asked, grabbing his arm.

"I've always had it. I don't remember." He shrugged. "Delphi told me once it was the symbol of the gods."

"Who are you, Storm Smoke?" she asked. "That is the mark of the God protector, usually reserved for the royal guard in the Far Viscera. My dad would tell me stories of the Templars as a child. History was a passion of his."

"God protector, really? They picked the wrong guy. My gods are cruel, and I would never protect Lord Gorgon or Lady Anasazi." He shook his head.

"Well, those are your gods, Sumerian. I take my oath to my gods seriously." She leaned against the counter, crossing her arms.

"You seem like you would be a rule follower even if King Hunter cursed you like this ring." He picked up the opal ring to place it back in the display case.

"May I see that?" She pointed to the ring. He handed it over, and she examined it carefully. "How did you come into possession of this ring?"

"To be honest, there's no record of the purchase, which seems a little strange, because Delphi has a story for everything else in this store," he said, waving his hand like he was dismissing her question.

"What is the story she told about this?"

"The rings of our planet were used to forge this. It was one of a set that were wedding bands. They represent the perfect balance between good and evil. This opal, believed to be Queen Circe's wedding band, searches for its one true owner to balance the universe. It was always their fate to be together. Only one woman can handle its power." He sighed. "I have told that story a hundred times, and no one has worn the ring for more than a minute. I'm thinking she doesn't exist."

"Opals are a window into your soul and healing for your spirit. This one has the glow of the gods," she whispered.

She leaned her elbows on the counter as Storm did the same. He reached out and took her hand, his fingers lightly brushing against hers. She felt a magnetic pull between them. Their eyes locked, and time seemed to stand still as she became lost in his gaze.

With a gentle touch, he slipped the ring onto Talia's left ring finger. As the cool stone met her skin, a shiver ran down her spine, causing her heart to flutter with both excitement and trepidation. It was as if the ring recognized its true owner and responded with an ethereal glow, casting an enchanting light upon their intertwined hands.

The opal gem nestled in the white onyx band seemed to come alive in her presence. Its colors danced and shimmered, illuminating the room with an otherworldly radiance. The air itself hissed with an electric energy, as if acknowledging the immense power contained within this ancient artifact.

When he held her hand, she felt a warmth spreading from the ring throughout her entire being. It was as if the ring was not only a beautiful piece of jewelry but also a conduit for something far greater, an ancient magic that resonated deeply within them both.

Time seemed to blur as memories from a distant past flooded her mind. She could almost hear whispers carried on the wind, fragments of forgotten stories and forgotten lives coming together to form a cohesive whole. The mark of the God protector on Storm's arm suddenly made sense, as if it were a symbol meant to unite them in a greater purpose.

As she looked down at the ring, she noticed her reflection in the opal's alluring depths. It was as if she were peering into a window to her own soul, seeing not only her desires and fears but also the vast potential that lay dormant within her. The ring seemed to whisper to her, beckoning her to embrace the power it offered and to embark on a journey that would shape her destiny.

The room fell silent as they stood there, their hands still joined, their hearts beating in sync. This moment marked a turning point, an awakening of something extraordinary. Their shared connection went beyond words or explanations; it was a cosmic bond forged by fate itself.

He whispered, "You are the one. Circe."

"I don't know what you're talking about." She tried to play down the moment.

"The ring belongs to you." He pointed down at her finger. "It chose you. Your finger didn't burn."

"That's impossible." Her heart pounded in her chest as she desperately tried to pull the ring off her finger. It felt as though it fused to her skin, refusing to budge no matter how hard she tugged and twisted. Panic welled up inside her, causing her to pull frantically at the ring, her fingers growing increasingly clammy and trembling.

The room seemed to close in on her, the air becoming thick with a sense of unease. As fear took over, Talia stumbled back, unintentionally colliding with a large display. Shelves toppled over, sending a cascade of items crashing to the ground. The sound of shattering pottery and tumbling trinkets filled the air, magnifying the chaos that now surrounded her.

Embarrassment overcame her as she turned to flee from the store, hoping to escape the overwhelming situation. However, just as she reached the spiral staircase, he stepped in her way, his arms outstretched. Rather than finding solace in his presence, she felt trapped, her anxiety intensifying.

In a desperate move to create a diversion for herself, she swiftly ducked behind a spinning card display near the counter. With unexpected force, she "accidentally" tipped it over, causing a deluge of greeting cards to flutter through the air like colorful confetti.

They scattered in all directions, creating a momentary distraction amidst the chaos.

As she made her escape through a path obscured by floating cards, she felt a mixture of relief and guilt. She knew running upstairs in such a manner was impulsive and reckless, but the overwhelming emotions caused by the stubborn ring on her finger had clouded her judgment.

The burden of the ring on her finger was a constant reminder of the mysterious power it held. It appeared the ring had chosen her, binding her to a destiny she was not yet ready to comprehend. She was not prepared to admit to herself or the world that she was human and the one to unlock the full prophecy from the Book of the Dead.

It's just not possible. How am I going to take on the gods to restore the balance of power? I haven't even made it through my second day of college.

"Wait," he begged as she disappeared up the staircase. "Who are you, Talia Trismegist..." His voice trailed off.

She tried to steady the panic in her breathing at the top of the stairs, leaning against the wall around the corner. She heard the beaded curtain rustling from the doorway that separated Delphi's store from her personal living space. She held her breath to listen, waiting to hear Delphi's voice. She bent down to see if she could get a glimpse of what was happening, but she couldn't see anything.

"What happened?" Delphi asked.

"Trismegist means three times great. That's what her last name means. Talia is the one," he said, the words rushing out of his mouth.

"Yes, I know," Delphi said softly.

"You knew and didn't say anything. She's the human. She's Queen Circe."

Delphi corrected him. "She is the prophecy."

"Talia has the key. She can translate it."

"She doesn't know she has the key," she warned. "Storm, you can't push her. It will only drive her away. Let her come to you and tell you who she really is. Be patient, my child. She will come around."

Talia's heart raced as she leaned against the brick wall with her palms pressed flat against its rough surface. She couldn't hold back the tears any longer as they blurred her vision and slid down her cheeks. She slumped to the ground, unable to bear the weight of who she truly was any longer. Storm's words echoed in her mind, revealing a secret she had been too afraid to accept or even acknowledge. All of it threatened to crush her as she wondered what would happen next.

She cursed under her breath as she tugged and twisted at the stubborn ring on her finger. She sensed the blood rushing to her face, as if it were constricting her, suffocating her, and taunting her with its inflexibility. Each attempt left her fingers sore and tingling with frustration. With a final grunt, she gave up her efforts. She couldn't believe something so small could reveal a secret so big.

As her fear surged, the lights in the house flickered. Tiny sparks danced and sizzled from her trembling fingertips. Desperate to stop the rising panic, she rubbed her hands together to calm her racing heart and soothe the tingling sensation radiating from within.

"Talia, what happened?" Olivia said as she opened the door to their apartment wearing only a robe. Talia looked up at her sister's worried face through the tears in her eyes. She immediately dropped to her knees, and Talia reached out for comfort as they embraced each other tightly.

Barely able to choke out the words between sobs, she whispered, "I messed up. He knows."

"I am here," Olivia said in a calm, faint voice. Talia lowered her head to recoil within herself as she felt her sister softly stroke her hair. "I need you to breathe with me. Take deep, slow breaths."

Her chest heaved as she tried to match Olivia's pace. In the narrow hallway, they swayed together. Each breath felt from Talia like a struggle, a battle for air and control.

CHAPTER SIX

HUNTER

King Hunter, a once formidable ruler of the Far Viscera, now found himself consumed by grief within the confines of his judgment chambers. The haunting memory of that fateful night when his beloved wife, Circe, left behind nothing but a swirling white ball of light plagued his every waking thought. Determined to reunite her spirit and soul, King Hunter had become overtaken by an all-consuming obsession.

As the nights grew darker, his restlessness only intensified. His footsteps echoed through the dimly lit chambers as he paced, his mind consumed by thoughts of Circe. Candlelight flickered, casting long shadows on the marble floors, mirroring the turmoil within his heart. The air in the room was heavy with a sense of loss and longing. With each breath he took, he felt a painful reminder of the void left by his beloved.

In his relentless pursuit of reconnecting with Circe in the living world, he had exhausted every avenue available to him. He had consulted seers and sorcerers, seeking their guidance and divinations, yet their attempts proved futile for so many years. Circe's spirit and soul had left the Far Viscera twenty-one years ago, by his calculation.

He adorned the walls of his chambers with maps and diagrams, each one representing a failed attempt to locate her spiritual presence. She could be anywhere in the living world, on the planet Niberia. Her soul and spirit could be roaming around the body of a Sumerian prostitute, or an Anunnakian homemaker, or even an Enochian pastor.

Day after day, Hunter neglected his duties as ruler of the kingdom. His focus rested solely on finding Circe, unable to tear himself away from the overwhelming desire to be reunited with her. In his absence, matters of government suffered, leaving his daughter and subjects feeling neglected and adrift.

The consequence of failure weighed heavily on his shoulders as he grappled with self-doubt and guilt. He felt he had let down Circe, his daughter, and the kingdom. Regret gnawed at him incessantly, fueling his reason for succeeding where he had previously faltered.

Despite the darkness that surrounded him, his resolve remained unyielding. He was a man driven by a love that surpassed time and space, a love that refused to be extinguished. With each passing moment, he clung to the hope that one day he would feel Circe's presence once again, her spirit intertwining with his own.

"King Hunter," Commander Jitatma greeted him, bending on one knee, bowing his head, and placing his left fist across his body to his heart, as was customary. "I am concerned about the restlessness in the kingdom."

"What is your concern, Commander Jitatma?" he asked, signaling for him to stand.

"We have an overcrowding problem in the village. The souls are waiting for their judgment from you," he said, reminding Hunter of his duties.

Niberians believed the Far Viscera served as the judgment grounds for the dead. They considered the soul to be the conscious mind of who they were and the spirit to be the subconscious mind of what they were in life.

When a Niberian died, the soul and the spirit became separate. Far Viscera received the released soul, while the spirit remained with the physical body. The spirit had three days to find the soul, guided only by the known passages from the Book of the Dead, which Niberians lost thousands of years ago. Once the spirit and the soul had reunited, the deceased had to face judgment for the way they lived their life.

Before each departed soul could enter, Hunter weighed their heart against a feather from a Saqqara bird over his pool of blood. If the heart weighed less than the feather, they would receive rewards for all the good deeds they had done in their life. Emperor Anu, God of the Afterlife, and his wife, Empress Ki, Goddess of Happiness, would welcome them into the Afterlife. If the heart had a greater weight, the punishment in the Underworld would be eternal. The pool beckoned the damned with shimmering blood, subjecting them to the chilling grip of Lady Anasazi, Goddess of Misery, and the subsequent torment inflicted by her husband, Lord Gorgon, God of the Underworld. If the scale was equal, then King Hunter and his wife, Queen Circe, Goddess of Magic, would imprison them in Far Viscera until the scale tipped in either direction.

"They have an eternity to wait," he remarked, only partially listening to his commander.

"We will have to expand the city limits to accommodate the extra souls." Jitatma took a step toward his king. "Your Majesty, I don't think you understand the gravity of this situation. The souls are restless. There are whispers in the city of mutiny." He straightened his back and spoke with confidence. "Sir, the kingdom needs your attention. I'd advise you to resume your judgment duties before it's too late."

"It's her, Commander," Hunter insisted, rushing over to the pool of blood. He waved his hand, and the large judgment scale moved on its own. It slid across the room as if it didn't weigh a thousand pounds. He commanded the three inward swirls to separate over the pool of blood with three swift raps of his staff on the marble floor. The red sapphire gripped by the Saqqara bird's claw glowed when Hunter waved it over the pool. "Circe, it's a weak connection." He noticed the sapphire was not glowing brightly. It was enough to sense her spirit, but not her soul.

"Are you sure after all this time?"

"Talia, that's her name," he whispered. "It's only her spirit, so they must have separated. Her soul can't be far." He felt hopeful. "I will have to make the connection stronger."

"How you do plan to do that, Your Majesty?"

"I will have to try to pull out Circe's spirit from her subconscious. I will have to invade her dreams."

Struggling to make sense of the darkness enveloping her, Talia rolled over in a bed that was not hers. The silkiness of the sheets beneath her wandering feet was foreign and jarring compared to the familiar feel of cotton that typically welcomed her skin.

She realized that she was not in her room.

Her eyes fluttered open to reveal a shadowy room lit only by the dying glow of embers in an enormous marble fireplace. Stoked memories lingered in the air along with the scent of charred firewood. Something about this place felt eerily familiar, yet she didn't feel quite at ease. She wasn't alone; uneasiness murmured up her spine as if whispering that she was being watched.

A rush of wind, an unwelcome guest, swooped into the room, causing goosebumps on her bare arms. Something sinister descended upon her. Invisible hands coiled around her neck, simultaneously lifting and strangling. Its uncanny grip stole away breaths until all that escaped was a trembling whistle through clenched teeth.

Inching closer with each choked gasp was a phantom face, defined by dread more than features, its masculine silhouette framed by moonlight streaming through the parted curtains. Horror seeped deep into her soul, steadily draining the life force from her paralyzed body.

She could neither fight nor call for help, breathless and panicking. Darkness wormed its way into her fading vision while strands of disheveled hair blocked out what little light there was remaining from reality. Just before consciousness politely excused itself from this ordeal, the last morsel left untouched, a chilling voice danced past her earlobe, calling out, "Queen Circe."

CHAPTER SEVEN

TALIA

Talia jolted awake with her peaceful sleep disrupted by a wave of fear. She frantically searched the darkness, her eyes wide with alarm. Gasping for air, she felt a tight grip around her throat, strangling her. Her hands tried to relieve the pressure from her neck, but all she could feel was the ring on her finger, the opal glinting menacingly.

An evil red mist seeped in from under the closed door, casting an eerie glow on the surrounding walls. Her body froze in terror as her arms hung at her sides, unable to move a muscle as the paralysis took over. It was as if an inferno had consumed her room, yet there were no visible flames. Her heart raced as she fought for air.

Her powers were useless against the invisible assailant.

As she lay on the bed, she struggled to escape the invisible force holding her down. She wanted to scream for help, but her voice was trapped in her throat. Her fear grew as she reached out to her sister for support, only to feel panic and desperation. She couldn't sense Olivia's presence in her mind, and the realization left her feeling even more alone and helpless.

"Talia!" Olivia shouted through her door.

She felt a strong sense of relief upon hearing her sister's voice from the hallway.

It was short-lived when her sister yelled, "The door is too hot to open!"

Her body lifted off the bed, her limbs flailing helplessly in mid-air. She felt like a marionette controlled by an unseen force, her muscles tensed with fear and confusion. The sensation of weightlessness caused her stomach to drop as she struggled to understand what was happening to her.

She heard a deafening roar that shook the very foundation of the house. The sound was primal and fierce, like a beast awakening from a long slumber. With a thunderous crash, the bedroom door splintered and shattered into pieces, revealing a massive Minotaur standing in the doorway. His hulking frame filled the space, casting a dark shadow over everything in his path. His muscles rippled beneath his fur-covered skin, and immensely ridged horns sprouted from his skull. Glowing with intensity, he fixed his piercing blue eyes on her.

Fear gripped her heart as she realized the terrifying reality standing before her—a beast—had come to take her away. His eyes blazed with an intensity that was both terrifying and mesmerizing, pupils dilating into fathomless pools of darkness. His powerful legs propelled him forward, supported by diamond-hard hooves that thudded against the floor. She stared at the Minotaur in front of her, instinctively braced for an attack, but instead she saw a glimpse of vulnerability in his eyes.

"You can't have her!" The Minotaur let out a guttural growl, the sound echoing through the room. She immediately recognized the voice as Storm's, but it was deeper with a tone of harshness. She felt a surge of reprieve as she realized the truth. He wasn't there to harm her; he was there to protect her. "Give her back to me. She's mine."

Storm grabbed her arms, trying to pull her toward him. His grip was strong and rough, yet filled with an underlying tenderness. She felt the heat radiating from his body, his muscles tensed as he held her tightly. The unseen entity released her, causing her to fall onto her bed with a bone-jarring impact with Storm still holding on.

Momentarily, silence enveloped the room, except for Talia's relieved gasp and Storm's labored breaths. The burn in her throat grew ever more intense with each breath. An enormous sense of contentment overwhelmed her as she registered his protective presence, but it was briskly replaced by the awareness of his proximity. His hard muscles, coated in a slick film of sweat, were pressed against hers.

"I'll shield you." His voice rumbled, rich like dark chocolate and smooth as velvet — an unexpected gentleness beneath the harsh exterior. Still sprawled on the bed, feeling the jarring impact against her spine, she nodded mutely.

Her gaze traveled down his beastly form, taking in his brawny limbs and bulging biceps that had come alive to protect her. Her gaze slid farther down toward the V-shaped ridges leading to his groin. The thought of him being rock-hard underneath that fur intensified the throbbing sensation between her thighs.

His intense blue eyes looked darker under the dim light, burning with an undeniable animalistic lust. His chest moved rhythmically against hers with each ragged breath. He lowered his face toward hers; they were so close that she could feel the hot gusts of breath escaping from his lips.

A low growl erupted from deep within his throat. That sound. She felt an inexplicable pull toward the Minotaur, almost like he was calling to her. She slipped her arm under his left shoulder, pressing her palm hard, pulling him toward her. Despite her defenses, she couldn't deny the powerful connection she felt. The sound of his growl seemed to vibrate through her entire body, igniting something raw within her. It was a fierce reminder of the Minotaur's true nature, one that both scared and exhilarated her at the same time.

As Storm's horns receded into his forehead, she watched him transform into his Sumerian form, towering over her. A mischievous smile danced upon his lips as he hovered, taunting her with his presence. Her fantasy shattered, and she was left staring at the man who constantly aggravated her, stirring up emotional chaos within her every chance he got.

"I thought you had no interest in sleeping with me," he said.

There's the narcissistic, skirt-chasing, self-centered pirate. He's back.

"I don't, so get off me, Pirate," she managed to say through the soreness in her throat, pushing him aside. He adjusted his torn sweatpants to cover himself. The sudden shift of his weight off her left a coldness on her skin. She longed for the warmth and protection of the Minotaur's presence.

"It seems you prefer the Minotaur. I can bring him back." His lips curled into a smirk, his head tilting slightly as he inhaled deeply through his nose. "He loves the smell of your sexual awakening."

She crossed her legs, desperately trying to conceal the dampness between them with the thin satin of her nightgown. "I like him more than you," she blurted, regaining her voice. As soon as the words left her lips, she wished she could take them back.

"Well, at least one of us does something for you."

"When you two are done, I could use some help," Olivia said as she stood in the broken doorway, her right hand pressed against her chest.

Talia immediately sat up, a look of concern etched on her face as she motioned for her sister to come closer. "What happened?" she asked with her voice beginning to return to normal, noticing the redness and blistering on Olivia's hand.

"I burned it on the door handle," she explained, holding out her injured palm for Talia to examine. "I'm so sorry. I was so scared. I couldn't sense you or get to you."

"I'm not upset." She shook her head and took her sister's injured hand.

Talia placed her other hand on top of her sister's. Storm furrowed his brow in confusion as he propped himself up on his elbows to get a better look. She attempted to turn away, but he leaned in, determined to get a closer view.

She called upon her healing powers, forming a warm white light over the burn. She waved her hands back and forth, generating new skin. The burn completely disappeared in a matter of moments.

"You are getting great at that," Olivia commented when she inspected her hand.

"I am glad I don't have to use that one too often." She sighed.

"I want that power. That is so badass," he said.

Rolling her eyes, Talia said, "Glad you approve."

"Talia, what happened to your neck?" Olivia asked.

"My throat hurts. Something was choking me."

"You have handprints around your neck," she said as she brushed aside her sister's hair to get a closer look at her injuries.

"I have a protection spell around this entire house. I do not know who or what that was," Talia said.

"You're the one who did that." He tilted his head. "My tattoo glowed when you did."

"Tattoo?"

She grabbed Storm's right wrist, lifting his arm for Olivia to get a close look. "He has a tattoo of my Chakram on his forearm with a shield."

"He's your shield."

"I thought when Dad told me that I would find my shield someday, it was an actual metal shield." She nodded toward him. "He never told me it would be a Sumerian Minotaur Templar living in this guy."

"He saved your life, so now you are bonded to him." Olivia smiled. "Do you know what this means?"

Talia sprang off the bed, her feet pounding against the floor as she paced. She shook her head vigorously, muttering, "This can't be happening. Not you." Her arms flailed in frustration as she turned to Storm, exasperated. "Out of all people on Niberia, why did it have to be you?"

"You're lucky, I guess." He laughed, flipping onto his back and crossing his arms behind his head as if he were settling into her bed for the night, his eyes clung to hers, analyzing her reaction.

Talia's gaze narrowed at the thought of him making himself at home like he claimed a side to sleep on. "You have no idea what it means to be bonded to someone. It's for life! Forever." She ran her fingers through her hair and released a long, slow breath. "I know Sumerians are incapable of such a commitment."

"I'll agree to be your shield," he said, turning his head to wink at her, "but only if I can still have sex with other women. It's only fair since you refuse."

"Ask the Minotaur's permission." She stopped pacing, folding her arms in front of her chest. "I would like to know what he thinks about you fucking other women."

The room was silent except for the sound of Talia's foot tapping impatiently, waiting for his response. Despite being in the safety of the Minotaur's embrace for only a moment, she could sense a strong connection between them. She had a hunch that the Minotaur would always be on her side when it came to arguments with Storm, but she wanted to put her theory to the test. She was curious to see how much control she had over this creature.

Storm's facial expressions changed rapidly, his eyebrows furrowing in confusion and his lips parting in surprise, with a subtle shift in his breathing. As his face settled into a scowl of frustration, she could hear slight grunts and growls escaping his lips.

That's my good boy, Minotaur.

"He doesn't like that idea." She smirked with satisfaction. She curled her bottom lip. Her voice dripping with sarcasm, she said, "Oh, I'm sorry. Did I cause a fight between you two?"

"That's not fair." He sat up, his voice laced with frustration and his face contorted in a mask of anger. "You tricked him."

"I didn't trick him." Talia closed the distance between them like a warrior taking the kill shot. She reached out and placed her hands on the bed, leaning closer to him. Her voice was low and steady as she said, "He chose me. Now the only way you are going to get your dick wet is when you take a cold shower."

As the anger dissipated, a hint of a smile tugged at the corners of his lips. His gaze drifted down to the neckline of her nightgown. "Now, that's a lean."

Talia's heart raced as she quickly straightened, feeling a wave of heat rush to her face as she became acutely aware of his gaze lingering on her. She could sense the flush of embarrassment coloring her cheeks as she realized that in her haste to confront him, she had unwittingly exposed more of herself than intended. Her eyes widened in mortification as she glanced down, confirming that he had been granted an unobstructed view of her breasts through the neckline of her nightgown.

A soft gasp escaped her lips as she instinctively brought a hand up to cover herself, the delicate fabric of her nightgown suddenly feeling inadequate in preserving her modesty. Her mind raced, trying to regain control of the situation and conceal her vulnerability.

I asked for that one. He's good at this game. Damn it, I am going to have to be more careful.

"I am feeling the tension in the room. Let's take a step back," Olivia suggested.

"What the hell is going on?" Brutus asked as he appeared in the doorway, with a hint of green flashing in his eyes. Confusion etched deeply across his face as he took in the scene before him. "What happened to the door?"

"Brutus, I can explain," Olivia begged, her voice laced with urgency.

Olivia, was he in your room the whole time?

He sleeps like he's dead.

"Who is this guy?" he asked, pointing at Storm.

"Storm. Storm Smoke." Storm swung his legs over the edge of the bed. He extended his hand to Brutus as an introduction, but Brutus rebuffed him by crossing his arms.

Sensing the growing panic within Olivia, Talia stepped toward Storm, wrapping her arms around his neck. Playing along with the façade she had started, he wrapped his arms around her waist. "Pirate, I told you to be quiet when you come upstairs. I guess our secret is out."

Brutus's initial bewildered expression faded as he took in the sight of Talia and Storm together. "Talia, you got yourself a man. It's about time." His eyes softened. "I see you are engaged. Congratulations."

"Yeah, I can't take the ring off since he put it on my finger," she said, looking down at the opal ring, her voice filled with irritation as the ring had become a source of tension for her.

She felt his hand traveling down her spine, a sly grin forming on his mouth. He playfully smacked her ass before saying, "She's my little maverick."

CHAPTER EIGHT

HUNTER

"I know she's the one. She's wearing Circe's ring. I don't understand why I can't make a strong connection. I can only get to her when she's asleep," Hunter said, frustrated after the first night of trying to connect with his wife's spirit. He paced around the pool of blood the next evening, contemplating his next move. "My magic is limited. I need the Book of the Dead. It has all my wife's magic."

The Book of the Dead held a crucial prophecy written in the divine language of the gods and great magic within its pages. It foretold the birth of a human on the planet of Niberia after three thousand years. This human would have no Nibmarks. They would restore the balance of power among the gods, possessing supernatural abilities never seen before. This human would be three times the greatness of any one god. Without knowing the full text of the prophecy, the Niberians and the gods feared the coming of this divine being.

"Circe never let that book out of her sight. She protected it," Emperor Anu reminded his brother. "She was the only one who could read it."

"I am a god, and she was my wife." Hunter's voice echoed through the walls of his judgment chambers. "That book has the spell I need to bring her back, and it's gone!"

Empress Ki stepped forward. "Hunter, I think you should listen to reason. Talia is not your wife, and she doesn't remember you."

"I will make her remember."

"Circe would never want to see you this way. She would want you to move on," Anu said.

Hunter stepped closer to Anu, his anger close to the surface. "I did not come to this fucking planet and create this world to be here alone. She was the one who convinced me to leave Earth. I had accepted our fate of dying on our home planet, but she couldn't. She couldn't do it. She wanted to tempt fate to become immortal."

It was during the twenty-first century when humans discovered a celestial body entering their solar system on a collision course with Earth. Upon closer examination, the humans named this celestial object Niberia. Scientists estimated that it was three times larger than Earth. Although they did not anticipate a direct hit, they believed it would cause irreversible damage to Earth and its inhabitants. Over the years, it was Gorgon who had predicted Niberia would brush against Earth, causing a polar shift. Earth would experience tidal waves, devastating earthquakes, and changes in weather. Humans feared the predicted event would wipe out half of the population.

"Before you were a god, you were just a human. Circe convinced all of us to volunteer for the mission to come here," Ki said.

"I still don't know how she talked Gorgon into being sober long enough to get on the spacecraft for takeoff." Anu chuckled and shook his head. "We had no idea what we were doing on this planet. She always had big dreams for all six of us, and dying on Earth wasn't one of them."

In preparation, they sent six explorers to Niberia, but because of complications, they had to make an emergency landing and lost communication with their home planet. Finding that Niberia had similar features and landscape to Earth, they could maneuver to the center of the enormous land mass that covered a third of the planet's surface. It was a primitive planet with an unlimited amount of freedom.

The explorers built a new civilization from the crash site. They quickly realized something in the atmosphere caused them to feel younger and stronger, giving them superhuman abilities. For hundreds of years, they developed their powers, mastering the art of magic. They were alone on the planet, long forgotten, doing what they could to survive.

"You forget, brother, all that we have built. Two worlds. A whole modern civilization that worships us, and an oasis in another dimension for us," Anu said, calmly stepping back, holding out his arms.

"It was Circe's magic that built the Far Viscera, your Afterlife, and Gorgon's Underworld. If it wasn't for her, we would still be on planet Niberia living with the constraints of that world," Hunter said.

"With or without Circe, this was all worth it. For three thousand years, we have ruled over the Niberians. Do not allow this woman to destroy all of that. She may look like Circe, but she is not your wife."

Hunter pointed at Ki, never taking his eyes off Anu. "You still have your wife. You have no idea what it's like to have her disappear and have nothing to grieve. It's a loneliness that I would never wish on anyone, not even Anasazi. That cold-hearted bitch killed my wife. I want my wife back. What did you expect me to do?"

"I expect you to do your job and judge the souls!" Anu yelled.

"You can't bring her back, and you can't replace her," Ki insisted.

"Give it up, brother. You wife is gone!"

"I will make Talia my wife! Even if I must drag her to this world, she will love me."

"You can't make someone love you," Ki pleaded.

"She will destroy our magic. I have worked too hard to hold on to it when the others fled Earth, seeking refuge on Niberia," Anu insisted. "We kept it from the other humans for a reason. I will not allow this human to take that away. If I have to, I will send her to the empty void. I will do what I have to do."

Hunter remembered the day the spacecrafts arrived. The planet was approaching Earth, so one by one, over hundreds of years, humans fled to Niberia, bringing with them their technology and the largest DNA bank ever collected. The population grew so quickly, the original six explorers were a little resentful. The cities and suburbs began building up around the larger rivers and lakes that cut through the landscape. It was becoming more like Earth, as they created rules, laws, and order.

He convinced Circe to build them a new world in another dimension, away from the human refugees, a gateway to the Afterlife and Underworld. A world they could control, which would never be taken over with modern buildings, frozen in time. This world they envisioned was a realm where they could use their magical abilities without any constraints or repercussions, offering them boundless possibilities and freedom. The very fabric of this alternate reality resonated with such energy, pulsating with raw power that only the explorers could harness and shape to their will. Hunter and Circe named their realm Far Viscera because it was their escape into the center of each other.

On the day of the collision, the remaining humans watched their home planet become engulfed in the shadow of Niberia, taking the debris within the rings. The debris from Earth created the three rings that were visible on a clear night. Humanity was no longer human. That day, they became the Niberians, and the six explorers became their gods.

"So will I, dear brother," Hunter warned.

Talia opened her eyes, trying to focus on her surroundings. She was comfortably curled up in a soft chair, wrapped in a cozy blanket. All she could hear was the crackling from the fireplace. She was back in the room with the four-post bed, adorned with an elaborately carved headboard and draped with sheer fabric. The room was warm and inviting. She watched the flames dance around the wood burning in the marble fireplace.

She felt kisses on the back of her neck, enjoying the softness of his lips and the warmth of his breath. She imagined his touch would be so tender, waiting for him to come to her all night. Now he was there.

"Minotaur," she whispered, "I've been waiting."

"I'm here." His voice was sultry in her ear.

She had tried to picture this moment in her mind since she first saw him, his chest calling to press her body against him, teasing her with his broad shoulders and powerful arms. Wondering what it would be like to be in the Minotaur's bed, staring into his eyes. She had waited for so long, and now he was there.

She wanted him.

Storm kneeled before her, surrendering his body to the Minotaur within him. He lowered his head as she watched, transfixed, as his horns emerged from his forehead. She traced their growth with her fingers, fascinated by the transformation. As his arms grew, she admired the bulging muscles straining against his skin.

The moment the Minotaur's gaze fell upon his mate, his snarling expression softened into a small smile. That smile. There was love and desire behind his sweet lips. She reached out for him as he took her into his arms, lifting her from the chair. She drowned herself in the smell of musk and cedar as he held her close to his chest, wanting to be near him, in his arms.

She watched the fire crackle as sparks flickered into an invisible breeze that drifted upward and out of the chimney. She nestled into his arms, his chest warm against her cheek. The soft glow from the fire silhouetted him against the dark wall. He was home. She felt her heart flutter in anticipation.

He laid her down on the bed with her white nightgown spread across the quilt like angel wings. He was to be her first and only. Taking his time, he unbuttoned her gown down the front, revealing more and more of her naked skin. She had never felt so desired in all her life, becoming aroused as he touched her body with such gentleness.

He moved himself onto the bed, hovering above her body. His brown hair fell over his forehead around his horns as he leaned in and kissed her lips lightly, tasting the sweetness of her mouth. His eyes met hers, pouring out love and tenderness. She gasped as he pressed himself against her, pushing their bodies into one passionate embrace.

She opened herself to him completely, letting go of everything that was holding her back from experiencing complete bliss together. They moved in a perfect rhythm that seemed to increase until they both reached their peak at the same moment in a powerful explosion of energy that left them trembling in pure satisfaction and comfort by being together at last.

CHAPTER NINE

TALIA

Talia's body thrummed with the memory of Storm's kiss lingering on her lips as she sat up in bed. Her fingers traced the curve of her waist, where she could still feel the heat of him inside her from her dream. She felt a feverish flush cross her cheeks, and sweat dampened her skin, but she couldn't help the thrill that coursed through her veins. The opal ring on her finger pulsated with an otherworldly light, illuminating the room.

"Talia," Olivia rushed into her sister's room, "are you okay?"

She brought her hands up to her cheeks, gently wiping away the last remnants of sweat from her face. "It was just a dream," she explained between her heavy breathing.

"You never have dreams like that." Olivia sat down on the edge of the bed. "I could feel everything. I mean, everything."

"Sometimes I hate you're an empath," she mumbled, feeling embarrassed.

"Don't be embarrassed, sis. Sex dreams are normal." Olivia nudged her.

She shifted her body to rest on her elbow. "There was nothing normal about that sex dream. Do you dream about having sex with a Minotaur?"

"No, but I'm jealous that you have one." She giggled. "I wish you could have seen his transformation in the hallway. If I wasn't so terrified of what was happening to you, that would have made my panties wet."

Talia collapsed onto her bed, her body sinking into the soft mattress as she relived the image of Storm's horns emerging from his forehead. She could still feel the rough texture on her fingertips. She knew it was just a dream, but the vividness of it lingered, haunting her thoughts. The image of his burly form, the intoxicating scent of him, and the hard muscles created a yearning ache within her that refused to subside. She could no longer deny it. He had filled her with a desire she'd never known before, awakening a hunger so intense she couldn't control it.

"Now I'm jealous I didn't get to see it." She gave her sister a playful shove.

"Who is winning the game? What is the score?" Olivia asked.

"It depends on who you ask, I guess." She shrugged. "I would like to say I'm winning, but I don't think that's true. I really thought I had him. I mean, he looked so angry when I used the Minotaur against him."

"I think you had him convinced he was going to live without sex for the rest of his life. If the rumors are true, Sumerian men would rather cut off their dick and bleed to death than have to give up their pleasure." She shook her head.

"I thought I was going to die when he saw straight down my nightgown and slapped my ass." She raised her hands to her face, remembering how hot her cheeks felt when she gave Storm full access to her naked breasts the previous night. The feeling of intense shame and embarrassment still lingered, raw and vulnerable, ready to resurface at any moment. She hit the mattress with her fists in frustration. "I don't get it! Why is this happening?"

She was typically the mature and composed one, but that was not what she needed. In a rare moment, Talia allowed her inner child to take over. She kicked her feet and thrashed around on her bed like a child throwing a tantrum. With a loud yell of frustration, she released all the pent-up emotions inside her.

Sometimes, you just have to.

"Feel better?" her sister asked.

"No, I can't separate the man from the beast," she said, the frustration still lingering in her tone. "If I want the beast, that makes me feel warm, safe, and secure, then I have to deal with the asshole who makes me so...Ugh!" She stopped, unable to find the words. With one last good punch to the mattress, she yelled, "Fucking Pirate."

"Keep your voice down or he is going to hear you from the basement," Olivia warned.

"I don't care. He's probably downstairs all smug and cocky, laughing at me."

Olivia lowered her eyes and smiled. "That's not what he's doing right now. I am pretty sure you two are thinking about the same thing but having two completely different emotional reactions."

Talia immediately sat up, her expression filled with curiosity. "Is he by himself, or is there someone else with him?" But as soon as the words left her mouth, she shook her head and changed her mind. "Actually, never mind. I don't want to know."

Olivia narrowed her eyes. "He is feeling lonely and aroused." Then her eyes widened, and she giggled when she said, "Could you image what it would take for him to jackoff? He's a Minotaur, so his dick has got to be enormous."

"Stop." Talia rolled her eyes.

"I have to know." She grabbed her arm and gently shook Talia. "I heard Sumerian men are gifted in length and girth. Storm's also a Minotaur, so that's like a double bonus." She begged, "Please, tell me. Were you able to tell?"

"How would I know?" Talia asked.

"He was on top of you."

"I can't tell size, and I have nothing to compare it to," she said. "I don't have any experience with men, but it felt large."

"Babe! Where are you?" Brutus called from the hallway.

"I hate it when he calls you that." Talia rolled her eyes.

"I'm in Talia's room," Olivia called back.

Brutus appeared in the doorway, in only his underwear, showing off his almost naked body like it was something to behold. He leaned against the doorframe, crossing his arms to flex his muscles. Talia immediately diverted her eyes, feeling uncomfortable.

"This is why you pushed me off you. You needed to talk to your sister," he said, sounding irritated. "I didn't get to finish, babe."

"Seriously, Brutus, you have no idea what is going on. You show up here out of the blue and expect my sister to drop everything to cater to you," she snapped, finally able to look him in the eye. "Do you ever wear clothes? I am tired of looking at your man boobs."

"What has gotten into you, Miss Prude?" He chuckled. "Don't you have a man now to shut you up?"

I swear, Talia looked at Olivia. *I am going to shock his dick just for fun.*

You can't, Olivia responded. *I am not finished with it.*

CHAPTER TEN

TALIA

S leep continued to evade Talia, and as dawn broke, a persistent
soreness still nagged at her throat with every sip she took from
her morning brew. With no sight nor sound of Storm, she made
her way to campus.

Once outside, a cold wind greeted her. The blinds hung motionless behind Storm's windows, very much like off-stage curtains refusing any peep into an actor's solitude. A hollowness lingered around his patio door, speaking volumes about his absence.
Hitching up the collar of her jacket against the morning gusts that
nipped playfully at her cheeks, she felt winter's sneaky approach.

Her warm coffee fought hard but failed to dissipate the foggy
sleepiness cloaking her eyes. She tightened both hands around the
comforting warmth radiating through the cylindrical mug, a small
sanctuary in the chilly morning. Her footsteps echoed through the
courtyard as she hurried toward her first class. A curious crowd
had gathered to follow her, their eerie forms floating in her wake.
The spirits felt drawn to the enchanting opal and white onyx ring
as it shimmered on her finger. As more and more spirits became
captivated by the ring's allure, the radiance intensified, creating an
iridescent beacon that illuminated the path before them. It was as if

a magnetic force compelled them to follow this mysterious figure, and word quickly spread among the spiritual realm that they were in the presence of none other than Queen Circe herself.

She tried to block out the whispers and hushed conversations that seemed to echo in her ears wherever she went. The stress of their expectations pressed upon her, and she felt overwhelmed by the stories and legends that had entangled themselves with her existence.

While she sat in class, attempting to focus on her professor's lecture, the words seemed to float aimlessly in the air before her. Thoughts of the recent nightmare that had plagued her sleep and the tantalizing dream that had ignited a fire within her consumed her mind.

The nightmare, with its shadowy figure and relentless attack, had left Talia feeling vulnerable and exposed. She knew she needed to protect herself from such unseen threats. She prayed to Circe for strength and courage. How did one defend against an adversary they could not even see? The question gnawed at her consciousness, tugging at threads of ancient wisdom buried deep within.

With each passing hour, she became more attuned to the whispers of spirits around her, their voices blending into an ethereal chorus that stirred her curiosity and trepidation in equal measure. She yearned to uncover the truth behind her connection to this hidden realm, to unravel the secrets that seemed to be woven into the very fabric of her being.

As winter's icy grip tightened its hold on the world outside, she knew she would need to delve deeper into her own mystical heritage to find the strength and knowledge necessary to navigate the challenges that lay ahead. The opal ring on her finger pulsed with a mysterious energy, resonating with the echoes of ancient queens and forgotten magic, urging her forward on a path she could not yet fully comprehend.

The early evening air was keeping her awake as she hurried through Middle Park on her way back from the campus. She wrapped her coat tightly around her to protect against the cold winter winds that blew through the town. On the other side of the park, she spotted Storm practicing archery.

He stepped up to the line and loaded an arrow onto his bow, drawing it back before aiming for the bullseye. His arrow flew straight toward its destination, just slightly missing the center point. As he lowered his bow, a satisfied expression spread across his face with a nod of approval. He grabbed another arrow and readied his aim, but she had different plans. She attempted to sneak up behind him, hoping to break his concentration.

Before she could get anywhere near him, he said, "He was able to pick up your scent as soon as you entered the park." With a deep inhale, he released the arrow and watched as it hit even lower than the previous one. His expression became irritated at the missed shot. "It's useless to try to surprise me. The Minotaur seems to know when you're around. It's kind of annoying."

My scent. What do I smell like? I hope it isn't a bad smell.

"What's my scent?" she asked.

"It depends on your mood, but he always knows." He sighed. "I guess I'll have to get used to it."

"I didn't know you could handle a bow," she said, a little surprised, looking at his target. "You are a good shot."

"There is a lot about me you don't know. I doubt you rushed over to talk about my archery skills," he said, slightly sarcastically.

"If I am being honest, you drop your elbow slightly before your release." She held out her hand. "May I take a shot?" He handed over his bow for Talia to step onto the line. With arrow in hand, she drew it back, taking only seconds to aim. Once released, the arrow hit dead center. Trying to remain humble, she just handed the bow back to Storm.

As a child, Talia was like fireworks in the night sky, full of zest and a dash of unpredictability, her violet eyes sparkling with excitement. Still quite young, her own energy often swept her up. Her dad, ever patient and easygoing, served as her calm anchor amid her fury. She discovered their backyard adventures were the perfect outlets for her electric spirit.

Armed with patience peppered with love, Dad taught her how to handle a bow when she was merely knee high to him. She remembered seeing the surprised look on her dad's face with her natural talent like straight out of an archer's fable. Her dart-like precision produced unusually accurate shots even then.

Her favorite part was waiting with bated breath and a tickling anticipation that danced on her fingers, holding on to the grip and pulling back the bowstring. In those moments of stillness wrapped up in soft murmurs of wilderness, it felt as though tranquility grew wings around her, offering rare pockets for quiet reflection and a newer understanding of herself.

"That was incredible. Did you rush over here to show me up?"

"No, I didn't rush, but I wanted to see you," she said, feeling shy.

With irritation in his voice, he asked, "Do you want to see me, or would rather see him?"

The usual naughty grin that danced on his lips was now replaced by a sober expression. His playful demeanor was gone. He kept a noticeable distance from her, his body language signaling a struggle. As their eyes met, she could see the pain and hurt he was desperately trying to conceal. She wondered if it was something she had done to cause this sudden change in him.

A flicker of fear crept into her mind, wondering if she had pushed him too far during their encounter two nights ago, when the Minotaur had been unleashed. Her guilt surfaced for using the Minotaur in their game of control.

Maybe I don't know a lot about him.

"I came to see you," Talia said quietly.

As he moved closer, she saw the intensity in his stare, his usually playful eyes now dark. His jaw was set, and his brow furrowed as he said, "I have to know." She could feel the Minotaur's heat radiating from his body, but she couldn't look at him. He walked tall, turning in circles around her, as if he were examining her.

Her body froze as a low growl emitted from his throat. The sound was deep and resonant, like a love song meant only for her. It made her ears tingle with warmth. She couldn't tell if the growl came from Storm or the Minotaur. As he stood before her, he lifted his hand to gently touch her chin, lifting it to meet his eyes.

"Stop doing that," he demanded.

Stop what? I was just standing.

"I thought you said that you had no interest in me, especially sleeping with me. Have you changed your mind, Maverick?" That voice, so smooth and confident. He stepped closer for her to feel his hot breath on her neck.

She fought back the urge to taste his lips, steadying her stance. "I didn't say anything."

"You don't have to. I can smell your hormones emanating from your body. I can taste your arousal in the sweetness of your perfume. I know a woman's awakening, but yours is different. It's primal to match my own," he said, taking a step back, leaving her with the coldness between them. "That's your scent. You've got my attention now."

"That was the most honest thing you've said to me," she said, desperately trying to adjust herself.

He let out a deep, frustrated breath and ran his hand through his hair. "I apologize," he said sincerely a moment before the playful Storm resurfaced with a smirk and a twinkle in his eyes. "I promise it won't happen again. I suppose I'll have to settle for either another icy shower or a hearty burger. Since you'll only accompany me for one of those options, my choice is somewhat limited."

I guess I only get a moment with the real Storm.

"Welcome to the Burger Shack. What can we make fresh for you?" the waitress asked as they settled into a booth in the back corner of the restaurant. In the early evening, it was nearly empty, which gave them the privacy they needed.

"I will have a double cheeseburger with fries and a cherry soda," Storm ordered confidently.

"The Storm Special." The waitress smiled, winking at him.

"That sounds good. Make that two Storm Specials," Talia said. After the waitress walked away, her posture straightened and her expression grew serious. "I will make you a deal. If you tell me one honest thing about yourself, I will do the same."

He propped his elbows on the table and leaned over to ask, "Are you changing the rules of our game?"

"What game?"

"Oh, come on, Maverick," he said, sitting back, shaking his head. "This little dance you and I have been doing of making each other uncomfortable. Your last move took me two days to recover. That was not fair on so many levels."

"Why is that?"

"I've been playing this game for a long time, but I have never had a woman be such a worthy opponent." He tilted his head to the side with a smile tugging at the corner of his lips. "I can't decide if you know what you're doing, or you don't. If you don't, you're damn lucky. Your turn."

"Truth. It was about half," she admitted. "I failed to do the first rule of my training, which is to know my opponent and never let them see my weakness."

"If your lean is your weakness, I wouldn't mind seeing it again."

Talia felt her cheeks flush with embarrassment as she sank into the booth. She wished she could disappear and hide from the awkward situation. The vulnerability of that moment was still raw in her mind. Thankfully, the waitress brought their sodas, giving her something to focus on and help ease her hurt. She took a long sip of her drink, savoring the cold liquid as it cooled her throat. As she nibbled on her bottom lip, she could still taste the lingering sweetness of cherry from her soda.

"Truth." He broke the silence. He fidgeted in the booth, downing his soda in one long gulp and wiping the sweat from his brow. "I meant that as a compliment, so I apologize if I upset you."

Did I just get a sincere apology from him?

Talia braced herself for a snarky back-handed comment to follow. It never came. As the heat of humiliation slowly dissipated, she was finally able to meet his gaze. Her eyes searched his face for any trace of judgment or amusement, but all she found was a calm and understanding expression.

Storm reached up to his chest, grabbing it tightly as his face contorted in pain. He winced and clenched his jaw, his breath coming in short, erratic bursts. His skin turned pale, and sweat lined his forehead.

She sat up. "Pirate, what's wrong?"

"Fine, I'll do it," he grunted. "Would it make you happy if I told you about the Minotaur? It seems he won't go away."

His beast, my joy.

She nodded in agreement. As her lips curved up into a slight smile, Storm released the tension in his chest and sank back against the booth. She struggled to contain her excitement and keep the high-pitched squeal from escaping her lips. She rubbed her hands together under the table, trying to suppress the need to clap and bounce like a child about to burst. Her mind was in a sugar rush, buzzing with questions, making it difficult to choose which one to ask first. She was eager to learn all she could about the Minotaur.

"Well, I'm not the Minotaur all the time, but he has been more active lately. He has never been like this before. Fear or anger usually triggers the Minotaur's transformation, but I found something else that has been stirring the beast," he said in a hushed voice with his eyes low.

As he took a deep breath, she heard the distinct sound of heels clicking against the tiled floor. She didn't want the conversation to be interrupted. Frustration boiled up in her until she saw the waitress approaching their table, balancing two plates full of steaming food and a bottle of ketchup on a tray. The savory aroma filled her nostrils as the waitress carefully placed their meals in front of them. With the ferocity of a starving man, Storm devoured his burger in just a few bites. It was as if he had gone without food for days and now finally had a chance to satisfy his hunger.

"If you haven't noticed, I have a large scar on my left shoulder over my Nibmarks," he continued. "It was the moment that changed my whole life, good and bad. It was also the first time I transformed into the Minotaur beast in public."

"What happened when the Minotaur came out in public?" she asked, leaning over the table to hear the entire story.

"As I am sure you can guess, I was not an innocent teenager."

"I'm sure, Pirate." She smiled.

"I got myself into trouble, and I went to Prison Island. I was trying to keep my head down and just do my time." He waved a fry in the air before putting it in his mouth. "Not long after I took my Sumerian oath, this prisoner attacked me from behind in the courtyard for no reason. He wrestled me to the ground. I thought he was going to beat the life out of me. Instead, he got really close to my face and said the weirdest thing to me. He said he knew who my father was, and no one could find out who I was. He showed me his right forearm, and he had the same tattoo." He pulled up his sleeve to show Talia his tattoo. "Then he said he was sorry, but he had to protect me. He pulled out a blade and cut across my Nibmarks."

"I went into beast mode to protect myself. I threw him off me, and he flew twenty feet in the air. As he landed, he hit his head hard. When the adrenaline wore off, I passed out from the excessive loss of blood. I woke up in the hospital with Delphi standing over me. She was my nurse, and she helped me get my strength back. Once I was able, she helped me escape. We disappeared to Grand View, and I haven't looked back since."

"What happened to the other prisoner?"

"You already know the ending to that story," he hinted.

"The other prisoner was Commander Jitatma. It's not a rumor. The story is true. Of course, the part about you turning into a Minotaur was left out," she said with wide eyes.

"Someone removed me from the courtyard and took me to the hospital so quickly, I must have had an angel that day."

"I would say Delphi was your angel."

"She saved my life in so many ways. She gave me the chance I needed when no one else would have. I owe her more than I can ever pay back in my lifetime. She is the mother I wish I had. My real mother was not very nice."

"I'm sorry to hear that."

"Don't be sorry. She is who she is, and I choose not to be like her." After he swallowed a few fries, he shifted the focus to Talia. "I told you the truth about who I am. Now, tell me who you really are. I can take a guess, but I want to hear it from you."

"I don't know what you are talking about."

"You can't say it out loud," he said. "I know the truth, and you still can't admit it. You are wearing the proof."

"I have never said it out loud. I only found out a few months ago, and I haven't really accepted it," she admitted.

"When I first realized I was a Minotaur, it was hard for me to accept, too. I get where you are coming from. The Minotaur is only a part of me, but not all of me. I still choose who I am," he explained. "Who are you, Talia Trismegist?"

"I can't," she said just above a whisper, knowing the family secret haunted her parents. When the outside world was shrinking around her growing up, they tried to keep her isolated. Now faced with Storm, she couldn't betray all the hard work they had done.

"Admitting it out loud doesn't change who you are at your core, Maverick. It helps you to accept that it's a part of you," he said softly, reaching across the table to touch her hand.

She remembered as a child spending the six months of winter being cooped up inside with only her sister and spirits to talk to, but it wasn't so easy during the six months of summer. She wanted so desperately to make friends during her youth. It took only five years of volunteer imprisonment to seep into normalcy for her. Even when she started going to school at age five, she could not connect with the other students around her.

Now that she was in college, Talia wanted to change that fate to break free of that subtle captivity she felt, but something was holding her back. He had awakened her warrior spirit, filling her with the need to be challenged and pushed. What had started out as a playful game had become a battle of wits and strategic moves. Storm was pushing her.

The Minotaur's presence was drawing her in, and she assumed it was due to his alluring and mysterious nature. However, after witnessing Storm's vulnerable side, she realized the Minotaur provided a sense of comfort and security. That was something she had been yearning for ever since she arrived in Grand View. She felt a deep connection with the Minotaur and knew he accepted her instantly.

She could establish a connection with Storm, but it meant revealing the most private part of herself. She dreaded the thought of going to sleep and waking up to find that the cruel side of him had returned. It would mean that this day was just a fantasy, and his kinder side did not truly exist. If that were to happen, she would have to go back to separating the beast from the man, something she desperately wanted to avoid.

"You have to swear never to tell anyone. Only my family and Delphi know the truth," she warned.

"I swear I never heard a word," he promised. "You are safe putting it out into the universe with me."

"I'm the reincarnation of Queen Circe, born to restore the balance of power to the gods." A sense of relief drifted over her, as if someone had lifted a burden from her chest, allowing her to breathe again. The air was so sweet. "I grew up hearing about the lost prophecy and the legend. I've trained for it my whole life, but I honestly don't know how."

"I knew you were the one, and you will know what to do when the battle comes. Besides, I will be right next to you. I'll shield you," he assured her as he squeezed her hand.

CHAPTER ELEVEN

TALIA

"I'd like to show you something," Storm said as they approached the edge of Middle Park. The setting sun cast a warm blush over the empty park, and a cool breeze rustled through the trees. He reached for her hand, his grip strong and reassuring as he led her across the park. She had to quicken her pace to keep up with his long, purposeful strides, feeling a sense of exhilaration as they moved forward together.

"Where are you taking me?"

In the distance, she caught a glimpse of flickering light. She had never ventured into the park after sunset before, and it felt like a completely different place now. As they passed the archery range, Talia's senses sharpened, and she began to recognize their surroundings. They were heading toward the source of the light, growing ever closer with each step.

When the round stone cauldron finally came into view, she realized they were approaching the Eternal Flame. Stepping onto the black-and-white tiles surrounding the structure, she was surprised to find the biting wind was no longer as cold as before.

The Eternal Flame stood tall and strong with six small stones that encircled it. Each stone was carefully carved with intricate symbols representing the different gods. Beyond them stood towering eight-foot bronze statues of each deity, their powerful forms radiating authority and divinity.

"My friend, Scooter, says this place has the strongest readings on all of his devices," he said, pointing to the white tent just beyond the statue of Emperor Anu. "He's been studying it for months. I've been helping him when I can."

"I have to admit it's impressive," she said with a hint of awe as she gazed at the mesmerizing dance of the flames on the intricately patterned tiles. She was impressed by the skill and artistry that went into creating such a spectacle.

"The flame isn't why I like to spend time here." Storm placed his hands on her shoulders and gently turned her in the opposite direction. He guided them toward the statues on the outskirts. He stopped her at the statue of Circe and asked, "What do you see?"

She gazed up at the statue of Queen Circe, bathed in the warm light of the Eternal Flame that illuminated her features. The bronze sculpture captured her in a moment of divine grace and power, frozen in time as if caught in the middle of a celestial dance. Her flowing gown billowed around her as if stirred by the wind, intricately carved to perfection, creating an illusion of movement frozen in time.

Circe's outstretched hands ready to release lightning, her expression was one of serene confidence and fierce determination, embodying the essence of a goddess who wielded both beauty and strength in equal measure.

As Talia took in the breathtaking sight before her, she felt a sense of awe and admiration for the skill and artistry that had gone into creating such a masterpiece. The play of light and shadow on the bronze surface further emphasized the intricate details of the sculpture, defining every curve and contour with a delicate balance of highlights and shadows.

"She is everything. She has a graceful beauty that could only be matched by her warrior spirit." Her voice was barely a whisper, filled with tears of awe that threatened to spill over her cheeks. She couldn't tear her eyes away from the statue's piercing gaze. "She radiates a wisdom and inner strength that only a true goddess could. Her eyes appear to be looking into the distance, holding knowledge beyond mortal understanding."

Talia felt his hands move from her shoulders down to her waist, and he pressed his chest to her back. She fell back against him. A gasp escaped her lips as he dipped his head to whisper, "You are Queen Circe. That's how I see you. That's what the Minotaur thinks about you. He wanted me to show you who you really are, Maverick. You are a free-spirited, fierce warrior with a great destiny. I wish you would believe."

She shook her head, breaking out of her trance. She tore her gaze from the statue and stepped away from Storm, trying to regain her composure. She turned to meet his gaze, still feeling the unshed tears in her eyes. The pressure of his words weighed heavily on her, evident in the slight tremble of her lips and the way her hands shook at her sides.

In the fading light, she could see Storm's face contorted in pain. The strain on his features was evident, with furrowed brows and clenched jaw. Beads of sweat rolled down his forehead, glistening in the evening light. His breathing was harsh and ragged, almost like he was gasping for air. Each breath was accompanied by a low groan of pain. He bent over, trying to take in air.

"Pirate, what's wrong? What is happening?"

Between facial contortions, he managed to say, "I'm fine."

"You don't look fine, Pirate. What can I do?"

"Smile."

"What?"

"I need you to smile."

A soft giggle escaped her lips, causing his expression to soften as he looked at her. "That is the second time today that has happened. Should I be concerned?"

"Absolutely not. Please, it only makes it worse," Storm said as he tried to stand.

"How does that make it worse?"

"I can't tell you that."

Crossing her arms with a scowl, she asked. "Why not?"

His face contorted in pain again. "Shit, make it stop."

"Make what stop? I don't understand."

As he motioned her over, Talia approached him with a sense of curiosity, wondering what he had in store for her this time. Expecting him to lean on her for support, she was surprised when he enveloped her in a tight embrace. The warmth of his body against hers was comforting, and she relaxed as she leaned into his chest.

She felt the fast pace of Storm's heartbeat close to her ear, matched by the rapid rise and fall of his chest with each breath he took. As she lingered in his arms, the steady beat of his heart began to slow, and his breathing returned to its natural state. In his strong arms, she felt safe and at peace, a feeling she never wanted to end.

A giggle escaped her lips into his chest. "Are you having an argument with the Minotaur?" She felt his muscles untense. "He's protecting me. Is that why you've been moody all evening? When you upset me, you're in pain? Is he the reason for your sudden change in behavior?"

"You have no idea."

She lifted her head to meet his gaze. "Is this what you've been going through the past two days?"

"I don't want to talk about it," he said, pulling away from her. "The game is over." He turned away. "Know your opponent and never let them see your weakness. You win."

"No, you don't get to do that, Storm." She grabbed his arm, and he turned to face her. "You don't get to put me in an emotional tizzy, get me all hot and aroused, and then convince me to open up to you. You don't get to shut down on me."

He took a bold step to her, with a low growl in his throat. His eyes bored into hers with an intensity that made her retreat. "You're my weakness, but so damn worth it."

He grabbed her by the shoulders to press her back against the Circe statue, trapping her between his body and the cool bronze. As he towered above her, his eyes burned with an unmistakable longing, and the strong aroma of sweat mixed with his customary musky cologne overwhelmed her senses. She felt his arousal intensify as her body molded to his, her curves pressing against his hard muscles.

His lips found hers. The taste of him was intoxicating, raw and untamed. He explored her mouth slowly yet firmly, each stroke promising more erotic pleasures than the last. She struggled to keep from completely melting into him. She had lost herself in that kiss, forgetting everything else around them. It was dirty and animalistic, but so damn perfect.

With his deeper, harsh beast tone, he said, "My Maverick."

The sound of the Minotaur's voice made her wet with desire. It sent a rush of heat pooling between her thighs, making her insides slick. She found herself drowning in the deep, baritone resonance of the Minotaur's voice. She sensed the primal energy pulsating between them as she traced his muscles up his arms.

His hands explored her curves with a hunger that ignited her senses, drawing her closer to giving in to her desire. A gentle gasp escaped her lips as his touch traced a path down to her ass, squeezing one side firmly, pulling her even closer to him. Her hips bucked, involuntarily seeking more of his touch.

"Damn, you are so beautiful," he breathed against her skin, causing goosebumps to erupt all over her body. Her mouth descended onto his once more in a raw kiss filled with pent-up desire. Their tongues tangled fervently, delivering sweet torment.

He withdrew abruptly, catching her off guard.

"If we don't stop, I won't be able to control him," he said with the sound of labored breathing between them, with his hands on his knees.

Her heart raced as she heard heavy, purposeful footsteps echoing on the smooth, cold tile floor. Her breath caught in her throat, anticipating who might be approaching. Slowly, she turned her head to see a figure striding confidently toward them.

"Mr. Smoke, what are you doing in the park so late?" a female voice asked, her tone dripping with confidence and authority.

"Agent Suit, I mean Markson," Storm said, straightening and running his fingers through his hair. "So good to see you, again."

"It's Enforcer Markson, Mr. Smoke." She spoke with a dry wit, her hands confidently planted on her hips as she pushed back the edges of her suitcoat to reveal her shiny badge and holstered firearm. The glint of authority in her eyes matched the gleam of metal at her side.

Enforcer Markson's eyes sparkled with an intense shade of umber, drawing attention to her sharp gaze that hinted at her keenly observant nature. Her luscious strawberry blonde hair fell in elegant waves around her shoulders. The sleek dark pantsuit she wore stressed her slim figure, giving her a polished and authoritative presence. A subtle hint of perfume lingered in the air around her, adding to her commanding aura as she stood with conviction.

"Right. Have you been demoted again to park patrol now? Are you sure your new title isn't Regulator Markson?" he said sardonically.

She scoffed. "Cute." With her fingers clenched tightly around her holstered firearm, she said, "Your little experiment with that weasel last summer got me in trouble with my boss. That stunt you two pulled got me bumped from regional agent back to local enforcer." Her voice was sharp and clipped, her words like daggers. "I will ask you again, Mr. Smoke. What are you doing in the park?"

He pointed to Talia and said, "I was escorting this lovely lady home."

"Really? Just a minute ago, it looked like you were thinking about violating the sixth law." Markson turned to her. "What's your name?"

"It's Talia Trismegist, ma'am."

Talia felt a twinge of nervousness at being caught. She shifted her weight as she tried to think of a way to explain without incriminating him. She couldn't deny his intentions were questionable, but she didn't want to get him into trouble.

"I assume she's Anunnakian." Markson stepped closer to him, her body language hinting at a readiness to act. Despite the height difference, Storm remained unfazed, standing his ground. "For a Sumerian to mate with an Anunnakian is a violation of the sixth law, Mr. Smoke. I hope I don't have you remind you to keep your damn hands off this sweet woman."

"No, ma'am."

Markson said, her tone stern and serious, "I would suggest you take her home and behave yourself before I arrest you."

"Yes, ma'am." He nodded. "It's always a pleasure seeing you, Enforcer Suit."

With a final warning glance in his direction, Enforcer Markson continued her patrol through the park. "Have a good night."

Once they were alone again, Talia turned to him with an exasperated expression. "Now I feel guilty for almost getting you in trouble."

He shrugged nonchalantly. "It's not a big deal. Sully is always looking for excuses to bust me." He grinned mischievously. "Besides, it's always fun seeing you squirm, and I didn't even cause it."

She smiled. After the hectic day they had, it was a relief to see him letting go and being his carefree self. She playfully rolled her eyes at his antics before continuing their way back home. As usual, he stayed close by, scanning the shadows for any potential dangers as they walked through the park. She shook her head affectionately at his protective nature.

"You know, I can take care of myself," she said, breaking the silence between them. "I'm not a helpless damsel who needs an escort."

"What can you do?" he asked as they came to the edge of the park. "Do you have powers?"

"Are you afraid I would melt your face in your sleep?" she joked.

"I would hope not, but it would be good to know what to expect in case I do make you mad."

"I can do a few party tricks." With a determined look on her face, she clasped her hands, centering herself and focusing her thoughts.

As she released her grip, a surge of electricity erupted from her palms, forming a small ball of vibrant lightning. The ball glowed with a captivating mix of colors, shades of blue and purple swirling. It crackled with a ghostly energy that seemed to dance and pulse with a life of its own.

Talia delicately encircled the ball with her hands, harnessing the raw power as if it were an extension of herself. He marveled at her ability to control the force and size of the lightning ball simply by adjusting the distance between her palms. The closer her hands came together, the smaller and more contained the ball became. As she stretched her hands farther apart, the ball grew larger and more majestic, its brilliance illuminating her surroundings.

A hissing sound filled the air, accompanied by faint sparks that danced around the ball like tiny fireflies. She felt the electric charge buzzing against her skin, tingling with an exhilarating rush. With each passing moment, she grew more attuned to this extraordinary power flowing through her.

Time seemed to stand still as she held the lightning ball, feeling its raw energy surging within her grasp. It was both thrilling and humbling to have command over such natural forces, to witness her own potential come alive in a display of dazzling brilliance.

Finally, sensing that she had fully embraced and controlled this manifestation of power, she brought her hands together once again. As if responding to her will, the ball of lightning dissipated into thin air, leaving behind only a faint scent of ozone as a reminder of its existence. "It took me a long time to control the lightning. An old friend taught me how to channel and focus my energy. Before, there wasn't an appliance in our house that was safe."

He laughed. "I bet your parents had to replace a lot of toasters. So, does this mean if I touch you, I will get an electric shock?"

"No, it doesn't work that way."

"I would like to test that theory." He gripped her hand. A sudden charge of raw, visceral energy broadcasted through the intensity of his touch. His other hand traced the curve of her neck, finding its way stealthily to where her Nibmarks would be—if she were not human.

His fingertips danced lightly across the inked skin, sending shivers down her spine despite herself. The tension in her body ebbed away in response to the comforting rhythm of his cascading touch, replaced by a throbbing anticipation that pulsed within every fiber of her being.

A low growl rose from his throat as he leaned in, his hot breath tickling her earlobe before he murmured, "Just checking for shocks." His voice was a sensual whisper, filled with raw, masculine promise and smoky undertones that made her heart pound in sync with the thrilling sensation coursing through her veins. "Are you sure it doesn't work that way?" he probed further, pressing his luck.

Their bodies were inches apart now, close enough for her to feel the heat radiating off his skin. She caught her breath as he closed the gap between them, teasing her bottom lip with the tip of his tongue before finally claiming it in a fierce kiss.

"If you are looking for my stimulant, I don't have one. My Nibmarks are fake," she said, trying to back away, but his hold on her was strong. Physically and emotionally, he was pulling her in, and she only made half an effort to resist.

"I was hoping you had one trait of the Niberian sexual stimulant to make this easier for me," he admitted.

"I would never make anything easy for you or anyone else."

"I like a challenge." He leaned in for another taste of her lips. "You're worth it, Maverick."

"This isn't right, and it's illegal. We're breaking the sixth law," she reminded him.

"It's only illegal if we get caught. Besides, it's a stupid law that's three thousand years old."

"I'm sure you tell yourself that with all the other girls," she said, pushing him away.

"Only I don't have to use that line with you. It's not truly illegal because you are not an Anunnakian." He winked and pulled her close to him again.

"We know that, but no one else does. It was a good try. I'll give you that." She winked back jokingly. "Pirate."

"Maverick."

CHAPTER TWELVE

HUNTER

Within the Far Viscera, a dimly lit and foreboding realm, Hunter paced within his ominous judgment chambers. His dark presence cast an unsettling aura as he sought to manipulate Talia's dreams. Standing near the deep pool filled with blood, the surface rippled with an eerie light, showing the power it possessed.

He was determined to establish a stronger connection to Talia, to infiltrate her subconscious thoughts and desires. He had tried to use dark blood magic to bend her will to his own, but his efforts were in vain. As he gazed into the swirling depths of the blood pool, fragments of her dreams taunted him. He yearned to taste the sweetness of her lips, a memory that ignited a fierce jealousy within him. It should be him, not Storm, she should dream about.

With a wave, he attempted to banish the image from the blood. Talia's bond with Storm, her beloved, was far too strong. In her subconscious mind, she resisted Hunter's intrusion, denying him access to her deepest desires. Frustration gnawed at him as he realized he could never replace Storm in her heart.

In his quest for complete dominance over her mind and body, he harbored a twisted desire to experience the intimacy Storm and she shared. The thought consumed him as he yearned for a taste of their passionate connection. But no matter how hard he tried, he could not break the impenetrable bond between them.

As agitation brewed within him, Hunter let out an exasperated sigh. His heart blazed with anger as his plans seemed to crumble before him. Seeking solace in his solitude, Hunter turned his attention to Gorgon, who flashed through the imposing double doors of the judgment chambers.

"Ugh! What went wrong?" he growled, his frustration seeping into his words. "That should be me she desires."

Intrigued by Hunter's distress, Gorgon approached slowly, his presence commanding attention. "You are trying too hard, brother," he said, his voice laced with a chilling tone as he took a drink of his wine.

His eyes narrowed as he absorbed Gorgon's words. He realized his pursuit of Talia's affection would require him to unravel the mysteries surrounding her connection to Circe.

He ran a hand through his hair, a smile playing on his lips as he relished the power he held over the scene before him. "I will break her soon," Hunter declared confidently, his voice echoing off the stone walls of his judgment chamber.

"You are not even close, brother," he scoffed. He lounged casually on his brother's throne, exuding an air of menacing wisdom, observing Hunter with a knowing glint in his eyes. "I torture souls for a living. I can tell from here that you've only scratched the surface."

"What do you suggest I do? I have tried haunting her and arousing her," he said, turning around to glare at Gorgon, annoyance dripping in his tone.

"You are new at this. You must find out her fear and use that against her. If you use both fear and desire, you will control her. Once you control her spirit, it will be easy to find Circe's soul." His voice was smooth, yet laced with malice as he imparted his counsel to Hunter.

"Talia doesn't desire me. She wants that Minotaur," he reminded him, his gaze drifting back to the image of Talia and Storm reflected in the pool. "I can't make her want me. Their bond is too strong. It's becoming unbreakable."

"That's because you did it wrong. If she doesn't want you, then make her want him even more. Make her love him."

"Why would I ever want to do that? I want to tear them apart."

"I believe your words were that you wanted to break her. If you break her, she will never love you like Circe did," he warned. "There is still a way to have her, but that is the price you must pay. You must decide what is more important to you. Do you want Talia to love you? Or do you want to own her? You can't have both. Which is it, brother?"

"I want to own her."

"Then make her realize how much she has to lose," Gorgon suggested with a wicked grin. "If you give her a glimpse of what that is, she will begin to break."

"You might have something." He pondered, looking back at Gorgon, eyeing him warily. "What is it going to cost me? You never give out advice for free."

"Let's just say I have a vested interest in your success," Gorgon said with a sly smile.

"Are you still in love with my wife?" he asked suspiciously.

"No. You can have your wife back. I have moved on from wanting Circe. I seek something else." He pushed himself up from Hunter's throne to the pool of blood. With his perverse charm, he stood tall beside the pool. His sly smile hinted at his motives and a web of intricate schemes yet to unfold, which only made Hunter more suspicious. "Although I can see the intrigue with Talia. She is like a warrior princess version of Circe."

"I will have her as my queen."

Talia felt the biting chill of the unyielding floor under her. A strange sensation crept into her mind. Something was off. Her heart raced as she struggled against the invisible restraints holding her in place within the transparent glass cube.

Her eyes fluttered open to a scene far removed from the familiar clutter of her bedroom. She tried to convince herself she was just caught in some fever dream. But everything felt too vivid, trapped within a glass prison that seemed harder than a diamond, bathed in intrusive, white light that danced down upon her like an unfriendly spotlight. The only sound punctuating this bizarre silence was the soft, wavering hum of an overhead fan providing oxygen.

Suddenly, another harsh, bright light cast its glare onto a disturbingly similar glass cage next to hers. As she squinted through the intense radiance adjusting her vision, realization dawned on her. Storm, with a bewildered, lost expression, had also been captured. Strangely enough, he didn't appear to see her at all.

Aching with every move she made against the paralysis that held her captive in her body, she forced herself in his direction. Despite her efforts to move closer to him, she remained frozen in place. Each attempted motion met with resistance, as if the very air around her conspired to keep her trapped.

"Storm!" cried Talia, voicing a desperate plea that filtered through clenched teeth. "Look at me! Storm!" All attempts proved futile; he showed no sign he'd heard or seen anything at all.

Struggling against the invisible force that held her captive, she forced herself to move toward him, her muscles aching with every effort. She could only move an arm, stretching it out toward their shared wall, but not far enough. As she reached out, her fingers brushed against the cold surface of her cage, longing for a connection in this strange and unsettling place.

Storm was right there.

She could not bear to be separated from him.

Her heart craved with an intense longing as she felt the bond between her and Storm slipping away. Her muscles screamed in agony as she dragged herself to the glass wall that separated them, pounding with all her might to catch his attention. But her feeble attempts were nothing compared to the overwhelming weight of their bond, threatening to shatter into a million pieces. Tears fell down her face as she realized there was no escape from this cruel separation.

His gaze tilted slowly upward when suddenly, without warning, the telltale hum dwindled away before dying completely, snapping off his direct supply of breathable air. She could do nothing but watch helplessly as every molecule of life-giving gas siphoned away from him, leaving behind nothing but chilling silence.

He dropped to his knees, gasping for air that wasn't there.

"No! Not like this! Storm!" she wailed as she continued pounding helplessly against their shared barrier of unforgiving glass, all instincts screaming at her to stop what was happening. "Don't do this! Don't take him away from me!" All words shattered into the cold, silent space. She hoped someone would hear her plight. Too soon came her worst nightmare.

"You wanted to love him so much." Hunter's commanding voice reverberated, sending a shiver down her spine. As he entered her glass prison, his imposing figure cast a long shadow that seemed to stretch ominously across the cold, unforgiving floor.

Hunter's piercing gaze locked on her. His presence exuded an aura of malevolent authority, and as he leaned in closer, his breath felt like icy tendrils brushing against her skin. Hunter's voice echoed with a cold authority that commanded attention and obedience. The tone in which he scolded sent a chill down Talia's spine, evoking a sense of foreboding and apprehension about what his next actions might entail.

"You can't do this," she demanded.

Hunter sneered. "I'm not doing anything, Talia. You are."

"That's not possible."

"You wanted to love him so much that you are taking the air he breathes. He is your weakness." He viciously laughed.

Her eyes widened in horror as she witnessed Storm's struggle for breath, his once vibrant and powerful form now reduced to a gasping, helpless figure on his knees. Each gasp from Storm felt like a cruel echo of hope fading away, leaving only a sense of impending loss hanging heavily in the sterile air.

As she pressed her palms against the unyielding surface of her own transparent prison, her heart twisted with agony at the sight of Storm's suffering. Her cries of anguish cut through the stillness, reverberating with a hollow ache that seemed to bounce off the unfeeling walls of their confinement. With every futile attempt to reach him, to comfort him, her own strength wavered against the invisible force that held her back, aching to be by his side in his moment of need.

In that fleeting moment of defiance against fate, she refused to let go of her love for Storm. She refused to accept the suffocating reality closing in around them, clinging to the belief that their bond was stronger than any obstacle thrown in their path. With tears streaming down her face and a heart filled with devotion, she whispered words of solace and reassurance into the void between them.

Storm collapsed, completely motionless, as Hunter snuffed out his life. "Pirate!"

CHAPTER THIRTEEN

TALIA

"Pirate!" Talia screamed, waking up in a daze back in her room. "Storm!" she yelled one last time before she realized where she was. Her opal ring was glowing once again.

"I heard you screaming for me from the basement," he said as he stood over her. "It was a nightmare."

"You're here." She touched his arm, making sure she was awake. "No one took me anywhere. I'm right here."

She was panting, her chest heaving, adrenaline pumping through her veins. The sight of him, alive and unharmed, sent a rush of relief. In an impulsive act of joy, she sprang forward, launching herself into his muscled arms. She brought her hungry lips to his, initiating a passionate kiss that was more than just grateful—it was fiery and raw.

Storm stepped back at her sudden onslaught of affection, adjusting his stance, but it didn't last. She felt his instincts kick in without missing a beat. He deepened the kiss, wrapping his bulky arms around her waist, drawing her closer, letting her feel his hardened muscles pressed against her softness. The warmth radiating from Storm's lips ignited a fire in her, and she succumbed willingly, melting against him like wax in the face of a flame.

They lost themselves in an intimate world of their own until he gently pulled away, his rough hand cupping her flushed face. He looked at her like a man dying of thirst would gaze at water with an intensity that burned even in the dimly lit room.

"Storm," she gasped between short breaths.

A slow smirk spread across his rugged face. "I'll shield you," he reassured her with an undeniable promise laced with raw desire. To seal this intense moment, he brought their lips together again, this time in a slow, sensual kiss—a real one that screamed 'I'm here, and I'm not going anywhere.'

"We haven't slept in days, so now it's a pattern." Olivia said, standing in the doorway of her sister's bedroom, half asleep. "If you two are done sucking face, we should figure out what the hell is going on. I made some coffee."

"Since I put this ring on, I haven't slept." She sighed, following her sister into the living room. "Something is invading my dreams." She accepted a fresh cup of coffee from Olivia. Storm sat on the couch next to Talia and accepted the second cup Olivia was holding.

"I can't take another night. Your emotions are all over the board," Oliva announced over her shoulder as she went into the kitchen to pour herself a cup of coffee. "Last night, one minute I am throat punching Brutus, and the next I'm having hot sex with him."

Storm looked confused.

"We share dreams." She shrugged, trying to downplay Olivia's comment, feeling the embarrassment rise to her cheeks.

"Talia had a sex dream about you," Olivia mumbled into her coffee cup.

"Really? How was I?" He chuckled, making Talia more uneasy.

"With that performance, I wouldn't kick you out of bed." Olivia smirked with a wink.

"Wait. You have powers, too?"

"Yes, but my powers aren't physical like Talia's. I am an empath. I can sense emotions, and sometimes I can communicate telepathically, mostly to Talia," she further explained. "Right now, I can feel the attraction between you two. I am having a hard time focusing."

"You can feel that?" he asked.

"I don't need to be an empath to feel all the emotions in this room," Olivia said, taking another sip of her coffee.

"I think this is beyond us. We need help. I need these nightmares to stop," Talia said, changing the subject.

"We need to figure out what is happening while you are dreaming. Do you remember anything?" he asked.

"No, only that it feels real."

"I might know someone who can help, but you have to keep an open mind about him. He's unusual," he said slowly.

"What? And we're normal?" Olivia said sarcastically. "We could start a campaign of weirdest in this room."

"I would like for you two to at least meet my friend Scooter. He'll know what to do," he said.

"How much do we have to tell him? I mean, I don't exactly run around telling everyone my secret," Talia explained, still feeling uneasy.

"If I figured it out, it would take Scooter about a minute to come to the same conclusion. He has been obsessed with the legend his entire life, and no one has more information than he does."

"Is Scooter the guy who runs around with a lab coat talking to himself? He almost knocked me over the other day. That crazy nut is going to help?" Olivia huffed, crossing her arms.

"Yes, that sounds like Scooter. He has a hard time with manners, social cues, and personal space, but he has the most brilliant mind."

"The first time he gets too close, I reserve the right to punch him," Talia warned.

"Don't worry. I will talk to him." He smiled.

"We do have one other problem," Talia said.

"What's that?" Olivia asked.

"Your houseguest."

"I know it's getting a little crowded in here. I think it's time for me to tell him to go home," she agreed. "I will talk to him."

"Who do you need to talk to?" Brutus asked, appearing in the living room in only his underwear.

Talia groaned. "Do you ever wear clothes? Did you bring any with you?"

"I sleep in the nude. You're lucky I have anything on in the middle of the night." Brutus smiled. "Do you guys ever sleep?"

"Not lately." Storm shook his head.

"I see you spend a lot of time here, Sumerian," he said.

"Well, when Talia needs me, I am there," Storm said, leaning in toward her, his voice carrying a touch of arrogance.

"Right? Talia, just Talia," he said suspiciously. The tension built in the air as he locked eyes with Storm. "Somehow, I don't believe that."

"Well, believe it," Storm said as he stood from the couch. He purposefully closed the distance between him and Brutus. His muscular frame appeared even more imposing at that moment. His chest subtly puffed out as if to assert his authority. He met Brutus head-on, refusing to back down from the challenge. "It's the truth."

Brutus took a step closer, his own chest expanding with new-found defiance. Unfazed by the brewing hostility, Storm calmly took a sip of his coffee. Olivia stepped between the two.

"Before I have to hold your coffee, let's put away the masculine measuring sticks, gentlemen," she requested. "Brutus, can I talk to you in my bedroom?"

"Can you put some pants on too while you're at it?" Talia said to Brutus, rolling her eyes.

"We can talk right here," Brutus insisted.

"Fine, but you're not going to like it." Olivia took a deep breath. "You have to leave. You can't be here right now."

"Babe, it's barely the weekend. I have two more days until I have to be home," he said, softening his eyes and taking a step back.

"I'm sorry, but it's not a good time for you to be here. You showed up at our door without warning," she said, trying to keep her voice steady and calm. "Then you played the part of the jealous boyfriend, running around in your underwear, threatened by a man who is not interested in me. Storm is clearly lusting after my sister and only looks at me if he has to be polite. Otherwise, he is staring at Talia." Her anger rose in her voice. "If you can't see that, you are blind and dumb!"

Storm looked over at Talia, a mischievous smile playing on his lips. In a low, smooth voice, he whispered, "True. I do stare at you, Maverick."

She felt her cheeks flush, sinking back into the couch.

"Wow, babe, if that's how you feel, I know when I am not welcome," Brutus said, backing up, shocked.

"I didn't mean it like that," Olivia said, reaching out for him.

"Sure, you did. I'm glad I know where you stand, Olivia. I will get my things." He disappeared into her bedroom. He returned a few moments later wearing a pair of jeans and carrying his backpack. Without a word, he stomped out of the apartment.

Talia broke the silence. "Hey, he finally put on pants."

CHAPTER FOURTEEN

TALIA

"Pirate, it's so early and you know I haven't been sleeping," Talia said, still groggy from her restless night. She found herself reluctantly being dragged by Storm through Middle Park in the early morning light. Her protests fell on deaf ears as he persisted in his mission, tugging harder on her arm with each step. The sun's golden rays began to filter through the trees. She fought back a yawn as she said, "For Circe's sake, I only had one cup of coffee before you dragged me out of the house."

He abruptly halted their brisk walk and thrust a travel mug toward her. "Here, have some of mine if it makes you stop whining."

Warily eyeing the steaming liquid within, she hesitated before tentatively taking a sip. The taste that hit her tongue was far from what she had expected — a bitter concoction that resembled more of a dark, sludgy mess than the comforting warmth of coffee. With a grimace, she recoiled at the unpleasant flavor, feeling it linger on her palate like a bad dream. Voicing her dissatisfaction, she said, "This isn't coffee. This is a cup of black sludge." She smacked her lips, trying to take the taste out of her mouth. "Where is the cream and sugar? Blah."

Talia glanced at him beside her, his usually mischievous eyes conveying a hint of concern as he watched her reaction to the coffee. His demeanor had been rough and brash since her complaining had begun at the house. The cold morning air was an unwelcome reminder that winter would come soon.

He yanked her arm fiercely, bringing her closer to him. His breath escaped his lips in small puffs of mist in the cold air. His frustration was evident in the way his eyebrows furrowed and his jaw clenched tightly. The intensity of his gaze made her heart quicken, and a slight gasp escaped her mouth.

"Listen, Miss Whiney, you don't get to complain."

"I don't like this crabby, intense Storm."

"I'm crabby because of you. Do you know what's it like for me to be around you?" With the fury rising in his voice, staring down at her, he admitted, "You have been teasing me with that ass of yours and flashing me your tits." His hand balled into a fist at his side. "I spent two days in the basement arguing with the Minotaur. I could smell your arousal, wanting to taste the sweetness between your legs. It's all because the Minotaur in me decided to mate with a woman I can't have. I will be arrested for fucking you, and trust me, Talia, I want to fuck you so badly it hurts. It's my Quickening. My Nibmarks are like knives stabbing me in the shoulder, and cold showers aren't going to help. If that isn't bad enough, whenever I upset you, the Minotaur reminds me to knock it off by grabbing my heart and squeezing." He ran his hand through his hair. "I lost my damn mind, and I couldn't control myself last night. You are my weakness."

"How do you think I feel? Do you think this has been easy for me?" She met his gaze, tilting her chin up, trying to hide her quivering lip. "I'm in love with the Minotaur and in lust with the man. I've been trying to reconcile the difference between you two, and it's driving me mad." She pushed herself closer to him, a rebellious act that surprisingly stimulated her. "Let's not forget the thing that's trying to control my mind in my sleep. It tried to kill me, filled me with desire, and then scared the shit out me. You are the only thing keeping me from falling apart. Tell me, Storm, does the Minotaur control the man or does the man control the Minotaur?"

"You really haven't figured it out, have you?" A smirk slowly crept across his face as he finally relaxed his iron grip on her arm. "I'm not doing anything. You are."

Where have I heard that before?

"Come on, Maverick. We have to get moving or we are going to miss Scooter."

Olivia, what is Quickening?

Oh, shit, is Storm crabby?

Yes, he is unbelievably crabby. He called me by my name and not Maverick.

Whatever you do, don't piss him off. Don't be like your usual Talia self. I will explain everything when you get back.

Well, too late for that.

Without another word, she followed him deeper into Middle Park to the white tent at the Eternal Flame. When they arrived, Scooter was hard at work, moving between two long tables. One stocked with instruments and monitors, and the other covered with tools and parts. He had a tablet in hand and was writing something as he focused on one of the six rocks.

"Holy Anu!" Scooter shouted as he fell back, finally noticing Storm standing beside him. "You scared the life out of my heart! What are you doing here so early?" he asked but didn't wait for the answer. He stood to brush himself off and went back to what he was working on.

His appearance stood in stark contrast to the controlled chaos of his work area. Vibrant red hair framed his face in untamed waves, accentuating his slightly disheveled appearance. Dark circles underscored his vivid green eyes, a testament to long hours dedicated to his research. To appear presentable, Scooter had donned a neatly pressed lab coat. However, it was an uphill battle against his unruly hair and sleep-deprived countenance.

As Scooter turned his attention toward a monitor, his tie fell haphazardly onto his tablet, partially obscuring the notes he had been jotting down. Dismissing it with a flick of his hand, he resumed shuffling between the two tables with an air of urgency. His movements were swift and purposeful as he reached for a handheld device atop the adjacent table. Frustration etched across his face as he tried unsuccessfully to power it on. A few frustrated taps later, he resorted to using a screwdriver to disassemble the device.

"There must be a loose wire. It was working yesterday. Hopefully, it's an easy fix."

"Gentlemen, what do we have here?" Enforcer Sully Markson approached the tent with her hands on her hips, showcasing her badge and gun on her waistband with pride.

Scooter avoided eye contact with the attractive enforcer, turning away from her intense stare. He continued fidgeting with the device in his hands, each movement calculated yet betraying an underlying unease that manifested in how tightly he gripped it.

"Enforcer Suit," Storm said, stepping in between them. "So good to see you again."

"This looks like another experiment. Do you have permits for this equipment, Mr. Harris?"

"Of course, Scooter has permits. This experiment has been sanctioned by the university and approved by your boss," he explained, since Scooter could not speak for himself. "The equipment is used for fact finding only."

"I don't believe that. Whenever something weird happens in this town, you two are always involved." She looked at Scooter and then back at Storm.

For a moment, Scooter looked at her from the corner of his eye, but quickly diverted his attention back to his device. He let out a little frightened squeak.

"I am watching you two," she warned before walking toward Talia.

"Yep, we know, since the day I got here. Thanks for the reminder, Enforcer Suit," Storm said.

"Miss Trismegist, I trust that Mr. Smoke got you home last night." Markson turned back to Storm.

"Yes, Enforcer Markson."

She angled her body toward Talia, hand confidently planted on her hip as she whispered, "That's two days in a row with Storm Smoke. You broke some kind of record."

"What do you mean?" she asked, looking at the Markson's profile.

She nodded in his direction and said, "I've never seen him with the same woman twice. You're the first." She turned to face Talia. "Let me give you some advice about that guy. I've seen him bring women before, but never the same one twice. Don't waste your time on that heartbreaker. He's not worth the jail time."

I don't know if I should be happy or hurt.

"I would rather not." Talia smiled. "I appreciate the advice."

"You seem sweet. Take care of yourself," she said before she walked away.

"That enforcer scares me," Scooter mumbled. "That is all I need, for her to be nosy."

"Forget about Enforcer Suit. We have more important things to worry about." Storm waved his hand in front of his friend's face. "Scooter, I need you to stop for a moment."

"Storm, I only have two more hours to work in complete silence before this place is filled with people and their gossip. Ugh! It's so distracting the way they carry on about their lives. Blah. Blah..." He carried on. "The snow is coming, and I am getting cold out here."

"I found her," Storm interrupted.

His words seemed to fall on deaf ears as Scooter continued his rambling monologue, oblivious to the urgency in Storm's voice.

"I don't have time for this. I told you I am on a deadline. This is probably the last day I can work outside unless I want to do this during winter, which I really don't. I will have to wait another six months until summer." He removed the small screws to look inside. "This machine is not working for me. I have to figure out why. I'm already behind schedule." He vented his frustration, lost in his own world.

This guy is going to be fun. I'm already annoyed by him. Storm looks like he has so much more patience.

Ignoring Scooter's obliviousness, he repeated himself in a calm and unwavering tone. "I found her."

Scooter stopped.

Finally, he halted his ceaseless muttering. Setting down his broken device, he locked eyes with Storm, his expression transforming from absentmindedness to rapt attention. Storm patiently allowed the importance of his statement to settle upon Scooter's mind. A flicker of uncertainty danced in his widened eyes as his entire body tensed with anticipation.

I can't image what is going on in Scooter's head right now. I think it might explode.

"Stop. I know your mind is racing right now, but I need you to focus on me for a minute. Are you still with me, Scooter?" he asked. "I know you have a brilliant mind, but you look like you are getting lost in your own thoughts. Come on, buddy, you can do this."

"You found her," Scooter said slowly, allowing the information to sink in. "Who is she? Where is she? Were you able to confirm her Nibmarks were fake?" His right eye was twitching rapidly, and his words were pouring out of him just as fast. "I need to meet her. I need to study her. I need to ask her questions. I have so many questions."

Oh. fuck, no! For the love of Ki, he is not getting near me.

"Scooter, she is real." He grabbed Scooter, shaking him with excitement as his face lit up.

Is that what he looks like when he talks about me?

"Which one is she? Is she the tall blonde or the red-haired one with the big eyes? Is it any of those? What were their names again?"

"No, it's not. Don't freak out," Storm begged as he motioned for Talia to come closer.

He reached out and grasped Scooter's arm, turning him to meet Talia's gaze. Scooter's eyes widened in shock as he caught sight of her. Gradually, his eyes rolled back into his head and his legs collapsed beneath him. Reacting quickly, Storm lunged forward and caught his fallen friend before he hit the ground.

Great, he faints.

As Storm propped his buddy up again, Scooter opened his eyes and said, "Storm, I had the best dream. I was standing in front of Queen Circe."

"Yeah, Scooter, that wasn't a dream." Storm nodded in Talia's direction.

"She really looks like Queen Circe." He pushed Storm aside to get up close to Talia. He walked around her. "It's like looking at a moving statue of her."

Storm shook his head and chuckled. "Scooter, it's called personal space. I wouldn't get that close."

As Scooter took another step closer, Talia felt a hint of unease growing within her. Small sparks of lightning danced on her fingertips as she lightly shocked his shoulder to give him a subtle warning. The unexpected jolt sent him jumping back, rubbing the spot where she had made contact. "If you get that close again, it will be a full lightning bolt."

"I warned him." Storm smiled. "We need your help. Grab some of those fancy toys and come with us to the house."

With a loud clatter and thump, Talia, Storm, and Scooter burst through the back door, their arms laden with equipment. The cold air seeped into the apartment as they struggled through the door. Their footsteps echoed across the floor as they headed into the living room.

"Nice lab coat," Olivia said sarcastically, referring to Scooter's bland form of wardrobe as she sipped on her coffee at the kitchen table, still wrapped in her robe.

"Its standard university issued."

Olivia scoffed a little. "I can tell."

Storm officially introduced everyone. "Scooter, this is Olivia."

Talia dumped her armful of equipment on the couch, returned to the kitchen, and asked, "Do you have any more of that coffee? I need some cream and sugar."

"This place isn't very big, but I can make it work as a home base. We'll have to move all this furniture so I can have room for my workstation. Do you have a projection board? If not, I have a portable one. Let's clear this place out," Scooter said.

"Scooter, we are not clearing out their furniture. This is their home, and we are going to have to work around them," Storm said.

"How am I supposed to work?" Scooter asked as his body shook. "I can't work this way."

"Is he having a seizure?" Olivia asked with a lower brow and a wrinkled nose. "He doesn't look so good."

"I guess he does that," Talia said as she poured herself a cup of coffee.

"He's fine. It's his natural response to anxiety when he doesn't get his way," Storm explained. He grabbed Scooter by the shoulder, turning his friend to face him. "You can do this, and I am going to help you. We can work around this current setup and still make you feel comfortable. Do you trust me?"

"We will have to sterilize everything. I can feel the germs in here. I hate germs," Scooter said.

"Do you trust me?" Storm asked again.

Scooter stopped shaking when he said out loud, "You've never let me down. I trust you."

"I'll help you get set up," Storm promised. "Olivia, I need your help to wipe down all the surfaces."

"I don't dust," she quickly replied.

"By the look of this place, that's obvious," Scooter said, looking around at the layers of dust.

Don't kill Scooter. We need him.

Before she could enjoy any of her fresh brew, Talia's arm was suddenly in Olivia's grip as she was pulled into her sister's bedroom. "Help me pick out an outfit."

"What is a Quickening?" Talia asked as soon as Olivia shut the door.

Olivia's sparkling eyes were wide with anticipation, and she couldn't contain her excitement any longer, letting out a high-pitched squeal that echoed through the room. Her entire body seemed to vibrate with energy as she bounced on her toes, barely able to contain her joy. She curled up on her bed with a pillow in her lap. Talia sat at the foot of bed like they were teenagers about to have a girls' night to talk about cute boys.

"Quickening is a man's sexual climax, and it ranges in intensity for each region. For Enochian men, like Scooter, they don't experience anything. He wouldn't know it was happening. Anunnakian men will have a mild intensity level, but it's manageable." Olivia brought the pillow up her chest to hug it and let out a little squeal. "Brutus said he was in the first stage, and Anunnakian men stay there for a long time. It was such good sex. I mean, it was spine tingling, toe curling, and then tell all your friends about it."

Talia rolled her eyes. "Is that why he was naked all time?"

"Brutus could not get enough of me, and he lasted for a long time. Of course, we kept getting interrupted, and that's why he left so frustrated. I am sure he's enjoying his Quickening with some other girl back home." She shook her head. "Let him have his fun. There are other men who are having their Quickening. I heard it's even better with a Sumerian man because it's intense. It's like slam me against a wall, rail my pussy, spank my ass, and call me your good girl until I tap out."

Talia's eyes widened in shock as her mouth fell open in a gasp as if someone had punched her in the stomach. She leaned back quickly, her body tensing as she tried to process her sister's words. She realized she was too close to the edge of the bed, but it was too late. Her body twisted and flailed before landing hard on the floor with a jarring, loud thud. She shifted onto her back, catching sight of her sister's face peering over the edge of the bed, her hair cascading around her features.

Bringing her hands to her face, not really wanting to know the answer, Talia asked, "How often does it happen? Please, tell me it's a one-time thing."

"It happens every month." She giggled.

"Every month! I have to put up with this every thirty days?"

Olivia reached out her hand to help her off the floor. "Sex with a man during his Quickening is the best you'll ever have."

"That's great, but I don't have anything to compare it to, sis." She paced the floor, rubbing the side of her thigh that took most of the impact of her tumble. Feeling a dull ache on her right side, she was sure a bruise was forming. "I haven't had sex yet with any man, let alone a man in his Quickening. It sounds painful and gross."

"You let me know what it's like to have hot, feral sex with a Sumerian."

"After what you just told me, I won't be having sex with Storm." Talia stopped pacing, squaring her shoulders and narrowing her eyes, trying to convince herself that would be possible. "I will just have to learn to control myself around him from now on. Let him deal with this Quickening on his own." Her brow began to relax, and she stared off at nothing in particular. "That means no more kissing his delicious lips, no more touching his gorgeous body, no more smelling the scent of musk and cedar in his cologne, and no more sweet sound of his growl." She fell back next to Olivia, letting out a soft sigh as she hit the mattress. "That last one is going to be hardest to resist."

"Do you hear yourself? You're using words that you hate when I say them." Olivia giggled. "You just described Storm using 'delicious lips' and 'gorgeous body.' There is no way you are going to resist him during his Quickening. What stage is he in right now?"

"I don't know. What are the different stages?"

"There are five stages of the Quickening. Stage one is his heightened arousal. The second stage starts with food cravings and appetite."

"I swear, he ate a double cheeseburger in three bites, so he's at least to that stage. What is stage three?"

"That is when his Nibmarks are sensitive, especially the stimulating ones. If you don't want to turn him on, don't touch those." Talia looked confused, so Olivia went on to explain, "I forgot you don't know where a man's stimulant Nibmarks are. Storm's would be on his deltoid muscle on his left shoulder just above where his scar begins. I heard a rumor there might be one behind his left ear where his Nibmarks start, so don't go whispering sweet things in his ear."

"He did complain about his Nibmarks being like knives."

"Storm is for sure in his fourth stage, which is irritability. You said he was crabby earlier. Even though he didn't show it on his face when he walked in the apartment, I could sense anger and frustration from him. The only way to fix it is for him to move to the fifth stage, and he needs help. He can't do it by himself, if you know what I mean." Olivia put her hand on her arm and said, "He must be satisfied. If Storm doesn't satisfy his sexual tension in the six days, I heard Sumerian men are in pain until the cycle starts all over again."

"Oh, great, no pressure. The Minotaur chose me as his mate and won't let Storm have sex with anyone else. If I don't give him my virginity, he will keep going through this every month for the rest of his life."

"Talia," she said as she lay down beside her sister, her tone grave and concerned, "you only have your first time once. You get to decide when that is and who that's with. Don't let anything or anyone, especially me, pressure you into doing something you don't want to. If feel you like you're not ready, wait until you are." She reached out and squeezed Talia's hand. "I know I give you a hard time, but I mean well. You're my favorite sister."

"I'm your only sister, and I love you too."

CHAPTER FIFTEEN

TALIA

S cooter installed his technology in the living room, careful to avoid too much disruption to their lives. He placed cameras with night vision and infrared capabilities in Talia's bedroom and the hallway. He positioned thermal sensors around the apartment to detect sudden changes in temperature. Scooter carried a portable EMF meter with him as he took readings to establish a baseline for his equipment. As she watched Scooter complete each task, Talia's anxiety grew.

She pressed her palms together, feeling the warmth pulsing between them. With each rub, she focused on containing the swirling power within her before it exploded. She could feel the walls of control starting to crumble as the pressure grew stronger. Focusing her emotions, she took long breaths.

"How are you doing?" Storm asked.

"I'm used to spirits watching me before I learned to create boundaries. I'm not used to having cameras watch me," she admitted quietly to him. "It seems strange to me. Will they be recording me sleep all night?"

"We will monitor things like temperatures and changes in pressure in the room. The night vision cameras are for things we can't see in the dark. It's more than just watching you sleep. This equipment serves a purpose. I need you to be safe," he assured her. As if he was tempting the Minotaur, that playful smile spread across his face. "If you prefer, I could always watch you sleep from your bed," he said, closing the gap between them, "especially after that taste you teased me with yesterday."

"I swear, Pirate, if you growl, I'll throat punch you." Talia held up a finger as a warning.

How can he be so sincere one moment and then such an ass the next? Is that his magical power?

"What does this stuff do?" Olivia asked as she pointed to the laptop screen with the cameras and the monitors giving readouts.

"It's measuring thermal changes, pressure changes, electromagnetic fields, and electronic voice phenomena. I have infrared and motion sensor cameras," Scooter explained as he pointed to each monitor and the laptop. "I've got every aspect covered. If there is something in that room, we will know it."

"I don't know what a lot of those words mean, so I will take your word for it. Are you, like, a ghost hunter or something?"

"I prefer paranormal investigator," Scooter corrected her.

"Have you ever seen a ghost? How do you know they exist?"

Olivia, they don't have to know everything about me. You only know because you're in my head all the time.

"I just know they do," Scooter said, sounding a little unsure.

"That sounds like an Enochian. You have a blind belief just to have a belief," Olivia said dryly.

"Actually, my beliefs aren't blind because they are proven by scientific studies, which I believe makes me a defector from the Enoch region," he admitted.

"Your parents must be so proud," Olivia said sarcastically.

Leave the Enochian alone.

"My parents don't know. They believe I am here spreading the good news about Emperor Anu and the Afterlife to all the dammed souls of the young students." Olivia looked surprised by his deception. "I pass out a few brochures a month, and it doesn't make it a lie." Scooter was scribbling notes on his tablet. "I have a theory about who is controlling your dreams, and I have to adjust this equipment to prove my theory."

Scooter jotted some notes on his device. Everyone in the room waited for him to express his point of view.

After an eternity, Talia finally broke the silence. "Are you going to tell us?"

"Oh, right. It's more powerful than a spirit. It has to be a god. That ring is cursed with blood magic to make sure the true owner could never take it off," Scooter said. "Once you put on that ring, King Hunter established a connection with you."

"Is that why the ring glows?" Talia asked.

"Hmm..." Scooter continued to scribble notes, not making eye contact.

"What?" Olivia asked.

Scooter could not take his eyes off his notes. The room filled with a heavy silence as everyone stared at him, waiting for a reply. Talia finally broke the silence with a light shock on his arm to jolt him up from his deep thought.

He jumped back and grabbed his arm as he yelled, "Holy, Anu! That hurts."

Storm chuckled. "Scooter, can you please share with the rest of us?"

Scooter continued to rub his invisible wound. "With the blood magic, it must be a two-way connection. When does it glow?"

"Usually when I wake up," Talia said.

"Hmmm..." Scooter paused and wrote some more notes.

Great. Another long, dramatic pause.

"Scooter!" the trio shouted together.

Startled, Scooter nearly dropped his tablet but quickly recovered it. "So sorry. I usually work alone. I'm not used to sharing information." He regained his composure. "With the way King Hunter has connected with you, the ring must be an early warning device."

"We all know Talia is Queen Circe reborn, so why does King Hunter invade her dreams? He's a god. He should be able to communicate with her directly," Olivia pointed out.

"Because he can't. Our spirits are the subconscious part of what we are. Our souls are the conscious part of who we are. He can only connect with you when you're unconscious," Scooter said.

"Why?" Talia asked.

"We've been under the assumption that Queen Circe was reborn into Talia completely, spirit and soul. What if that weren't true? What if Queen Circe's spirit and soul were separated? King Hunter could only find her spirit, and he was still looking for her soul. The ring has identified with Talia because she looks like Queen Circe."

"Where is Queen Circe's soul?" Olivia asked. Everyone in the room turned to lock eyes with her. "Why is everyone looking at me? You think it's me?"

"I would have to test this theory with my observations tonight," Scooter said.

"It would make sense. You have visions, and you're empathic," Storm said. "Those are both powers Queen Circe was believed to possess. We just have to keep King Hunter from finding Olivia. He isn't going to stop searching. He wants his wife back. We're going to have to slow him down until we can figure out how to fight back."

"King Hunter is our god. He wouldn't hurt me," Talia said, disbelieving her own words. "Gods are not supposed to harm or interfere with Niberians. That is not what we are taught. It must be something else."

"You are not an Anunnakian, Maverick," he reminded her. "What else could it be?"

"I don't believe it," she said firmly. "I have a protection spell on this house."

Mom always said we should thank King Hunter for the gifts in our life. What kind of gift is this?

King Hunter's role was to observe the development of the Niberians and to judge their dead. He has been the one she prayed to for guidance her whole life. Whenever Talia was struggling, it was Hunter she had relied on to show her the way.

"King Hunter is more powerful than a spirit. Your protection spell is not working," Olivia pointed out.

"Believe what you want about King Hunter, but I know first-hand that our gods are not as innocent as we think they are. They have been interfering in our lives since the beginning of our civilization. Think about it," Storm said, looking around the room. "We would not be standing in this room together if our gods had left us alone. Some of us would not exist if our gods had kept to themselves. I don't know what your parents have been telling you all these years, but it's not true."

"Our gods are not cruel. I don't care what you say, Pirate," she said, her anger pushing to the surface. "Just because your gods are assholes doesn't mean mine are."

Talia's devotion to her deities went far beyond admiration. She was convinced of a strong spiritual connection that influenced her beliefs and behaviors. She firmly believed in the benevolence of Circe and Hunter, considering them vital figures in the lives of the Anunnakian. Her faith was deeply ingrained from teachings passed down by her parents.

Why would Hunter test my loyalty like this?

Circe, her hero, represented strength, while Hunter acted as her guiding light. In a world where she felt rejected, she turned to them for support. As a child, she cried out to them when her powers became overwhelming. Her pleas were answered on the night of the fight with her sister thirteen years ago.

"I didn't mean it like that, Maverick," he pleaded, but she wasn't listening.

As she remembered that fateful night, the urge to run overcame her once again. She craved solitude and desperately wanted to escape. Storm reached out for her arm, but she recoiled, not wanting him to touch her. She grabbed her jacket, wrapping it around her as the cold air hit her face when she ran out the back door. As her footsteps retreated down the steps, she heard him call out to her with regret and desperation in his voice.

Fuck you, Pirate!

As she ran to Middle Park, she thought about that night so many years ago. It had changed her life. Her mind flowed with memories of running out of the back door of her childhood home. It stuck with her like an old legend.

As soon as Talia unleashed her powers on her twin, she sprinted outside. Electricity still sparked from her fingertips. She caught a glimpse of Dad emerging from his workshop in her peripheral vision but avoided looking directly at him. The fear in her eyes was something she didn't want him to see. However, when he called out her name, a bolt of lightning shot from her hand and struck his workshop, setting the old wooden structure ablaze.

The sheer force of her power made it difficult for her to maneuver through the complex thicket. Branches thrashed and quaked under the relentless barrage, their wooden limbs contorted and splintered from the sheer intensity of the electrical assault. She tried to avoid the falling debris, dodging with a mix of agility and instinct, but the faster she ran, the more treacherous the obstacles became. Twisted roots reached up from the ground like gnarled fingers, threatening to trip her at every turn. Vines slithered deceitfully along the forest floor, attempting to ensnare her fleeing form and binding her to this chaotic upheaval of nature.

Despite the elemental chaos surrounding her, she could faintly hear her mother's voice echoing in the distance, calling her name with a mixture of worry and desperation. But there was no time for reassurance or solace. Talia knew as long as she remained near others, they would be in danger. Her power roiled within her like a temper, yearning to be released upon anything or anyone unfortunate enough to be nearby.

With conviction, she pushed herself harder, every stride taking her farther away from home, from safety. Sweat mixed with tears streaked down her flushed cheeks as she fought against both her own physical exhaustion and the unyielding storm brewing within her. The air popped around her like an electric shroud, charged with a tangible tension that seemed to vibrate through her very core.

As she continued her desperate escape, the forest seemed to groan under the mass of her power. The once tranquil woodland transformed into a surreal landscape of twisted trees and smoldering ground. The scents of singed wood and burning foliage mingled in the air, creating an acrid aroma that underscored the impending danger. The nocturnal creatures that called this place home fled in fear, their cries blending with the chaotic symphony of crackling energy.

Talia's resolve hardened as she distanced herself from civilization, from the people she loved. Her steps became more purposeful, fueled by a mixture of fear for the others and self-preservation. She couldn't bear the thought of causing harm or destruction to those she cherished most. With each passing moment, her desperation grew, urging her to find a haven far away where her powers could harm no one.

Amid this tumultuous flight, a whirlwind of emotions clouded her mind. Guilt gnawed at her conscience as she left her sister behind, hoping Olivia was safe and unharmed in the chaos she had unleashed. But above all, there was a deep sadness, a longing for control and understanding that weighed heavily on her heart.

As she disappeared into the depths of the wilderness, she knew finding solace and redemption would not be easy. The road ahead was uncertain and fraught with challenges, but she would forge on, driven by a determination to protect those she loved from the tempest that raged within her.

She decided this was her destination upon reaching the white sand beach and hearing the flowing river. She had hoped this place would give her the peace she desperately sought. With a cry of sorrow, she dropped to her knees, burying her hands in the white sand. "I don't want to hurt anyone. I need help." From the heat of her hands, an image burned into the sand surrounding her, beginning with three inward swirls connecting her to the gods.

With the sun setting, the inner ring of the planet shone across the sky as the two moons rose. Talia's cries triggered the glowing of light within this inner ring. In the chaos of her emotions, Talia had a moment of clarity when the right words came into her mind. "I call upon the powers that be. Come to me, I summon thee. Spirits from the other side, cross now the great divide." The glowing light descended upon the beach. Talia witnessed an angelic creature flying on white wings stretching across its back. As the creature approached, Talia realized it was not a creature. The angelic figure was a girl not much older than Talia bearing wings like an angel.

Upon her descent, the young girl's magnificent wings folded in around her, enshrining her in an ethereal cocoon. Each feather was a marvel to behold, an exquisite blend of silvery hues that shimmered under the moonlight, giving the illusion of a liquid silver cape. This celestial cape formed a radiant halo of feathers around her head, enhancing her otherworldly beauty.

A regal crown, glimmering with an inner light, sat majestically on her head, clasped just behind her delicate temples. From the center of the crown dangled a single teardrop-shaped blue sapphire. Its mystical glow was as bright as her radiant skin, a sight that even the darkness of the night couldn't mitigate.

Talia found it somewhat challenging to behold such luminescence, compelling her to squint under the brilliance. In response to Talia's discomfort, the winged girl did a subtle bow of her head and transformed into a more Niberian form. She assumed a pale skin tone, eyes that were as clear and pure as water from a mountain spring, and hair that faintly glowed with an optic white radiance. In this form, she appeared just like any other young girl. She was petite, yet enchanting, with an air of mysterious elegance.

"I heard you, Talia. I am here to help."

"Who are you? How do you know my name?" she asked, stumbling to her feet.

"I am Princess Johara."

"Your Majesty," she greeted her, bowing her head. "I didn't know it was you. Can you help me? I don't want to hurt anyone."

"I know you don't want to hurt your family," Princess Johara agreed.

"What can I do?" she pleaded.

"Your emotions control your powers. They come through your hands. Let me show you something." Princess Johara reached for her left hand, but Talia hesitated and took a step back. "Trust me. You won't hurt me. Give me your left hand."

She held out her left hand, as instructed.

Turning her hand palm upward, Johara explained, "Anger and frustration control your left hand. Now focus and channel that energy into your palm."

Talia's veins boiled with rage as she thought back to the fight with her sister. The room spun around her, and time seemed to stand still, suspending all the game pieces in midair. A fiery force surged through her body, from the top of her head to the soles of her feet before it focused itself on her left palm. With a trembling hand, she opened her eyes, and what she saw made her heart jump. Hovering just above her palm was a brilliant white ball of light that seemed to have grown from within her.

"Did I create that?" she asked.

"Yes, that was all you. You did it. That was a great start. Hold on to that light and give me your right hand. Fear and sadness control your right hand. Keeping your anger and frustration in your left hand, focus, and channel that energy into this hand," Johara instructed.

Talia tightly shut her eyes and felt herself being enveloped in the memory of the fight. The wall now had a gaping hole, and the game pieces lay scattered in broken shards on the bedroom floor. Olivia and Mom stood paralyzed with terror. A chill ran through Talia as she felt energy raging inside her, from head to toe and radiating out of her right arm. An electric shock blazing from her right hand caused her palm to quiver. When she finally opened her eyes, a glowing orb of light hovered above each hand, burning like fire.

"I did it." Talia became eager.

"We're not done yet. Now comes the hard part." Sensing her joy, Johara put Talia's hands close together, joining the two balls into a larger one. Talia held the glowing sphere in both hands, admiring her accomplishment. "Love and happiness together control both hands. Now you can aim it at that rock over there."

Cradling the pulsating, radiant sphere against her chest like a cherished keepsake, Talia promptly turned right and thrust it ahead. It tore through the velvety curtain of the night sky with astonishing speed before crashing loudly against a jagged rock face. An explosion unfolded, brilliant shards splintering from the sphere, showering out and dissolving on impact like incandescent confetti vanishing.

A burst of exhilaration shot through her veins as a triumphant squeal bubbled from her throat. Riding this victorious high, she had impulsively wrapped Princess Johara in a bear hug tight enough to rival a boa constrictor's squeeze. As reality knitted itself back together in the euphoric haze, embarrassment spread over her cheeks at an alarming rate. She hastily unwound herself from the princess and pulled back, treading on an invisible sea of mortification.

The crisp smell of spent magic still hung heavily in the air, mingling with traces of rocky dust triggered by the previous spectacular light show. Talia said sheepishly, "I'm sorry."

"It's all right. That was good."

"Please, teach me more," she begged.

"I will. There is a lot for you to learn. I will teach you," Johara promised. "When you need me, I will always know."

"Talia!" Dad called. "Talia!" He was getting closer. "Talia! Are you out here?"

"I'm over here," she answered. Talia turned to thank Princess Johara, but she was gone. When Dad emerged onto the beach, Talia was standing alone by the river.

"Are you okay?" He hugged his daughter.

"I am now," she said, feeling lighter.

"Your mother and sister are worried about you. Let's go home. There is a hole in the side of the house and a workshop that needs our help." Dad smiled. "Don't worry. It can be fixed."

CHAPTER SIXTEEN

TALIA

S nowflakes, like delicate whispers from the sky, dusted Talia's cheeks as she raced through the fading light toward the Eternal Flame. The iconic flame flickered with a persistence that belied the encroaching chill of the evening, casting a warm glow that seemed to reach for her with each hurried step she took. Ahead, the imposing presence of King Hunter's statue loomed, an eight-foot testament of bronze and reverence standing sentinel by the sacred fire.

Her breath formed ghostly plumes in the air, her heart pounding with a beat that matched her hastening pace. The snow muffled the sounds of her boots against the concrete path that led through the park, creating an eerie sense of isolation as she approached the statue of her god.

With his gaze fixed eternally across the flame, King Hunter stood opposite his queen, Circe, their bronze forms embodying the divine union that had once inspired all Anunnakians. He stood tall, his left fist clenched over his heart.

She stopped abruptly before him, the soft crunch of snow underfoot betraying the turmoil that churned within her. Her eyes, bright with unshed tears, sought answers in the cold, impassive features of King Hunter's visage. She reached out, brushing against the icy surface of his carved cloak, tracing the intricate patterns of power and protection that had always instilled a sense of safety and guidance.

But now, betrayal seeped into every crevice of her belief, tainting the image of the god she had revered. The news that King Hunter could have been invading her dreams shattered the sanctuary of her sleep, breaking the trust she had placed in his divine oversight. She thought he was kind, a benevolent deity meant to guide the Anunnakians with wisdom and love. Yet this revelation painted him in a new, insidious light—one that cast long shadows over everything she had ever been taught about him.

"Kind? Guiding?" The words escaped her lips, a bitter whisper lost in the falling snow. "Was it all a lie?" The question hung in the air, unanswered by the silence of the statues and the solemn dance of the flames. The sense of betrayal clung to her like the cold—it wrapped around her heart, tightening its grip with every thudding beat.

The snow continued its gentle descent, the tiny flakes catching in her hair, on her lashes, as if nature itself attempted to soothe the raw edges of her shock. There was no comfort to be found in the quiet beauty of the evening or the steady warmth of the Eternal Flame. The realization that her god—King Hunter—could be capable of such deception cut deeper than the winter's chill, leaving her feeling exposed and alone beneath the watchful gaze of her once-beloved protector. How could she ever feel safe again?

Her breath formed a misty cloud as she stood before the towering statue of King Hunter, snowflakes settling on the furrowed bronze brow above eyes that seemed to pierce through her. She reached out a trembling hand, the cold metal unyielding beneath her fingertips, contrasting with the warmth she once felt in her heart for this figure of worship.

"King Hunter," she addressed the statue, her voice steadier than she felt, "why are you doing this? Why would you be so sinister?

All I ever wanted was for this world to accept me, so I looked to you for guidance. I needed you." Her words echoed softly around the silent square, as she took a step toward the statue. "This is how you repay me for my loyalty. You betray me. Please," her voice broke, a single tear carving a path down her cheek. "Help me understand."

She searched the statue's face for any hint of the kindness she believed in, any sign of the god who was supposed to protect and inspire his people. But the sculpted features offered no answers, only reflecting the harsh truth—gods, too, could be flawed.

With a heavy heart, she knew she could not unravel this mystery alone. She needed answers that only one person could provide. Closing her eyes against the sting of the cold, she recalled the incantation taught to her long ago. The words slipped from her lips with practiced ease, a spell woven into the chill air, a plea for an audience with royalty.

"I call upon the powers that be. Come to me, I summon thee. Spirits from the other side, cross now the great divide."

When Talia finished the spell, the Eternal Flame exploded six feet in the air, burning in a full blaze. She jumped back, shocked by the intense heat that lit up the park. Staring into the red flames, a figure formed until there was a blinding flash. The flame returned to its usual size, revealing a hovering figure with white feathered wings spread six feet across. The figure had skin glowing like sunlight and white fiberoptic hair. When Talia saw a sapphire crown on her head, she recognized her friend.

"I heard you, Talia."

"Princess Johara." Talia bowed her head. "I need you."

Johara folded her wings, wrapping her in a white cape. She gracefully floated down to the ground like an angel.

"I know, my friend. As promised, I am here," Johara said with a gentle smile.

Talia's hands shook as she held back the angry tears forming in her eyes. She took a deep breath and demanded, "I need the truth." Her voice wavered slightly, betraying her emotions. "I need to know if what Storm and Scooter said is right. Is King Hunter ruthless and controlling?"

"There is some truth in what you are saying, but there is also truth in what you believe."

"Tell me," she urged, her voice barely above a whisper. "Tell me what you know about King Hunter."

Johara's eyes darted to the statue of King Hunter and then back to Talia. "There is something important that I must tell you," she said, her voice carrying a hint of sadness. "I am the daughter of King Hunter, the very tyrant I have been fighting against all this time. Queen Circe was my mother." Johara nodded to the statue in the opposite direction of the queen. "He is the one who forced me to leave you. He sent his soldiers to Nothingness Forest to kill my tribe while I was training you. I couldn't leave the creatures of the Far Viscera defenseless again."

"That's why you stopped coming to Niberia," Talia said softly.

"I never told you before because I knew how much you revered him as a god, and I didn't want to shatter your belief."

"Is anything I know about Hunter true?"

"In the past, he was a compassionate and just ruler. Before my mother's passing, he was a noble king. He embodied all the qualities you admire. I have fond memories of him carrying me in his arms. He was a devoted husband and doting father. I know that's the god you would like to believe exists, but he is gone. My father died the day my mother did. I can't even call him my father now. He is Hunter to me, and he doesn't deserve to be king of the Far Viscera."

"How can you say that?"

"When my mother died, Hunter changed drastically. He became fixated with the idea of bringing her back, regardless of the cost." Her gaze locked on the imposing statue, with eyes narrowing in spite. "We've paid the price for his obsession and vengeance. He was willing to shred the fabric of our realities with dark magic for a mere chance to see her again. He is using a dangerous power he doesn't understand to get to you. He wants you back at his side as his queen."

"His queen," Talia murmured, her fists clenched at her sides. She stared up at the statue. The features of King Hunter that once inspired awe now seemed to mock her naivety. "I've been a pawn in Hunter's game, haven't I? Used for his dark purpose."

"Your light was never meant for darkness, Talia. Remember that," Johara said, placing a reassuring hand on her arm.

The comfort Johara offered was lost on Talia. Betrayal curdled within her, a bitter taste in her mouth. The gentle snowfall could not wash away the stinging revelation; the Eternal Flame could not warm the cold dread that settled in her bones. King Hunter had invaded her dreams, her life, twisting her path towards an end she could no longer recognize. Standing among the statues of the Niberian gods, her faith was shattered, her destiny was uncertain, and her heart ablaze with an anger that yearned for retribution.

"Those training sessions," Johara began, her voice a solemn whisper against the silence of the snowy park, "they were not just lessons in combat and magic. They were preparation for the inevitable confrontation."

"Confrontation?" Talia echoed with disbelief, her eyes never leaving the statue.

"Your destiny was set the day you were born," Johara confessed, her own eyes shadowed by the weight of secrets kept too long. "I trained you to be strong, resilient, a force not to be reckoned with, but you're not ready to face him. At least, not yet."

"Ready?" Talia's voice rose, frustration seeping through. "How could I ever be ready for this? To fight a god?"

"You are more than a trained fierce warrior, Talia." Her words were firm. "Before you can stand against Hunter's darkness, you must embrace Circe's light within yourself."

Talia shook her head. "I don't understand. How do I find this light when Hunter is filling my head?"

Johara took a step closer. "It's in your heart, Talia. You've been so focused on trying to fit into your world, you have been denying the human god you are. You have to accept you're human. You asked how to fight a god."

She nodded.

"Only a god can defeat a god. Unleash your warrior spirit and let that guide you. As long as you believe in yourself, Circe will never fail you. She lives in you, but you have to see it." She turned Talia to Circe's statue. "You are powerful, compassionate, and capable of great light. Do not let Hunter's darkness define who you are. Be the god you admire. Be Queen Circe."

She wanted to dismiss Johara's words, to refuse the identity thrust upon her, but the truth resonated deep within, stirring something she tried to bury. She was not an innocent, insecure pawn in Hunter's fantasy to possess his beloved wife. She wasn't going to let him have her.

She was a warrior goddess queen. She was three times great.

Talia looked back at the statue of King Hunter, her fists still clenched. The image of him, once a figure of awe and respect, now stood before her as a symbol of manipulation and deceit. His features, once noble and regal, now seemed to mock her very existence.

With a deep breath, she closed her eyes and reached within herself, searching for the light Johara spoke of. The warmth of the Eternal Flame seemed to pulse in time with her heart, and she felt a surge of power.

When she opened her eyes, the world around her seemed to sharpen, as if she were seeing it through a new lens. The air crackled with energy, and the Eternal Flame roared to life. She raised her hand toward the statue of King Hunter, the ground beneath it trembled, and lightning struck all around.

"Hunter, I hope you're listening," she yelled. "You can't have me. You will never have me. I'm not your wife, but I am three times great. Come and get me, asshole! I'm right here. If you want to fight, show your face." As Talia's challenge echoed through the park, the Eternal Flame roared higher, acknowledging her embrace of her inner goddess. It was the truth of her existence shining through like a beacon of hope. This was what she was destined for, the moment when she would rise above her insecurities and fears and claim her rightful place as a powerful force in the world. "I am human."

"Well, it's about time, Maverick. You finally said it out loud."

Her face twisted in fury; she spun to see Storm's smug expression. Without hesitation, she charged toward him with a fierce battle cry, launching herself into the air and delivering a powerful blow to his chin. The force of her punch sent him stumbling backward, his smile quickly fading into shock and pain.

He staggered, clutching his jaw as he struggled to regain his footing.

She had never before unleashed such raw power on anyone. Her chest heaved as she struggled to rein in her anger.

"That's for trying to make me jealous."

"Talia, wait!" he called, but she was already charging at him again, her fists clenched and her eyes still burning. He barely had time to react before she was upon him, delivering another blow with a strength and speed she didn't even know she had. He fell on one knee and tried to shake it off.

"That's for turning me on and making me all hot."

"Okay, we're doing this," he declared, standing and looking at her. "Let me see your fierce warrior, Maverick."

He braced himself for the third swing, muscles tensed and ready. Just as her fist whizzed toward his face, he sidestepped and caught her wrist in a firm grip. With a swift movement, he spun her around so that her back was pressed against his chest, imprisoning her in his strong arms.

Talia was not one to give up easily. She managed to wrench free and deliver a sharp elbow to his gut, causing him to double over in pain and loosen his hold on her. Breathing heavily, he stumbled back, giving her a momentary advantage in their sparring match.

She whirled to face him, her eyes blazing with anger and hurt. "That's for pissing me off and then being honest."

As she took in his expression, her jaw unclenched and her shoulders relaxed. Her lips parted slightly in surprise. In that moment, all her defenses melted away, leaving her vulnerable and exposed before him.

"This is for believing in me and seeing me for who I am when I couldn't."

Talia charged toward him once again, her steps quick, her eyes locked on him. He flinched, bracing himself for another powerful blow from her fists. Instead, she threw herself at him with surprising force, wrapping her arms around his neck as she pressed herself against him and sought his lips for a passionate kiss.

His hands found their way to her hips, pulling her closer as their tongues danced together. His lips tasted of salt and sweat, but also of something sweet and intoxicating.

As they broke apart, both were left breathless, their chests heaving as they stared into each other's eyes. His grip on her hips tightened, and he pulled her even closer, their bodies pressed together as if trying to become one.

Her eyes fluttered shut, and she rested in Storm's embrace, feeling his warmth surrounding her. For a moment, all the pain and confusion of the past few days seemed to melt away, replaced by a feeling of pure, unadulterated happiness.

As quickly as it had come, the happiness was replaced by a gnawing sense of dread. Her eyes snapped open. As she pulled away from him, her brow furrowed in concern.

"What is it?" he asked, his voice laced with worry.

"Forgive me for this," she whispered.

Before he could ask, she pushed him away. He stumbled back, seeming surprised by her sudden aggression. Her hand connected with his cheek in a sharp, stinging slap. The noise echoed through the park.

"You have some nerve, Storm, bring her here!" she yelled as she pointed to Johara. "What were you thinking?"

Markson approached to ask, "Miss Trismegist, is everything okay?"

"Yes, Enforcer Markson." Talia moved away from Storm and approached the enforcer, speaking to her. "You were right. He's not worth the heartbreak."

"Mr. Smoke, what did you do now?" Markson gestured to his face, where the bruises from Talia's punches were showing. "It looks like you fell on someone's fists."

"I guess I should be more careful not to trip."

Markson angled toward Talia, giving her a playful nudge. She said, "I knew there was something I liked about you. I see you can take care of yourself if he touches you again." She straightened and smirked, turning back to him. "Mr. Smoke, you better get some ice on that. It looks like it's going to be a nasty bruise."

"Thanks for the advice, Enforcer Suit," Storm said as she walked away.

Shit, I really kicked his ass.

CHAPTER SEVENTEEN

HUNTER

"She can't be in love with him!" Hunter announced in a jealous rage. "I don't know if I can take this."

In the dimly lit judgment chambers, he paced, his eyes filled with burning jealousy as he watched Talia and Storm grow closer. The image of them together, their affectionate embraces and passionate kisses, fueled his anger and obsession. It was a torment he couldn't bear.

Furious, he summoned his staff, a symbol of his power and authority. Gripping it tightly, he hurled it across the room in an explosive display of rage. As it soared through the air, the staff transformed into a deadly spear, its shaft glistening with malevolence. At its tip, a vibrant red sapphire gem radiated, pulsating with dark, mysterious magic.

The spear struck one of the double doors with a thunderous impact, narrowly missing Lieutenant Malta, who had just entered the chamber. The force of the blow left a deep indentation on the sturdy wood, a visible testament to Hunter's fury and the immense power he possessed.

Breathing heavily, Hunter's voice echoed through the chamber as he declared his sinister intent. "I must turn Talia against him," he said. He plotted to dismantle the love that had blossomed between Talia and Storm. In his twisted mind, he couldn't fathom that she could truly be in love with someone else.

The air in the room hissed with tension as his jealousy consumed him. He was driven by an insatiable desire to tear apart their connection, to sow seeds of doubt and discord within Talia's heart. In his pursuit of power over her emotions, he would stop at nothing to manipulate her affections and turn her against Storm.

As the sapphire gem continued to emanate a red hue, casting macabre shadows across the chamber, his determination grew stronger. His actions and intentions became darker, his resolve unyielding. Those entwined in this intricate web of desire and power would have their fate determined by a battle of emotions, where love and jealousy clashed.

"At least that little weasel scientist found Circe's soul for me." Hunter smiled. "I will have to thank him for that. He did the work for me."

"Olivia is an empath, so it should be easy to get in her head." Gorgon smirked. "It's almost too easy."

"King Hunter," Lieutenant Malta greeted him, kneeling on one knee, bowing his head, and placing his left fist across his body to his heart.

"Yes, Lieutenant," he said, turning away to take a seat on his throne.

"I come with word from Nothingness Forest. There are rumors of a rebellion," Lieutenant Malta said. "Princess Johara is leading the treason."

"Her tribe is defenseless with Princess Johara in the living world. If you can find where they are hiding in Nothingness Forest, you should be able to squash this rebellion before it begins," Gorgon suggested.

"Take care of those rumors. You know what to do with the Woobles," Hunter replied.

"Yes, Your Majesty. I will show them your true wrath."

"True wrath." Hunter sprang from his throne with the corners of his lip curling into a wicked smile. He had a plan, and it was clear he was eager to put it into action. Turning to the pool of blood, his gaze shifted back toward Talia and Storm as he sneered viciously at their blissful ignorance of his plans. "That gives me an idea. I will show Talia the true face of her beloved. I am done just reaching out in her dreams. I need to be near her."

"Are you sure that's a good idea, Hunter?" Gorgon asked.

"I need to stop these childish games with her and go to the living world. I will have to show her who Storm Smoke is. His truth wrath."

Calling upon the blood magic for his dark purpose, he chanted, "I call upon the powers that be to show the face of love to see. Unleash the beast from within to reveal his wrath of desire therein."

Feeling the intoxicating heat of Storm's presence, Talia snapped awake, her heart pounding as she locked eyes with a strikingly handsome man possessed by a demon. His red eyes glowed in the shadowy room, and a dangerous thrill shot through her as he pinned her to the plush bed. His hands were firm, his lips insistent and demanding on hers, igniting a forbidden desire she didn't dare to admit.

The ring on her finger cast an unnatural light, transforming Storm into a beastly silhouette on the wall. It wasn't him, she knew. Not really. He seemed to be under a spell, consumed by a power she didn't understand. As she tried to resist, Storm's transformation became more pronounced. His muscular frame grew, and horns sprouted from his head, morphing into a beastly Minotaur.

Her fear tinged with an unexpected ecstasy as she saw him tower over her, his bull-like face mere inches from hers. The gruff growl that rumbled from his chest sent shivers down her spine, and the sight of his muscular form made her pulse race. She closed her eyes, willing it to be just another sensual nightmare, but it wasn't.

As she trembled beneath him, a desperate plea passed her lips. "Please... don't hurt me."

"I want to taste you, Talia." His voice was deep and demanding, just like the rolling thunder in his name.

This was not how she'd imagined being with him, not wrapped in fear but in desire. She felt utterly ensnared, all control slipping from her grasp. In that moment, he was more than just the man she yearned for; he had transformed into an untamed beast, insatiably looking as if he were starving for her. She felt like his feast.

As he hovered over her like a predator stalking its prey, she couldn't ignore the visceral energy he emanated. The bulging muscles of his arms were a hard contrast to the softness of her own delicate form beneath him. His chestnut hair fell into his eyes, partially obscuring their dark purpose but adding to his savage appeal. She was hopelessly drawn to him, her body kindled with a carnal ache that only he could soothe.

He seemed transfixed; his hands started to explore. His rough fingers traced a path from her slender neck down to her supple breasts, relentlessly kneading the sensitive flesh through the thin fabric of her nightgown. Her breasts ached with need, the rosy tips taut and throbbing from the torturous tease of his fingers.

Her body arched instinctively at his touch, her back bowing and her muscles tensing. A low, sultry moan escaped her lips as his fingertips grazed over her nipples, sending a shiver of anticipation through her body. The fire within her blazed brighter with each passing moment, fueled by the intense desire that consumed her every nerve ending.

She surrendered to the overwhelming sensations, unable and unwilling to resist him any longer. With a deep breath, she opened herself fully to him, inviting his touch and giving in to the pleasure that awaited her.

"Oh, fuck, Talia," he growled, his voice laced with raw desire. His firm hand slid farther down, making its way to pull back the sheets. A gasp left her mouth as his fingers brushed against the warmth of her thighs, sending waves of arousal surging through her.

With sure-handed confidence, his hand slid up her nightgown, and his fingers grazed against the wet silkiness of her heat. She bucked against him as he took his time circling around that sweet spot, teasingly slow, before dipping into her slick folds.

"Storm..." She breathed out his name like a prayer, or perhaps a sin. Her breath hitched when he inserted two thick fingers inside her. A delightful whimper echoed in the room as he began to pump his fingers in and out of her slick entrance at a steady pace.

She squirmed under him, waves of pleasure crashing over her as his skilled fingers worked their magic on her throbbing core. Her legs instinctively spread wider for him to gain unrestricted access to have more of what she offered. With one final thrust of his fingers, he sent her over the edge. Her body convulsed around his fingers as she cried out in ecstasy. Storm pulled away from her, his gaze locked on hers. With a growl of desire rumbling deep in his chest, he moved back down, ready to taste her. She felt like she was a feast laid out before him, and he was famished.

She watched as he positioned himself at the end of the bed, staring at her. He wrapped her legs around his shoulders and teased her fiercely with his lips, letting his tongue dance across her clit, tasting her. He moaned against her pussy. She seized his horns, using them as leverage to guide him deeper into her pleasure. She sang the sweet song of uncontrollable short, hot moans to match the fury his tongue was unleashing on her, begging him not to stop.

"So sweet." He groaned.

When she leaned into her desire for him, an unsettling feeling came over her. Her hands flew above her head, pinned to her pillow by an invisible force. She couldn't move. Paralysis overcame her. Her moment of pleasure was turning to fright.

Across the dark room was a sinister presence, the unmistakable glowing red staff casting light on Hunter's leering face. He was observing their erotic dance. Fear caught in her throat when he crossed the room and leaned over her face.

Hunter mocked her. "Talia, love, I own him now. I can make him pleasure you or hurt you."

Storm continued his oral pleasure on her, grabbing her thighs with an iron grip. Arousal glazed her eyes, and she felt her hot cheeks as she threw back her head in ecstasy. Her legs quivered around his broad shoulders, trembling at each passionate assault from his skilled mouth.

While her body responded to Storm, Hunter, a reminder of their twisted dynamics, filled her mind with fear. Hunter observed them with a twisted smile curling his lips. Possessive pride flared in his eyes when he saw how frenziedly she squirmed under Storm's touch.

"This isn't a dream. I am real, and I am always watching you, my queen," Hunter declared. His laughter reverberated through the room, haunting and menacing. "Defy me again and I will turn your beloved beast against you."

The pleasure abruptly stopped as the Minotaur closed in on her, his hot breath mingling with the lingering scent of her own arousal. In a swift move, he grasped her delicate neck in his massive hands and squeezed. With her arms pinned and helpless, there was nothing she could do to stop Storm from choking the life out of her. Every sharp inhale felt like a stab, every gasp for air a futile struggle against the unrelenting grip of the beast. The world began to dim around her as she fought for survival, the sweet memories of their passionate encounter fading into a terrifying nightmare.

She heard a faint, menacing laugh.

As quickly as he appeared, she found Storm's monstrous form melting back into his Niberian shape, an irresistibly rugged

Sumerian. His crimson gaze softened, as if waking from a deep slumber. Storm seemed disorientated as he released his grip from her neck, the powerful weight of his toned body shifting off hers abruptly. His eyebrows furrowed in confusion, but then his eyes widened, and his mouth dropped open as the truth finally sank in.

She watched him with anticipation pooling in her belly. With the paralysis gone, she scrambled to the edge of the bed. A mix of fear and curiosity reflected in her eyes as she reached out to him. Their animalistic encounter had left her yearning for more. He wasn't just a man to her. He was a phenomenon whose very presence made her pulse race out of control.

He asked, backing away from Talia's gesture of kindness, "Did I hurt you?"

"That wasn't you."

"I don't remember. I'm so sorry."

"Storm, I know you would never knowingly hurt me." She reached for him once again. This time, he accepted her hand. She pulled him toward her to sit on the edge of the bed.

"I shouldn't be this close to you right now."

"This is exactly where you should be." She placed her hand on his chest. "I don't want this to happen again. Please, I beg of thee, just let him be. Cloak him from evil forces. Shield him from unseen forces." She surrounded him in a protective white light.

"That felt warm all over," he said.

"That was a protection spell."

"What do I need protection from, Maverick? What happened?" he asked with concern rising in his voice. "I can taste you on my lips."

"King Hunter. He has gone too far now," she said with anger boiling to the surface. "It's one thing to invade my dreams, but now he's manipulating my Minotaur."

Talia's blood boiled with uncontrollable rage as she seethed with anger at the mention of King Hunter. Her fists clenched, her teeth ground, and a primal yell escaped her clenched jaw. She jumped

out of bed. As she paced, her thoughts were consumed with revenge against the god who dared to manipulate her and her lover.
"I am not going to let that bitch get away with it. I don't care
if he's a god or not. No one messes with my Minotaur." A dark
fire burned in her violet eyes as she turned to face him, her body
trembling with contained fury.

With amusement evident in his voice, he said, "I like this Talia.
She's kind of hot."

Her world turned upside down. After years of blind faith in
the gods, she was now faced with the truth that Storm had been
trying to tell her. It shattered what she had always believed, and
she couldn't deny it any longer. The very beings she had trusted
and revered were selfish and cruel. She couldn't bear the thought of
being like them, controlling and manipulating her people for her
own amusement. They did not simply watch over the Niberians
and judge their dead.

A shiver ran down her spine as she finally accepted the full
truth. She was just like the gods, with the power to control and
manipulate her people. The realization hit her like one of her own
lightning bolts, for she never wanted this burden. She never asked
for this fate, given to her before she took her first breath.

These powers she believed were a gift, but now felt more like a
curse. She blamed the ring she wore. That only served as a reminder
of what she was. To truly confront the gods, she must first admit
she was one of them.

"King Hunter messed with the wrong goddess."

"Let the record reflect, you just admitted you're a goddess, Maverick," Storm said.

"You're damn right. I'm a goddess."

CHAPTER EIGHTEEN

TALIA

T alia's eyes fluttered open, and she found herself in the familiar comfort of her own bed. Storm was beside her, his strong arms wrapped protectively around her. She could feel his warm breath against her neck, and the sound of his steady heartbeat lulled her into a sense of peace.

Her body refused to budge, anchored by an overwhelming desire to stay in this moment with him. Every inch of her being craved his presence, and she longed to be lost in his embrace for eternity. This man who drove her crazy in so many ways now seemed so comfortable.

She molded her body to his, fitting like a puzzle piece against the strength of his chest. Her back pressed firmly against his solid frame, as if seeking refuge from the outside world. Her gaze fell to his forearm, where a bold purple and silver tattoo caught her eye. She reached out and ran her finger along the outline, feeling the raised lines and smooth shading.

My shield.

She was torn between the comfort of his presence and the realization of what had happened last night. As she clung onto him, her mind replayed the intense pleasure she had felt from the lips of the Minotaur and the fear from Hunter's control over him. She didn't know how to feel about the conflicting emotions swirling inside her. Was it wrong to find pleasure in such a frightening situation? She buried her face in her pillow, hoping to find some clarity in the chaos of her mind.

She pleaded with him to stay by her side after what had happened, on the condition that they keep their clothes on. She knew the risk of having him in her bed while he was in the middle of his Quickening, but she didn't want to be alone. Her desire for him was undeniable, but she wasn't ready to give up her virginity just yet. The idea of confessing to him that she was inexperienced with men made her stomach twist uncomfortably. It was her secret, one she held tightly to herself.

Storm muttered under his breath, "I really hope I'm not dreaming."

Talia turned over onto her back to face him. His eyes remained shut, but he had a gentle smile on his lips instead of his usual smirk. He held her closer, pressing his nose into her hair as he let out a contented sigh.

He whispered, "Please, tell me I'm lying in bed with a goddess." He slowly opened his eyes and gazed down at Talia, his expression filled with wonder. "You're real," he murmured, his voice husky with sleep. His gaze shifted to her lips. She thought he might lean in to kiss her, but he hesitated, as if unsure of what to do.

Talia smiled. "I'm real," she confirmed, reaching up to brush a stray lock of hair from his forehead. "This Pirate is very sweet. Where has this guy been?"

Sweet Storm. I didn't think it was possible.

"Well, let's see. I've had a beast raging inside, a Quickening making me crabby, and a god causing shit." He smirked, resting his head back on the pillow. "Let's not forget about the warrior goddess queen driving me mad and kicking my ass last night. This sweet side has been hiding. Not many people get to meet this guy."

"That was a little crazy last night."

"A little? I have a feeling life with you is never a little crazy, but I love chaos. It's in my name."

Her hand gripped his chin and turned it toward the light. A crimson welt stood out on his skin just below his facial hair, a result of her earlier punch. With a tightening in her chest, guilt washed over her as he groaned in pain.

She unfurled her hand and focused on the power of healing within her. Gently, she placed her palm against his cheek, allowing the warmth and light to flow from her fingertips into his skin. She could feel his tension melting away under her touch.

"That should help." Lowering her eyes, she said, "I'm so sorry for attacking you last night. I've no idea what got into me."

"It was an asshole god trying to manipulate you, but you didn't let him." Shrugging one shoulder, he said, "Besides, I needed it for my aggression. The Minotaur seems to be content for now." A playful smile tugged at the corners of his lips. "It's not because of our sparring match. I may not remember everything that happened last night, but he sure does. He's sending me pictures of his favorites moments since you asked me to stay." He released a low growl. "Since you asked for clothes on, it was a struggle to be a gentleman with your beautiful ass rubbing against my cock all night."

One more growl will get me in trouble. Must resist him.

When she shifted in discomfort, the smooth satin of her nightgown clung to her curves and offered little protection. She attempted to slide subtly away from him, feeling exposed and vulnerable in the thin fabric.

With a sudden movement, he pulled her toward him, forcing her to roll on her side and press her chest against his. Her breath caught in her throat as she felt the warmth of his skin against hers. "Oh, no, you don't, Maverick," he groaned. He gripped her firmly and possessively by the waist, pulling her even closer. His hand slid down to grasp her bottom with a firm hold, making it clear that he didn't want her to move. "You leave that beautiful ass right where I can reach it." His voice was low and husky.

Her body tensed. She couldn't bear to meet his gaze, knowing it would only intensify the heat building within her core. The dampness between her legs and her increasing heart rate gave her a physical reminder of the desire she was attempting to suppress.

He is making this so hard.

The comforting smell of his skin filled her nostrils as she lay there. She couldn't believe how bold and assertive he was being. It made her blood boil, and she felt herself responding to it, even though she knew what he wanted would go against everything she'd promised herself. As he held her close, it was becoming difficult to ignore the desires growing inside her.

"Pirate, I don't know if I can do this," she whispered into his chest. She bit her lip and glanced at him from the corner of her eye, taking in his powerful chest and defined abs. Her heart fluttered as she felt his warm breath against her neck.

"Do you want me to stop?" he asked, allowing his hand to wander down to her thigh, voice low and raspy with desire.

His fingers dug into her thigh with a bruising force, dragging her leg over him as if daring her to resist. His hand traveled up her body, greedily clenching the fabric of her nightgown and yanking it up, exposing her delicate skin.

She didn't answer for a moment, feeling conflicted between what she wanted and what she knew was right. Her fists clenched against his chest, fighting the need that coursed through her body. Finally, she shook her head softly, feeling him let out a growl of satisfaction that rumbled through his chest and into hers. He nuzzled into her hair again before speaking. "Good," he muttered hoarsely.

She gasped at the sensation, her body responding to his touch with an intensity she had never experienced before. She felt his arousal pressed against her, and it only fueled her own desire. Without hesitation, he pressed his warm, eager lips to hers in a passionate kiss that left her breathless.

Oh, shit. Good morning, Pirate.

Her heart raced as she felt Storm's warm touch against her bare thigh. She wanted to resist, knowing that she was not ready to give herself to him completely, but her body betrayed her. She found herself arching into his touch, her hips swaying in rhythm with his movements.

"No," she whispered, barely able to speak through her hushed, trembling voice. "I can't."

"You're right," he said, his voice soft and warm as he pulled back from their embrace. He slowly released her, fingers lingering on her skin before finally letting go. As they locked eyes, the space between them felt charged with an unspoken longing and desire. They both let out a shaky breath, unable to deny the overwhelming pull toward each other. They fell onto the bed. "I did promise to be a gentleman."

"One more growl, and I would have made you break that promise."

Oh, shit. Did I say that or just think it?

As her ears picked up the low rumble of a growl, she reacted instinctively, rolling over and hovering above him with her hand clenched into a tight fist. She pressed against him, ready to strike at any moment. She gave a warning, her voice low and intimidating. "Do you want a throat punch, Pirate?"

"No, I had enough of your punches." He chuckled, putting up his hands. Then his expression turned solemn. He gently took her hand and opened her fist, guiding it to rest against his chest. "Seriously, Maverick. If you need to take a break, just let me know. I assume you've never been with a Sumerian man before, and we have a heightened sex drive. It's different from being with an Anunnakian man."

I can't tell him that I've never been with any man, Anunnakian or Sumerian.

"I've heard the rumors."

"If you want to know about Sumerians, you can ask me any-thing. I'm not shy. I mean, I told you about my Quickening." He tilted his head to the side. "I promise I will set aside the humor and give you straight answers."

Since he brought it up, I am dying to know if what Olivia said was true.

"What's it like? Your Quickening?" she asked, hardly able to look him in the eyes. As she opened her mouth to ask, she felt a flush of heat spread across her cheeks. It was a simple question, but it made her feel like she was doing something wrong. She tried to swallow past the knot forming in her throat. "I mean, I know what it is. How many days do you have left? I heard that it could be painful if you don't make it to stage five before the cycle is over. It takes a month to start over..."

His voice was low and intense as he commanded softly, "Look at me." She met his gaze, her eyes looking into his as he placed his hand over hers. "While everything you said is true, I don't want you to worry over it. Maverick, I'll wait for you. I would rather endure a lifetime of pain than ever make you feel forced or pressured."

He picked all the right words.

Her ears perked up as she heard Scooter's familiar voice from the living room. She quickly disentangled herself from Storm, and they both rushed out of the bedroom, almost colliding with Olivia in the hallway. As they entered the living room, Talia's gaze fell upon Scooter sprawled on the floor, his lanky frame splayed haphazardly and a greasy bag from Burger Shack pinned under his body. Princess Johara sat calmly on the plush couch, a hint of amusement twinkling in her eyes as she observed the chaos before her.

Olivia let out a sigh of relief mixed with annoyance. "We really need to start locking that door."

Storm went to pick his friend up off the floor.

He uttered with excitement, "Storm, I had the best dream. Princess Johara was sitting on the couch." When he saw the princess, he stumbled and rested heavily against Storm for support.

With the distraction of Storm attending to his fallen comrade, Olivia grabbed Talia's arm and whispered, "Was it as good as you thought it would be?"

It wasn't sex, actually.

I guess he doesn't need to use this cock. Lucky you. That takes talent. Olivia smiled knowingly at her sister. *That's his magical power.*

"Storm, are you a magic pirate?" Olivia giggled.

"So much that I don't remember," he said, running his fingers through his hair.

"Scooter, what brings you here so early?" Talia asked, changing the topic.

"I brought breakfast burritos, but I can't guarantee their condition," Scooter said, holding up the greasy crushed bag, making his way to his workstation across the living room. "I wanted to check the footage from last night."

"No!" Talia and Storm both jumped for the laptop, frantically waving their hands and shouting at the top of their lungs. She felt panicked as they tried to get Scooter's attention.

Closing the laptop, Storm chuckled nervously. "I don't think that's necessary. Nothing happened."

"I wouldn't call that nothing." Olivia shook her head and giggled. "That was something else."

Olivia, open your mouth and I will melt it shut.

"What was something? What happened?" Scooter exclaimed, flailing his arms as he held a bag of burritos in one hand. "Clearly, something is going on. Princess Johara is sitting right there." Looking at her, his knees started to buckle, but he quickly recovered.

"Is he going to have a stroke?" the princess asked, looking concerned. "Is he okay?"

They nodded in unison.

"Scooter, you're way too innocent for that footage unless you're looking to add to your spank bank." Olivia giggled.

"What's a spank bank?"

"That fact that you have to ask tells me that you don't have one."

"I want one."

Storm walked over to his friend and placed a comforting hand on his shoulder. He leaned in close and whispered something in his ear. Scooter's face went from relaxed to alarmed, then twisted into a look of sheer horror. His eyes widened, and he took a step back, shaking his head in disbelief.

"Enochians don't do that!" he yelled. "Olivia, that is gross."

Storm patted his shoulder.

Olivia smiled. "You have no idea what you're missing. Maybe it'll make you a little less nervous."

CHAPTER NINETEEN

TALIA

"**I** have my Chakram," Talia said, patting her weapon on her hip as she followed Johara down the spiral stairs. "What else could I possibly need?"

Olivia said with a hint of sarcasm, "I tell her all the time that she shouldn't carry that thing so openly."

"You need one more important thing," Johara insisted. "The source of Circe's magic."

As Talia took the last step into the store, she noticed Storm straining under the weight of a wooden display stand, sweat glistening on his forehead. Scooter stood nearby, half-heartedly holding one end. Talia stepped in, hip checking Scooter out of the way, her muscles flexing as she took most of the load off Storm's shoulders. He let out a sigh of relief and a grateful smile spread across his face. She carefully moved the display where Storm was directing her.

"The source of Circe's magic was the Book of the Dead, but it's been lost for thousands of years," Scooter said. "We only have a few passages from the book."

"The book was never lost. My mother protected it. She knew it contained the most powerful magic. If you have my mother's ring, you should have the Book of the Dead."

Her voice strained under the physical exertion, she said, "I would remember if I had something like that."

Talia wiped the sweat from her brow and shifted the weight of the heavy display stand into place. As she caught a glimpse of Storm out of the corner of her eye, she admired his muscular arms as he leaned against the stand. Then her momentary distraction was interrupted by his loud sigh, and she turned her attention fully to see him slumped over with crossed arms and a downcast gaze. Something was clearly bothering him.

"She doesn't have the Book of the Dead," he said sharply. Storm avoided direct eye contact and bit his lip. His gaze darted around the room but never landed on her.

Olivia, are you watching this?

Well, that's a first. He can't look at you. I am sensing a little guilt like he's hiding something.

Talia planted her feet in front of him, blocking his path. She raised her chin and stared at him, determined to make him acknowledge her presence. Her hands went to her hips, tapping her foot, until his eyes lifted to meet hers. "Pirate, you can't hide anything from an empath."

"It's going to come out at some time, but it wasn't my secret to tell, Maverick."

Delphi stepped through the beaded curtains and calmly stated, "It was mine. Don't be mad at Storm. He was only doing what I asked." Turning, her hands went over to her heart and a smile spread across her face. "Is that my little Princess Johara? Oh my, you are so beautiful."

"It's so good to see you again."

The two women embraced like long-lost friends, their faces alight with joy and familiarity. Talia was surprised and curious about their connection, her mouth falling open in surprise. She had never known that Delphi and Johara knew each other before this moment.

"Delphi, it's time." Storm nodded.

Delphi vanished into the sequestered sanctuary of her personal living space. As the confusion spread across Talia's face, Storm grabbed her hand, leading her through the beaded curtains. Johara followed close behind. Hot on her heels, Scooter and Olivia kept up with them, their boot soles sounding soft thuds on the worn-out rug covering the hardwood beneath.

"Queen Circe said if anything happened to her, I was to bring the Book of the Dead to the living world and to give it only to the one who could wear her ring," Delphi said as she walked to her living room.

Delphi tiptoed to a massive bookcase looming in a dimly lit corner and adjusted an inconspicuous statuette of Circe. A soft, low growl emanated from the wall. The bookcase rolled aside to unveil a concealed room cloaked in shadows. A solitary podium harboring one majestic occupant commanded attention within this hidden universe, an archaic relic looking its age yet displaying intriguing charm. A dust-adorned Book of the Dead slept peacefully undisturbed for eons until now.

"She would have the key to unlocking the book, but only if she truly believed who she was." Flashing a smile, Delphi tenderly rescued the artifact from its cushioned throne by presenting it to her. "I believe this belongs to you, Talia."

"I can't believe you have been hiding this!" Scooter said excitedly, giving Storm a playful slap square on his granite-hard biceps. "This is *the* original Book of the Dead. I have been looking for this. Storm, did you know it was here this whole time?"

"We couldn't read it." Storm shrugged.

The weathered binding and yellow pages held strong. Talia felt the credence of the knowledge between the leather covers as she held the book. It emitted an ancient fascination held within. She flipped through several pages. She shook her head. "They are all empty. The pages are blank," Talia announced.

"What?" Scooter asked, shocked. "I hope not."

"Maybe you have to be dead to read it." Olivia shrugged.

"It has the symbol of the Gods on the cover, so this has to be the Book of the Dead. Why can't I see the text?" Talia wondered out loud. "I don't know a powerful enough spell to unlock three thousand years of magic."

"Maybe it just needs a password," Olivia offered.

"A key. My Chakram. Dad also called it the key to my destiny."

Talia carefully closed the ancient Book of the Dead, feeling a sense of awe and anticipation. She traced the familiar symbol carved on the leather cover with her finger. With a sense of purpose, she turned the Chakram to align its intricate design with the embossed picture on the book's cover. As she placed it down, she felt a subtle click, signaling that it had locked into place.

Suddenly, a vibrant light erupted from the Chakram, illuminating the room with a brilliance akin to a shooting star streaking across the night sky. The glow enveloped the entire book, causing it to levitate above her hands. Talia and her companions took a step back in awe as they witnessed this extraordinary transformation.

As the book floated in mid-air, its pages opened on their own, revealing once-empty spaces that were now adorned with an array of mystical symbols. The symbols gradually filled the pages from left to right, covering every inch with intricate markings and cryptic sigils. It was as if the book itself was unraveling its secrets before their very eyes.

However, she noticed that the first three pages remained untouched by the symbols. The significance of this omission intrigued her and added an air of mystery to their unfolding quest. She watched as the book slowly ceased glowing and settled back into her open hands. Closing the book, she gingerly removed the Chakram from its place on the cover.

With curiosity, she opened the Book of the Dead once more, running her fingers over each page as if trying to decipher their enigmatic language. The ancient script in the text felt both familiar and foreign to her. She studied each character intently, searching for any clues or patterns that might unlock its hidden wisdom.

The room fell silent as she immersed herself in the task, her companions watching with bated breath. As she turned each page, she realized the immense power and knowledge contained within this ancient book. It was a testament to Queen Circe's mastery over magic. Yet, in all its intricacy, it remained elusive, its secrets locked behind a veil, waiting to be lifted only by those who held the key.

"I recognize those symbols," Scooter said, looking over her shoulder. "It's the language of the gods. I've seen some of these symbols carved in stones at the Enteral Flame, but no one knows the key code."

"What is a key code?" Olivia asked.

"It's the symbols in order," Scooter said. "Twenty-six symbols for twenty-six letters."

"Like the symbols on my Chakram," Talia said. "It's the key code!"

"I knew you would figure it out." Johara smiled. "My mom used to read this to me."

"Since this book isn't digital, I will have to scan each page. This is going to take a long time to translate," Talia said, looking at how thick the book was. "By the time I'm done, I will read this language fluently." Talia turned to the first few pages of the book to point out, "The first three pages are still blank. I wonder if something was supposed to be there."

"It must be something special if it's not so easy to unlock the pages," Olivia said.

Talia was pouring over the Book of the Dead at the kitchen table. Suddenly, she felt a chill run down her spine as the room filled with a mysterious presence. Panicked, she looked around but found herself completely alone in the apartment. However, something still wasn't right. Then her ring captured her attention. It was emitting an unnatural light that seemed to get brighter and brighter. Suddenly, from deep within her, she heard a voice call from beyond. "Hunter." Fearful and awestruck, she whispered his name.

The book emitted a warm, golden radiance, captivating her attention. With anticipation, she carefully flipped to the first page to witness an enchanting sight. There, before her, gold symbols burned themselves into every fiber of the aged parchment. The significance of these words was palpable, and she intuitively understood they held great importance in unraveling the prophecy.

With a racing heart, she read the inscription aloud with growing wonderment. The words flowed from her lips like whispers from ancient spirits. "The Prophecy," she began, her voice filled with awe and reverence. "From the wake of darkest night comes the gleaming white light to labor the legend for which is told." Each word seems to resonate with power and meaning as they left her lips.

As she continued reciting, the significance of each phrase consumed her. "A human through the spirit of old, and a native with the soul twofold." The connection between humans and Niberians became even more apparent, a blending of two worlds that carried immense potential but also enormous responsibility.

"From the wake of darkest night comes the gleaming white light, to bear the legend for which is divine," she read on, feeling a profound sense of destiny. According to this prophecy, a radiant force for good would triumph over darkness in a pivotal moment.

"The veil between each will shine so they will all witness the sign," she continued, contemplating the symbolic imagery presented in these words.

Finally, the solemn words built toward a climactic revelation. "From the wake of darkest night comes the gleaming white light to destroy the legend for which has begun. The bond that cannot be undone. United as one, divided by one." Her heart skipped a beat as she pondered the implications of such a powerful statement. She flipped between the first three pages. "That's it? That can't be the whole prophecy. It doesn't tell us anything."

"What doesn't?" Olivia asked, walking into the apartment from the back door, listening to the end of Talia's conversation with herself. Johara followed close behind. They brushed the snowflakes from their jackets as the icy wind blew through the apartment. Olivia quickly closed the door to warm up, shaking the wind from the core of her body.

"I know, but I found out so much information. Remember how the first three pages were blank? Well, the first part of the prophecy appeared, and I think it's about the day we were born. As events happen, more of the prophecy will appear. I was hoping this book would tell me how I am going to restore the balance of power and reunite our societies. An instruction manual would be helpful. Maybe it's farther in the book."

"Well, Storm and Scooter are coming over with his scanner to set up a base camp. Scooter wants to help with translating the book," Olivia informed Talia.

"Where is he going to put it?" she asked. "This place isn't big enough for a base camp."

"I know, but I couldn't stop him."

"We are back," Storm announced as he swung open the door, carrying a large scanner.

Scooter trailed behind, a small projector in hand, while Storm carried the bulkier equipment. He focused on setting up the book for projection while leaving the door open, allowing a chilly breeze to swirl into the apartment. Olivia appeared annoyed as she pushed the door shut and assisted Storm with the scanner. She then slid Scooter's laptop down the long rectangular table in the living room, much to his chagrin, making space for Storm to unload his arms.

To speed up translating the Book of the Dead, he needed to set up his commercial scanner. He connected a projector screen with his laptop so everyone could easily share information between devices. The screen was touch-activated, which made it simple to interconnect all the tablets and laptops in the room.

"What did you find out?" Scooter asked, leaning much too closely over Talia's shoulder.

Talia held up her index finger, emitting a small electric shock as a warning for him to back away. "Scooter, I'm telling you, if you don't leave me alone, I'll fry you like bacon."

"Do you hear that?" Olivia asked.

Talia, sensing a shift in the atmosphere, turned her attention back to Olivia, finally noticing the faint glimmer emanating from her ring. Concern etched across her face as she reached out to comfort her sister. "Olivia, are you okay? Something feels off."

Trembling, Olivia shook her head, trying to clear the fog that clouded her mind. "I-I don't know," she stammered, her voice filled with vulnerability.

"Why don't you have a seat?" Johara said as she pulled out a chair for Olivia. "I can make you some tea."

The living room, now known as base camp, was coming together. A large wooden table stood proudly in the center, covered with an ancient relic, the Book of the Dead.

To the left of the table, a scanner hovered gracefully above the pages, its soft humming sound filling the room. It emitted a laser light that moved methodically from top to bottom, carefully copying each intricate symbol onto its digital interface. As the laser worked its magic, an image materialized on a projection screen across the room, revealing the hidden secrets within the pages.

Talia and Storm had curled up on the worn-out couch nearby, their eyes fixated on the book's transformation into a digital format. As each symbol translated, they watched with bated breath. The translated page would then elegantly find its place at the front and center of the projection screen, illuminating the room with newfound knowledge and understanding. Olivia sat at the kitchen table with a steaming cup of tea in hand. Johara joined her with her own cup of tea.

"Wait. Go back to that last page." Talia sat up straight when a word caught her eye. Scooter pulled up the previous page with the word *portals* at the top. "Portals are the gateway to and from the Far Viscera, and this book can be used as a guide for the living," Talia read out loud. "It gives a spell to open a portal."

"You can't open a portal just anywhere. The spell requires more than just a chant," Scooter said.

"It requires a lot of magic and power," Johara added. "It takes twice the magic of a summoning spell."

"Where do we get more magic?" Olivia asked, looking up from her phone.

"We would need something to amplify your magic, like an electromagnetic source," Scooter said. Standing, he paced, deep in thought. "How could we do that? It would have to be like a battery charger."

"It would have to be lightning." Johara looked up at Talia. "I know someone who can create it."

"I can't create that much power at will," she admitted.

"You did it the night of our huge fight when you blew up Dad's workshop and put a hole in the wall."

"Yes, you can. You just need a reminder," Johara said confidently. "You are more powerful than you know. You've been training for this battle all your life. I will be here to guide you."

"Now we have the Book of the Dead. It should be a wealth of information, but I don't think I am ready to face Hunter."

"Maverick, you won't have to do it alone." Storm squeezed her hand.

CHAPTER TWENTY

HUNTER

H unter continued to pace in his judgment chambers. He fixed his eyes on the mystical pool of blood that sat before him. An eerie darkness veiled the room, with the only source of light coming from the flickering torches affixed to the walls. Each step he took echoed through the chamber, resonating like a foreboding drumbeat, filling the air with tension and anticipation.

His staff, once a symbol of his power, now acted as a crutch, physically supporting him. It tethered him to his dark purpose. With each strike against the cold marble floor, sparks of energy crackled and danced along its length, further emphasizing the latent power that pulsated within.

The gem on his staff emitted a light, its vibrant red hue representing the potent magic it contained. The intensity of its radiance signaled that something significant had occurred, the awakening of the Book of the Dead. A cruel grin formed on Hunter's face as he reveled in the knowledge Talia had unlocked this ancient artifact. He knew her intellect was formidable, and she possessed a keen sense for deciphering cryptic prophecies.

As he approached the pool of blood, his gaze hardened, his eyes narrowing with conviction. He raised his staff high above his head and began an incantation, his voice resonating ominously throughout the room. "Reaching across the great beyond," he intoned, "make a connection to bond. The thought of mind intertwined, my love of spirit and soul to bind."

With each word spoken, intricate spirals etched on the surface of the pool glowed with a supernatural light. The crimson liquid stirred restlessly, swirling in a clockwise motion, until it parted in the center, revealing a vivid image of Talia in real time. He watched her immersed in her study of the Book of the Dead, meticulously scanning each page in search of clues.

The pool of blood served as a conduit between realms, enabling Hunter to peer into Talia's actions and witness the unfolding events. The connection he established allowed him insight into her progress, giving him an advantage in his relentless pursuit of Queen Circe's soul. His ability to sense her spirit fueled him, pushing him forward on his dark path.

As he observed Talia's dedication and curiosity, a thought crossed his mind. Perhaps he could use the revelations within the prophecies to further his own twisted agenda. A sly smile played on his lips as he contemplated the potential power that lay within those ancient texts. He knew if he could harness the information hidden within the Book of the Dead, he could tip the scales of their ongoing struggle in his favor.

As Talia delved deeper into deciphering the enigmatic language and unlocking its secrets, Hunter grew more determined to possess that knowledge for himself. His staff glowed brighter, pulsating with malevolent energy as he plotted his next move. Aware that time was not on his side, he vowed to stay one step ahead of Talia and her companions.

"Talia woke The Book of the Dead," Hunter announced. "I underestimated her abilities."

"She is more powerful than Circe," Jitatma observed.

"I think Olivia is ready. She was much easier to break." He smirked, changing the image in the pool of blood.

With his black hair neatly styled and framing his chiseled face, Commander Jitatma exuded an aura of strength and confidence. Standing tall and muscular, he commanded attention wherever he went. His soldier uniform, impeccably tailored, emphasized his powerful physique, adorned with a vibrant red cape that billowed behind him as if caught in an invisible breeze.

Bracers adorned his wrists, gleaming in the light, symbolizing his courage and commitment. His breastplate showcased intricate designs, reflecting his fearless spirit and dedication to his duties. Completing his attire were sturdy leather boots, polished to perfection.

He asked Hunter, "Is this necessary?"

"Don't allow Olivia to distract you, Commander. I gave you an order," he warned.

"Women are never a distraction for me," the commander said, straightening his stance and looking away from the pool of blood. "They are merely a means to satisfy my Quickening. For that purpose, I'll gladly take her." He cleared his throat. "I must advise you Emperor Anu will not allow this."

"Emperor Anu will not know," Hunter insisted. "My daughter has betrayed me. She has started a rebellion against me, enlisting the most powerful magic in my late wife, and turning my kingdom against me. I will not allow Princess Johara to be my downfall. I don't have the luxury of time to wait for my wife's spirit. I need her magic. She belongs to me."

"What are you planning to do with her?"

"I need to extract Circe's soul and then reunite it with her spirit in Talia." He smiled wickedly. "She may not be my wife, but she looks like her. I will make her be Circe."

"I will prepare for the arrival," Jitatma agreed, unable to sway Hunter from his plan, obeying his duty to his king and kingdom.

CHAPTER TWENTY-ONE

TALIA

Talia emerged from the bathroom with her long hair pulled back in a binder. She was preparing to wind down for the night, her body tired from a long day. She felt so comfortable in her long nightgown, even if it had offered very little protection from Storm's wandering hands. As she walked through the hallway, she nearly ran into Olivia, who was holding a towel loosely in her arm.

"Looks like you're changing in the bathroom again," Olivia teased with a playful smile. "Storm must be sleeping up here tonight."

A small sigh escaped Talia's lips as she nodded. "It's probably not the best idea, but I feel safer when he's close by."

Olivia's eyes twinkled mischievously. "The rest of us should be so fortunate to have such a strong and protective man in our bed. Let me know if you want to borrow something shorter, sexy, and see-through."

Absolutely not! He's having a hard enough time controlling himself, and I'm one growl away from giving in.

The thought made her cheeks warm, but she couldn't deny the comfort and security that Storm provided with his presence. She headed toward the lights of her bedroom as she prepared to settle in for the night. She could feel the weight of exhaustion in her bones, and the soft cotton sheets of her bed and Storm's arm would provide her with much needed sleep.

Storm was already nestled cozily in her bed, the soft covers pulled up to his waist. As she entered the room, he propped himself up on one elbow, his muscular chest and arms on full display, tempting and teasing her. The dim light from the bedside lamp cast shadows across his chiseled features, giving him an air of seduction. She felt drawn to him as he gazed at her with playful eyes.

"Now I can't get that image out of my head." Storm lowered his eyes as he stared at her. "I'm saving that one. I'll put it in a special place in my spank bank. Right next to the one of you in leather and a whip."

"That's not my style, so that's the only place it will exist." She shook her head, standing next to the bed. "I don't even want to know what else is in there."

"Nothing is better than this." In a swift movement, he reached out and took her hand, guiding her onto the plush bed. He leaned in and pressed a tender kiss to her forehead, his lips warm and soft against her skin. She felt a rush of warmth spread throughout her body as she gazed up into his eyes, knowing this was where she belonged. His touch was gentle yet firm, and the sweet scent of his cologne filled her nose.

She was lost in her moment with Storm when she realized there was a silence in her head like never before. She sat up straight, feeling a chill run through her body. Lowering her eyes, she turned to face the doorway, straining to listen for any sign of her sister's familiar voice in her mind.

Nothing.

Olivia.

With each passing minute, the heavy silence in the room seemed to grow thicker and more suffocating. Her heart raced as she sat on the edge of the bed, her gaze darting around the room for any sign of movement. She could feel the tension building inside her, like a balloon about to burst.

With a sudden surge of energy, she leaped from the bed and sprinted toward the bathroom door, her bare feet slapping against the cool wooden floor in a desperate rhythm. Reaching the door, she pounded on it with trembling hands, her knuckles turning white with worry. "Olivia! Olivia, are you in there?" Her voice was filled with panic as she waited for a response, her mind racing with worst-case scenarios.

No response greeted her frantic calls, and fear clawed its way up her spine. Her heart leaped into her throat, and she slammed her open palm against the door, her ring glowing. "Olivia, please, if you can hear me, just say something!"

Silence.

She couldn't sense her sister.

"Hunter! You can't have my sister."

Talia's vision became hazy as she frantically tried the doorknob. The door remained stubbornly locked, its handle refusing to budge. She took a step back, inhaling deeply before unleashing her electric power onto the door. The wood splintered and groaned under the force of her power, sending shards flying in all directions, blue sparks danced around the frame.

"Olivia!" she screamed, her voice hoarse with desperation.

As her heart continued to race in her chest, she couldn't believe the scene unfolding before her eyes. Olivia's lifeless form was cradled in the arms of a mysterious man. He had an air of otherworldly power about him, his eyes dark and intense as they locked on to Talia's. His features were sharp and angular, giving him a menacing and enigmatic appearance.

As Storm rushed into the bathroom beside Talia, his expression a mix of shock and anger, he yelled, "Jitatma! What are you doing?"

"I'm sorry, Storm. I had no choice." He raised his hand to open a portal. It swirled with dark energy behind him, with an unknown power that seemed to draw all light and warmth into its depths. "Hunter's orders."

A surge of desperation and disbelief swept over Talia. "No! No! No! This can't be happening," she cried, her voice raw with as she took a step forward. Her eyes filled with unshed tears of anguish as she clenched her fists at her sides, feeling the weight of responsibility pressing down on her shoulders.

As she watched in horror, she knew she had to act fast, to do whatever it took to save her sister from whatever dark fate awaited her beyond the portal. With a deep breath to steady herself, she summoned forth her powers with a fierce burning from her core, sizzling blue sparks dancing around her fingertips. Through sheer willpower, she channeled all her strength and courage into protecting her sister.

Before she could release her raw power, Jitatma disappeared into the portal, and a low rumbling sound filled the air. She sprinted to the dark opening, her hand outstretched in a desperate attempt to grasp her sister's limp arm. The tips of her fingers barely grazed Olivia's skin before the portal slammed shut, leaving her grasping at nothing. Her heart raced as she stared into the impenetrable darkness, wondering if she would ever see her sister again.

"I tried to stop him," she weakly admitted through tears, her voice a mere whisper, as she fell to the bathroom floor. Desperate, her fingers stretched and scraped against the smooth surface, searching for any sign of her sister on the other side. But all that remained was a cold emptiness and the lingering scent of magic in the air.

She felt Johara's arms wrapped around her shoulders. She curled into a ball, her body shaking from her uncontrollable crying. Her sobbing echoed off the bathroom walls, the only sound breaking through the heavy silence in the room and in her head.

"I promise, we'll get her back." Storm said.

Talia struggled to raise her head, breaking her embrace from Johara, her hand instinctively rubbing her chest as she asked, "How can you make such a promise to me?" Feeling the tightness in her chest. "He took her. Why? He should have taken me. I'm the one he wants."

With swift, confident strides, Storm approached her and scooped her into his strong arms. A sense of safety and warmth came over her as she nestled in his embrace. He gently swayed with her, his hand lightly brushing her hair as he spoke softly in her ear. "I don't know why Hunter does the barbaric things he does, but I am not going to let him hurt you anymore, Maverick."

"What can I do?" she asked determinedly as she wiped away the tears from her cheek.

"Everything. You are three times greater than any one god. My fierce warrior goddess."

"We are going to take that book in the living room and open a portal to the Far Viscera," Johara said. "Then you're going to find that asshole to unleash the most powerful lightning bolt that only you can create."

"We are going with you, Maverick," Storm offered. "You are not doing this alone."

any sign of her presence, but in the sea of wheat grass and shadowy figures, he could not discern her form.

Undeterred by the rising sense of urgency, he clenched his fists tightly around the reins and spurred his Caribrax forward. Determination burned brightly in his eyes as he vowed to find Olivia, for she was the key to his relentless pursuit and Talia's valiant efforts to save her sister.

After an hour, Lieutenant Malta galloped over to Hunter with frustration and impatience on his face. With an undertone of anger in his voice, he said, "They could be anywhere in the field."

"No excuses! Find her!" Hunter yelled. "I need Olivia."

As the grass parted with a gentle rustle, a sight unfolded before the king. He saw Jitatma carrying Olivia, a fragile figure lost amidst the sea of sorrow. Without hesitation, Jitatma mounted his steed and swiftly lifted Olivia's frail form in one fluid motion. He pulled out the iron cuffs and placed them on her wrists. He cradled her with a firm grip on the reins.

"Bring her to me," Hunter commanded, his voice booming with authority. Jitatma skillfully guided his magnificent Caribrax alongside Hunter's, their powerful beasts snorting and pawing at the ground. As Olivia hung in Jitatma's arms, Hunter leaned over and whispered, "Wake her."

Jitatma nodded, and with a swift motion, he pressed a button on the iron cuffs. A jolt of energy surged through Olivia, and her eyes fluttered open. She looked around, confusion and fear etched on her face as she took in her surroundings.

"Where am I?" Olivia whispered.

Hunter's voice was cold and frightening as he said, "Welcome to the Far Viscera, Olivia. I hope you enjoy your stay."

Olivia's eyes widened in terror as she realized who was speaking to her. She tried to struggle free, but Jitatma held her firmly in place.

"Please, let me go," she pleaded, her voice trembling.

Hunter chuckled darkly. "I'm afraid that's not possible. You see, you have something I want, and I won't stop until I get it."

Olivia looked at him with horror. "What do you want from me?" she asked, her voice barely above a whisper.

He leaned in closer, his face just inches away from hers. "You have my wife's soul," he said, his voice low and dangerous. "I want it back, and you're going to help me get it."

Olivia's eyes widened in shock.

He chuckled again. "Your sister will come for you. When she does, I will have Circe's spirit."

"What is going to happen to me?"

The words dripped from Hunter's lips like poison, a wicked grin spreading across his face as he spoke. "Oh, sweet girl," he sneered. He roughly grabbed a fistful of her hair, yanking her head back with a cruel grip. "That doesn't matter. Once I extract Circe's soul and place it in Talia, you will cease to exist. You'll just be another victim of the empty void."

Hunter yanked hard when she struggled against his hold. His power was too great, his desire for vengeance too strong to resist. He reached into his leather pouch and extracted the vial of water from the River of Forgetfulness. The liquid promised to wipe away all memories that it touched. He held her head steady, prying her mouth open with one hand while carefully pouring the liquid past her lips with the other.

"Drink this," he ordered. "I can't have you remembering who you are and communicating with your sister."

Jitatma let out a piercing whistle, signaling the men to return. They rode together across the solid stone bridge. Hunter pulled on his steed's reins, bringing them to a halt just as they reached the other side of Punishment Valley.

"What would you like to do with her until then?" Jitatma asked.

"Take her back to the castle. She can be a guest in our dungeon." Hunter waved his hand to dismiss them.

"May I offer a suggestion? I need a chambermaid." He kept his gaze on his king. "I could have some fun with one."

"Fine, but you are responsible for her. Keep her in your chambers," he ordered. "Malta and I will wait here for the rest of our guests. I have a welcome gift for them."

"Thank you, King Hunter."

Jitatma rode with Olivia with a relentless purpose toward the blue and purple trees that marked their return journey through the Nothingness Forest, followed by the guard soldiers.

Hunter turned to face Malta to read his expression. "Talia will not go down easily. We need every advantage to capture her."

"I agree, King Hunter," Malta said, eyes scanning the horizon. "She has proven to be more powerful than the queen."

"There are only two people I trust in my kingdom. You and Jitatma. He has Olivia under his command, so I am going to need someone to lead my army."

"I understand, King Hunter," he replied, his voice steady and his gaze unwavering. "I will lead your army with honor and will not let you down."

He nodded, satisfied with Malta's response. "I have a plan," he said, his voice low and serious. "Now that we have Olivia, Talia will come for her. I need Talia alive. Her friends are a different story."

Malta raised an eyebrow. "What about the traitor in the castle? How do we know they won't warn Talia of our plan?"

Hunter's eyes narrowed. "That is why I need you to find them. I have my suspicions, but I need proof. I need you to use her friends as bait to lure out the spy. Tell no one."

He nodded, understanding the gravity of the situation. "Understood, King Hunter. I will do whatever it takes to find the traitor and secure Talia's capture."

"I trust that you will, Malta. I have underestimated this warrior once. It won't happen again." He took a deep breath. "I'm finally going to get my wife back."

CHAPTER TWENTY-THREE

TALIA

"This is crazy. We are talking about ripping open the veil of time and space. There are so many things that can go wrong. I can't even imagine the effect this will have," Scooter warned, trying to keep up with Talia's quick pace across Middle Park.

Talia's heart pounded in her chest as she led Johara, Smoke, and Scooter toward the Eternal Flame. The flickering light in the distance loomed like a beacon of hope and despair all at once. Her palms were slick with sweat, but purpose fueled her steps. Olivia depended on her success.

"I'm doing this, Scooter."

With the words spilling out of his mouth, Scooter said, "What if we get caught? Enforcer Suit Demon will arrest us. I can't go to jail. I wouldn't do well in jail. Have you been to jail? I heard it's not a nice place to be. Scary things happen there."

"Yes, it is crazy, but this is my sister. If I don't save her, jail will be the only safe place you'll be able to hide. Hunter will keep coming to get me. I would tear down every veil across all dimensions if it meant I could have even a slight chance of bringing Olivia back. I don't care about the consequences."

Moonlight glinted off the freshly fallen snow. The air was thick with anticipation, their breaths intermingling like whispered secrets in the night. She knew she must open the portal to Far Viscera, but the spell's complexity left her uncertain. It was almost time.

"I understand your passion, but we have to think about this logically," he reminded her gently.

"No, we don't. This is my sister. I get you are an only child, so you will never understand what it is like to lose a sibling, especially a twin. Olivia is trapped," she replied, her voice heavy with conviction. "I can't stand by and do nothing. There must be a way to save her." She clenched her fists, the static energy crackling around her fingers like a warning.

"Scooter, she is on a mission, and there is no use trying to change her mind. Just go with it," Storm said, slapping him on the back. "Let's go on an adventure."

"I can't just go with it. T-that would be irresponsible," he stuttered.

Smoke chuckled, his deep voice rumbling like distant thunder. "Do you really want to pick a fight with a woman who has a deadly weapon and shoots lightning bolts from her fingers?" His teasing grin revealed an undertone of protectiveness for Talia.

As they reached the Eternal Flame, its warmth brushed against their skin, a stark contrast to the chilling uncertainty that gripped Talia's heart. She glanced at the princess, her eyes questioning. "Are you sure this will work?" she asked, a hint of doubt creeping into her voice. It wasn't every day one attempted to open a portal to Far Viscera.

"Trust in the magic," Johara reassured her, her tone steady and confident. "I've studied these spells for years. With our combined powers, we can do this. Remember, Talia," she said softly, placing a reassuring hand on Talia's shoulder, her voice like a soothing balm amid the tension, "focus on the incantation and let the magic flow through you."

She nodded, drawing strength from Johara's unwavering belief. She closed her eyes, trying to silence the whispers of doubt that threatened to consume her thoughts. With each breath, she focused on the love she held for Olivia and the hate for Hunter.

"I'm ready," she whispered, steadying herself for what lay ahead.

As they prepared to perform the spell, the scent of burning embers and the hum of energy in the air filled their senses. She knew there was no turning back now. The fate of Olivia rested heavily on her shoulders. But with her friends by her side and the power of their combined magic, she was ready to face whatever challenges awaited them beyond the portal.

Johara and Talia stood side by side, their hands clasped as they recited the chant in unison. "With these words, I call forth the gateway to allow us among the dead in a realm far away. With this key, I cross now the great divide and bring us to the bridge of the other side."

As the two women recited the incantation, the surrounding air popped with energy. They could feel the power rushing through their bodies, connecting them to something much greater than themselves. Talia could feel her heart pounding against her chest, her breaths coming in short gasps.

As they continued to chant, her body began to vibrate with the same electric charge that filled the air. It was as if every cell in her body was pulsing in harmony with the energy surrounding her. She knew this was the time. Talia focused her energy and channeled her powers of lightning, feeling the electric charge build within her.

When the final words echoed through the night, a bolt of lightning shot from her outstretched hand, striking the Eternal Flame with a deafening boom. The ground trembled beneath their feet, while the skies above roared with a primal fury. The portal shimmered into existence, revealing a swirling vortex of color that seemed to defy all logic. The sight was both intriguing and terrifying, unlike anything they had ever witnessed before.

Storm, who had been standing guard nearby, approached cautiously, his eyes wide with awe. "Is that the portal?" he asked, his voice barely audible over the maelstrom of sound and chaos before them.

"It is," Talia confirmed, her own voice trembling with a mix of fear and excitement. "We've done it. We've opened the way to the Far Viscera."

"L.I.A! Stop!" Enforcer Markson yelled from across the park, followed by an army of regulators.

"She is going to arrest me," Scooter said.

"Then there's no time to waste," Johara declared, her gaze fixed on the portal. She grabbed Scooter's arm, pulling him toward the swirling opening. "It won't stay open for long."

"*Damn it!*" Enforcer Markson screamed.

Storm held out his hand to Talia. As they prepared to jump, she stole a quick, nostalgic look at the world behind her, then firmly clasped his arm and they jumped side by side. Their hearts pounded with anticipation as they crossed the threshold into the unknown. And as they vanished into the swirling pool of light, the portal snapped shut behind them, sealing their fate and propelling them headlong into the realm of the Far Viscera.

As they emerged from the portal, they found themselves standing on a long, rickety dock that seemed to extend endlessly into the mist-shrouded distance. The wood beneath their feet creaked and groaned under their weight, as if echoing the eerie atmosphere that surrounded them. The air was thick with an oppressive fog, obscuring their vision and adding an ominous sense of mystery to their surroundings.

The River of Forgetfulness stretched out before them, its dark and murky waters reflecting the gloom of the realm they had entered. The surface of the river was calm, devoid of any ripples or movement. It appeared time itself had ceased to flow in this desolate place. The smell of death clung heavily in the air, a reminder of the perilous journey they had embarked upon.

As they ventured cautiously along the dock, they could hear distant echoes of haunting whispers carried by the breeze. Shadows danced strangely across the water's surface. An unsettling stillness suffused the atmosphere, only broken by faint rustling and creaks from unseen creatures lurking in the surrounding darkness.

The sky above was a murky blend of gray and black, devoid of any stars or moonlight. It felt as if a perpetual twilight had settled over this accursed land, heightening the sense of nervousness that gripped Talia and her companions.

As they took hesitant steps forward, each footfall on the decaying dock created a hollow echo that seemed to resonate throughout the desolate landscape. The air was heavy with an unspoken tension, as if the very realm itself was holding its breath, waiting to reveal its secrets or unleash its horrors.

"Where are we?" Scooter asked, his voice trembling as he took in their surroundings. He ventured closer to the edge of the dock, drawn to the inky black waters.

"Stay back!" Johara warned, grabbing Scooter by his lab coat and yanking him away from the water's edge. "This is the River of Forgetfulness. Touching the water can make you forget everything." Her eyes scanned the foggy landscape. "The river cleanses the souls of their past lives before they enter the Far Viscera. We must not touch it."

Scooter's wide eyes scanned the murky water, his body tensed as he took cautious steps toward the edge of the dock. "Right, I almost forgot, which, I guess, is the point. Speaking of forgetting," Scooter continued, patting his pockets frantically, "I think I've forgotten to bring coins for the ferryman. Isn't there something about needing to bribe him for passage?"

Johara laughed softly, her eyes twinkling with amusement. "Fear not, dear Scooter. I will ensure our safe passage across the river."

As if summoned by Princess Johara's assurance, an old, creaky, wooden longboat materialized out of the swirling fog, gliding silently toward the rickety dock. The mist clung to the boat's weathered sides. A mysterious figure stood at the helm, draped in a flowing black robe that billowed in the ghostly wind. The hood of their cloak obscured their face from view, leaving only a hint of a pale, skeletal hand gripping the long paddle. The ferryman remained silent, their presence adding to the sense of unease that hung heavily in the air.

Talia felt a shiver run down her spine as she locked eyes with the mysterious ferryman. However, her love for Olivia pushed her forward. She took a deep breath and stepped onto the boat, Storm and Scooter following suit. Johara was the last to board. The moment they were aboard, the ferryman skillfully guided the boat away from the dock, propelling them into the dense fog that enveloped the River of Forgetfulness.

As they ventured deeper into the murky abyss, she marveled at the ghostly souls that floated just beneath the water's surface. These incorporeal beings appeared as flickering lights of various colors, dancing and twirling in a ghostly ballet. Some glowed with a soft blue hue, while others shimmered in vibrant shades of green and purple. Each soul emitted a gentle glow that illuminated their surroundings and added a touch of wraithlike beauty to the haunting atmosphere.

The fog grew even thicker as they journeyed farther along the river, creating an unnerving and disorienting environment. Visibility became limited to just a few feet ahead, making it feel as though they were sailing through a void of shadows. The only sound was that of their boat slicing through the water, creating ripples that distorted the reflections of the floating souls below.

Throughout their peculiar voyage, echoes of distant whispers carried by the breeze intermittently reached their ears. These haunting murmurs seemed to emanate from all directions, their words indecipherable, but carrying an air of melancholy and forgotten memories. She wondered if these whispers were the voices of those who had lost themselves in the river's waters, trapped in eternal confusion and longing.

The ferryman's presence remained enigmatic, never uttering a single word as they guided the boat through the treacherous waters. They moved in a way that seemed almost choreographed. The figure's hidden face added to their air of mystery, leaving Talia with unanswered questions about their intentions and true nature.

As they continued their journey along the River of Forgetfulness, the gloomy, foreboding atmosphere intensified. The mist seemed to thicken, wrapping around them like a suffocating veil. Each breath they took felt heavy with the scent of decay and forgotten dreams.

Talia's heart quickened with anticipation as she realized they were venturing farther into the unknown, inching closer to the Far Viscera where Olivia awaited rescue. She fidgeted with her knees, anxiously twisting to find some sense of comfort in this unfamiliar world. Her thoughts were filled with darkness and sadness, missing the comforting presence of her sister's voice. She felt alone, surrounded by only her own mind.

As she sat on the rough wood bench, she could feel his hand gently slide down her back, coming to rest comfortably on her waist. Storm pulled her in for a small embrace and she gladly snuggled closer, relishing the warmth of his touch against the coolness of the bench beneath them.

"Look at them," Talia whispered, gesturing toward the swirling souls below. "It's hauntingly beautiful."

"Yes," Johara agreed, her voice tinged with sadness. "It is a necessary process, but one that is not without its own pain."

CHAPTER TWENTY-FOUR

TALIA

As the ferry completed its journey and gradually came to a halt, the temperature dropped noticeably. The thick fog that had veiled their surroundings began to dissipate to a somber gray sky overhead. It was as if the oppressive atmosphere of the River of Forgetfulness had settled over them, casting a spooky gloom upon their surroundings.

With cautious steps, Johara, Talia, Storm, and Scooter disembarked from the ferry onto the river's shore. Their feet sank into the soft, damp bank, leaving imprints that seemed almost fleeting. They could still hear the distant echoes of the ferry's departure as it turned back around, soon swallowed up by the swirling mist. Left alone in this desolate wasteland known as the Field of Sorrow, an overwhelming sense of isolation settled upon Talia.

The wind suddenly intensified, carrying with it a bone-chilling coldness that pierced through their clothing. It howled mournfully as it swept through the tall wheat grass that stretched out before them, casting dancing shadows against the barren landscape. The once-ominous grass now took on an almost ethereal quality, its slender stalks swaying and rustling as if whispering secrets only they could comprehend.

Shades of gray and dull tones dominated the color palette of this desolate scene. The sky remained perpetually overcast, its heavy cloud cover reflecting a world devoid of vibrant hues. Occasionally, a faint glimmer of light would break through the layers of mist, casting an uncanny shine that heightened the air of mystery and melancholy.

Amidst this barren tableau stood Johara, Talia, Storm, and Scooter - four figures whose presence seemed incongruous yet essential in this realm. Their faces mirrored anxiety as they gazed into the distance, where the tall wheat grass blurred the line between reality and the ethereal. In this desolation, they could almost hear the faint echoes of forgotten sorrows and long-lost hopes, beckoning them forward into the unknown.

Storm looked grim as he scanned the vast field before them. "We must find Olivia quickly." His deep voice echoed across the barren landscape, mingling with the ghostlike whispers of the wandering souls. Talia shivered at the sound, her eyes darting nervously from side to side as she tried to make out any sign of her sister amidst the swirling spirits.

As Talia and her companions ventured farther into the miserable Field of Sorrow, the scenery seemed to intensify in its haunting beauty. The wheat, once golden and vibrant, now appeared tattered and worn, its blades rustling like ancient paper as they brushed against their legs. Each step sent a gentle shudder through her body, as if the ghosts of those who had passed were warning her away from their desolate place.

As they walked deeper into the field, the air grew heavy with a musty smell, carrying the faint scent of death that mingled with the dampness of the surroundings. Her nostrils flared as she inhaled deeply, taking in the somber bouquet that permeated the atmosphere. Her heightened senses picked up on the presence of countless tormented souls, their despair weighing heavily upon her. It felt as though the spirits were pressing against her, their desperate pleas for help echoing in her mind.

Storm's jaw clenched tightly as he led the way, his broad shoulders acting as a protective shield against some of the restless spirits. The otherworldly whispers continued to fill the air, their haunting voices carried by the wind. Her heart ached as if it could hear their tragic cries. "Help us... don't forget us..." The weight of their longing haunted her every step, fueling her will to find her sister.

With each step, the spirits seemed to grow more restless, their gentle forms flickering in and out of sight. It seemed to be a vessel for the sorrow that permeated this forsaken realm, stirring the wheat grass into a dance that created ever-shifting shadows against the landscape. The slender stalks now possessed an almost gentle quality as they swayed and rustled.

Despite the hopelessness in the air, she refused to give up hope, calling out Olivia's name. The howling whispers swallowed her voice, but she continued to shout, driven by a desperate determination to save her sister. The princess followed suit, her voice adding to the cacophony of pleas for help.

As they trudged deeper into the field, the spirits grew more numerous and urgent, reaching out to them with cold, bony fingers. She could feel the blood rushing in her ears as she tried to focus on finding Olivia among the sea of restless souls.

Suddenly, a loud squawking sound shattered the silence. A flock of Saqqara birds descended upon them, their beaks and talons glinting in the moonlight. The massive creatures dove at them with a force that knocked all four to the ground. Talia scrambled back, fear igniting her instincts as she watched the red, yellow, and orange feathers swirl around her. She flinched at the sound of the discordant symphony of their deafening cries.

Her heart pounded like a drum as she realized these weren't ordinary birds. They were massive, twice her size, with long tails trailing behind them as they circled above like a swarm of predators.

As Storm half-turned to look at Talia, his eyes widened with shock for a moment before a transformation began to take place within him. She gasped as she watched in awe as his muscles rippled beneath his shifting skin, contorting and expanding. His form twisted and elongated, as if being molded by some unseen force, until he stood before her in the monstrous guise of a Minotaur.

The transformation was both mesmerizing and terrifying to behold. The once familiar features of Storm were now obscured by the beastly form of the Minotaur. His skin took on a dark hue, almost like charred wood, with patches of fur sprouting from his arms and legs. Massive horns curved menacingly from his skull, gleaming in the dim light of the desolate field.

As the Minotaur stood towering over her, its eyes locked on hers with an intensity that sent a shiver down her spine. The gaze held a mix of ferocity and sorrow, as if battling against the primal instincts raging within this monstrous form. Despite the fearsome appearance, there was a glimmer of recognition in those deep, dark eyes that hinted at Storm's presence lingering within the beast.

With a mighty roar, he charged at the Saqqara birds, his hooves leaving deep imprints on the soft ground. His strength and determination were palpable as he swung his massive fists, sending the creatures flying. Her heart raced as she watched Storm fight off their attackers, her mind racing to find a way to assist him.

Princess Johara cried out, shock reverberating through her voice. She reached for her wand, appearing from the air to draw it close as she formed a protective bubble around herself and Scooter. Scooter whimpered from behind her, trembling in fear. The princess's eyes darted between the attacking birds and Storm, who was doing an admirable job of holding them off but clearly struggling.

Talia's mind raced, a whirlwind of thoughts during the chaos. Her hand went instinctively to her Chakram, the familiar weight of the weapon comforting her in this moment of terror. She closed her eyes, focusing on her powers. The energy pumping through her veins felt more intense than she had ever felt before, building the electricity in more than just her hands to emanate through her entire body.

With her warrior cry, she released her Chakram, sending it through the air with a crack of lightning. It sliced through one bird, sending it plummeting to the ground in a shower of feathers and blood. The others hesitated for a moment before diving again, their beaks and claws aiming for their prey. She gritted her teeth, calling on her powers once more. This time, lightning danced along her fingers as she threw the Chakram, striking another bird mid-flight.

The fight unfolded in a flurry of action, with Storm's powerful blows shaking the ground beneath them. The Saqqara birds retaliated with beak strikes and claw slashes, their wings creating gusts of wind that whipped through the field. The clash of feathers against Talia's weapon echoed through the desolate landscape, adding an edge to the symphony of combat.

Storm continued to fight, his massive strength pushing back against the onslaught of birds. He swiped at them with his powerful arms, sending them spiraling away from him, but others quickly replaced them, their cries growing louder by the second. The air was thick with the stench of blood and death now, mixing with the scent of the tall wheat grass around them.

Despite the danger, Talia felt a surge of admiration for Storm. She'd never seen him fight like this before. His muscles rippled with each movement, his breath coming in sharp pants. He was beautiful in his Minotaur form. She found herself briefly turned on.

The atmosphere vibrated with tension as the battle raged on. She could taste the metallic tang of blood in her mouth, a result of exertion and the Saqqara birds' earlier attack. With every beat of the fight, her muscles burned with exhaustion, but she pushed through it, fueled by adrenaline. Storm's roars mingled with her warrior cry as they fought side by side, their teamwork evident in their synchronized movements and calculated strikes, like they had done this dance before.

Then, suddenly, the last bird fell. The sky grew silent again, and she let out a long breath. She turned to Storm, eyes wide with shock and awe. "That was incredible."

He lowered his head in acknowledgment, a small smile gracing his lips. One by one, the fallen creatures disappeared in a flash of white light. Something absorbed their existence. The Saqqara birds, only injured in the battle, squawked in a low tone to convey their pain.

"Where did they go?" he asked.

"A place called the empty void," Johara replied. "If you are killed in the Far Viscera, you cease to exist."

"That doesn't sound very pleasant," Scooter said.

"Don't get killed here, Scooter, and we will be fine," Storm said, a little unsettled. "Easy enough."

Slowly, the four companions pressed forward through the desolate, sorrowful expanse. Each step felt heavier than the last, as if the weight of their burden was physically manifesting in their weary bodies. Despite the overwhelming hopelessness that permeated the atmosphere, Talia refused to surrender to despair.

As they neared the exit, a glimmer of hope flickered in their hearts. Before they could fully embrace it, they froze in their tracks, stunned by the sudden rush of wings in front of them. More Saqqara birds materialized out of thin air, their numbers endless as they formed a relentless army.

Talia's breath caught in her chest as she took in the sight before her. "We can't possibly fight them all," she gasped, her voice laced with both fear and resignation. The flock of Saqqara birds swarmed them like a wrathful tempest, their sharp talons slashing with alarming speed and precision. She instinctively ducked and weaved, her body becoming a blur of agile movements as she sought to evade their relentless attacks.

Her strength began to wane under the incessant assault. She cast a frantic gaze around, seeking any glimmer of hope or assistance in the chaos. Then her eyes fell upon Storm, who was valiantly battling his own assailants. She watched in horror as a Saqqara bird's razor-sharp claw tore through his flesh, leaving a gash across his shoulder. The birds swooped down like a torrential downpour, pecking and clawing at anything in sight.

Fear surged through her as she rushed to Storm's side. "Are you okay?" she asked urgently, softly reaching out to touch his injured shoulder. In that fleeting moment of contact, a bright spark ignited between her fingertips, causing Storm to flinch in surprise. The electricity that crackled briefly between them was a testament to the immense power she possessed, a power she had only begun to tap into.

"I'm fine," he grunted.

With renewed fortitude, she redirected her focus on the Saqqara birds. She could feel the energy flowing through to her fingers, building with an intensity she had never experienced before. It was as if the very elements were responding to her call, ready to aid her in this desperate battle.

Expelling a cry of defiance, she unleashed her Chakram once more. The weapon soared through the air with a thunderous crackle of lightning, finding its mark and slicing through another bird, causing the corpse to fall near her feet.

Princess Johara stood nearby, her eyes hardened. "We need to find Olivia," she said firmly, her voice carrying over the sound of squawking birds.

"Where could she be?" Talia asked anxiously.

Princess Johara shook her head. "I don't know, but I do know we need to get out of here."

Talia took a deep breath, nodding in agreement. The Field of Sorrow was no place for them anymore. She stopped short when they heard a loud squawk from above. She looked up to see another Saqqara bird diving toward them, its blood-red eyes fixed on Princess Johara. With a cry of terror, Scooter bolted into action, breaking beyond the protective bubble, charging at the bird with all his might. But he didn't stand a chance; it swooped down and caught him in its talons before he could make it halfway there.

"No!" Talia screamed, rushing forward with her Chakram at the ready. She powered up her weapon, feeling the electric current through her veins. Her vision narrowed as she focused on the bird, feeling its despair wash over her like a tidal wave.

She let the Chakram fly, slicing through the air with a satisfying sound before connecting with the bird's wing, sending it crashing to the ground. Scooter fell with a loud thud, knocking him unconscious. Storm scooped up Scooter and easily threw him over his broad shoulder.

"We need to move," he said, his voice shaking slightly as he witnessed the aftermath of the downed bird.

Johara, still shaken from the attack, clung to Storm's arm as they walked. He stood tall, trying to keep her upright while he carried Scooter over the other shoulder, ready for any additional attacks. He was tense, his muscles coiled like wire, ready to spring into action at any moment. But the silence only unnerved them more. It was as if the field itself knew something terrible was happening here and didn't dare make a sound.

The rustle of the tall grass was the only sound they heard as they moved across the field. The air felt alive with an unseen energy that made Talia's skin crawl, as if it were watching their every move. She glanced over her shoulder constantly, paranoid that something else would appear out of nowhere to harm them.

CHAPTER TWENTY-FIVE

HUNTER

Hunter stood perched on the jagged edge of Punishment Valley, his staff in hand, humming with ancient power. The Saqqara claw pulsed like a living heartbeat, emitting a soft radiance. With a flourish of his wrist, he choreographed the movements of the Saqqara birds that circled above the Field of Sorrow, their cries piercing the air.

"Watch them dance, Malta," he murmured, his voice laced with dark amusement as he gestured grandly, feeling the raw energy of his command.

The birds swooped and dived with precision, an airborne legion bending to Hunter's will. His eyes, sharp and calculating, never strayed from the chaos unfolding below. He watched Talia, valiant even among the relentless assault, strike out at the feathered assailants with swift, practiced movements. Each parry, each evasion, spoke to him of her fierce spirit, and it ignited within him a perverse yearning.

Talia's hair, a cascade of black silk, whipped around her face as she confronted another dive-bombing predator. The Saqqara bird's talons gleamed wickedly in the dying light, but she dodged with grace, countering with a strike that sent the creature reeling.

A smug smile played upon his lips; this dance of predator and prey thrilled him more than it should have. In the excitement of the hunt, he found himself entranced by her resilience, her unwillingness to yield.

"Beautiful, isn't she?" he said aloud, though the question was meant for no one but himself.

"She certainly looks like Circe, but she doesn't move like her."

The woman before him was a far cry from the gentle Circe he had known. She moved with deadly grace, wielding her weapon with precision and power as she fought off the monstrous creatures that threatened them. Her beauty was untamed and wild. This was not the demure flower he had once loved, but a force to be reckoned with. He wondered how such a fierce being could be connected to the gentle woman he once knew.

As he gazed at her, he couldn't help but see his late wife in her features, but there was something more that captivated him. In Talia, he noticed a power and authority that mirrored his own. She was not just a carbon copy, but an amplified version. In some ways, she was even better than Circe.

He raised the staff higher, and the claw resonated with a surge of energy that rippled across the valley. The Saqqara birds responded instantly, their formation tightening as they prepared for another wave of attacks. Soon, he mused, she would look up and see the architect of her despair. When he could finally look this warrior in her eyes across the expanse of torment, he would savor the moment her indomitable spirit recognized its master.

"Again!" he commanded. The birds obliged, descending upon the field with renewed ferocity. From his vantage point, Hunter watched, entranced by the spectacle, his dark desire for Talia blossoming into something aggressive and uncontainable.

His gaze was as sharp as the birds he commanded, locked on the chaos unfolding in the Field of Sorrow. He watched with calculated detachment as one of his Saqqara birds swooped down, its talons outstretched like daggers, and struck Storm with a precision that sent a shiver of satisfaction through him. Another bird, obeying his silent command, grasped Scooter in its iron grip, lifting the small Enochian. The tableau below was one of pure pandemonium, but to Hunter, it was a masterpiece of manipulation.

"That's enough," he murmured, the words barely audible over the din of battle. With a deft twist of his wrist, he signaled the birds to retreat. They obeyed instantly, their silhouettes drawing back against the twilight sky until they formed a looming backdrop to his imposing figure. They were his army, as much a part of him as the staff in his hand, and he relished the power that surged within him at their return.

From across Punishment Valley, Talia and her companions began their weary approach. He could see the toll the attack had taken. Talia's shoulders slumped ever so slightly, helping to support Johara. Storm grabbed at his side, carrying Scooter over his shoulder. Yet, despite their injuries and exhaustion, their advancement irked him. It was as though they were challenging him, defying the very order he sought to enforce.

"Let them come," he whispered to himself, his voice a low hum that resonated with anticipation.

He stood statuesque, his silhouette rimmed in the fading light, staff raised like a scepter, the glow of the Saqqara claw casting eerie shadows on his features. His eyes gleamed with a dark intensity as he waited for the moment when Talia's gaze would find his own. He imagined the recognition, the realization, the resignation that would flicker across her tired face. That moment would be his triumph, the sweet culmination of his meticulous planning.

"I'm here waiting for you, my queen," he willed silently, his heart pounding with dark anticipation. "Look up and know who holds your destiny."

When Talia emerged from the Field of Sorrow, it was the moment Hunter had been waiting for. Talia's gaze, sharp and penetrating even from across the valley, finally met his. In her eyes, there flickered not resignation, but a defiant fire that stirred something unexpected within him. It was as though she was reaching into the depths of his darkened heart and igniting embers he thought long dead. A strange sensation twisted in his chest—a mix of admiration and an unsettling desire.

"Beautiful and fierce," he muttered under his breath, his smugness wavering for a fraction of a second before he steeled himself against the softness threatening to breach his resolve.

"Hunter! Where is my sister?"

With a swift, commanding motion, he lifted the staff higher, the Saqqara claw pulsating with a brilliant light, its power resonating through the valley. He set his jaw, his gaze never leaving Talia, and thrust the staff forward, releasing his command into the wind.

"Attack!"

The response was immediate; the sky darkened as a wave of Saqqara birds took flight, their wings beating in unison, a cacophony of feathers and fury came over the valley. They darted across the sky, a charge of beaks and talons aimed at the weary group below.

Talia and her friends braced themselves, their bodies tensing for the onslaught. The birds swooped and dived, their movements orchestrated by Hunter's will. Each strike, each screech, echoed across the landscape, a symphony of chaos that thrilled Hunter's senses. He could taste the metallic tang of fear on his tongue, smell the sweat and blood of the impending struggle, feel the rush of air displaced by the flurry of wings.

Hunter watched, a cruel smile playing on his lips as the Saqqara birds closed in on Talia and her companions. His heart thumped with exhilaration, savoring the power he wielded over life and death. This was his domain, his rules, and they would all bow before the might of the king.

His reign over the birds wavered when an ear-piercing screech cut through the din of battle, a sound so commanding that even the frenzy of birds halted in their assault. Hunter's eyes snapped upward, a surge of annoyance flooding him as he registered the source—a smaller Saqqara, her feathers a vibrant array of red, slicing across the Field of Sorrow. His grip on the staff tightened, his knuckles whitening. He had banished her from his realm, cast her out for her defiance. The Saqqara Queen had returned to defy him once more.

"Impossible. I banished their queen years ago," he muttered under his breath, the smugness fading from his face.

His nostrils flared as the scent of betrayal filled the air. How dare she return? The audacity of her challenge stoked the fires of his ire, and he could almost taste the bitterness of his own fury.

As he seethed, the regal avian descended with grace, landing squarely in front of Storm, who stood panting and wide-eyed. With a swift motion, the Saqqara Queen faced him, her wings unfurling in a display of splendor and authority. A single squawk, sharp and resonant, escaped her beak. It was an unmistakable command.

In that moment, the air seemed to still, and the Saqqara birds, once his relentless soldiers, turned their heads toward their queen. The connection between them was evident, a bond forged by nature that no magic could sever. With a collective rustle of feathers, they lifted off, abandoning the attack as quickly as they had commenced it. They soared away, leaving a stunned silence in their wake.

He watched, disbelief etched into his features, as his feathered army dispersed into the skies, shrinking dots against the vast canvas above. He felt the power of the staff wane, its glow dimming in tandem with the retreat of his birds. The queen had usurped his command, her presence alone enough to sway the allegiance of the flock.

"Traitors!" He spat the word like venom, his voice swallowed by the expanse of Punishment Valley.

His fingers clenched around the staff, the wood creaking in protest. This was not over; it could not be. But for now, he had to watch as Talia and her friends regrouped, their gazes locked onto him with newfound determination. The battlefield had shifted, and with it, the balance of power. The queen stood resolute, the echo of her defiance lingering in the air, a challenge that Hunter could neither ignore nor forget.

"You have my sister! I'm coming for you, Hunter," Talia yelled.

His jaw clenched at Talia's declaration, the muscles in his face taut with rage. He could taste the bitterness of defeat, a flavor he loathed more than any other.

"Come, then!" he shouted back across the valley, his voice laced with scorn. "Commander Jitatma is having his way with her by now!"

His grip on the staff tightened, knuckles whitening as he mounted his Caribrax. With a swift kick, Hunter guided the creature into Nothingness Forest in retreat, with Malta close behind.

"We'll be ready for her. I will make sure of it," Malta said as they rode back to the castle.

CHAPTER TWENTY-SIX

TALIA

"You have my sister! I'm coming for you, Hunter," Talia yelled.

"Come, then!" Hunter shouted back across the valley. "Commander Jitatma is having his way with her by now!"

Talia's heart pounded and her breathing was heavy as she watched Hunter vanish into the depths of Nothingness Forest. She longed to sprint across the rickety stone bridge and follow him, but her body was still recovering from the savage assault. She bent over with her hands on her knees trying to calm herself. She straightened to stretch her muscles.

If he touches her, I'm going to fry his dick.

Her gaze was drawn to the small red Saqqara, its vibrant wings slowly closing. The bird then turned to face Storm, who lay an unconscious Scooter on the ground beside him. Its beady eyes seemed to lock onto him with a curious intensity, as if studying each other intently.

With a protective instinct for her beloved beast, she swiftly positioned herself between them, brandishing her Chakram like a shield. Her hand trembled with adrenaline as she raised the sharp disc toward the intimidating bird, locking eyes with the creature. She prepared to strike at its neck if necessary.

She felt Storm's firm grip on her shoulder, and his commanding voice broke through the adrenaline rush. "Stand down, Maverick."

He stepped forward toward the bird and extended his other hand. The bird dipped its head, gently rubbing its sharp beak against his outstretched palm. Each smooth, calculated motion of the bird's head displayed its trust and affection. Her stance softened slightly as she witnessed this display of harmony unfold before her. It reminded her that even in a place of darkness and danger, there existed moments of unexpected beauty and connection.

With a deep breath, she felt a surge of conflicted emotions welling up within her. The thought of her sister in danger fueled a fire within her. Fighting to get her sister back made her feel the silence in her mind more keenly. She reached out and waited for a snarky remark or a cry for help.

Nothing.

The feeling in her gut was all too familiar. It was the same one she had on the night of their biggest fight, when she had shut her out. She put up a mental barrier to block out any communication. Now it felt like an eternity since the twins had spoken to each other, and she couldn't stand the deafening echo of her own thoughts in her head.

She longed to hear Olivia's voice, to feel that familiar connection that bound them together even across distances. The bond between the two sisters should have been unbreakable, a telepathic link that had always been a comfort and a source of annoyance in equal measure.

The scene before her with the Minotaur and the Saqqara bird sharing a moment of unexpected tenderness tugged at her heartstrings. It reminded her of the deep longing she felt to have her sister back by her side. The sight of the majestic bird finding solace and familiarity with the Minotaur stirred something within her, emphasizing the void that Olivia's absence had left in her life.

"A friend of yours?"

"Yes, she appears to know me. Her scent seems familiar, like I've met her before," he said, softly. "You saved us."

Johara took a step forward, struggling to steady herself. "That's Little Dragon." She smiled. "She was once the Saqqara Queen, but Hunter banished her many years ago. It seems she has found her way home."

"Little Dragon."

The Saqqara Queen gracefully took a single step back, her ethereal wings spread wide and shimmering even in the absence of sunlight. Little Dragon let out a small squawk before taking to the sky, disappearing into the vast Field of Sorrow.

She winced as Storm's strong grip on her shoulder tightened, causing her to feel the heat and strength radiating from his body transforming back. She turned and watched in awe as he slowly stood and began to shift back into his Sumerian form. His torn pants revealed his legs, while scraps of fabric hung from his broad shoulders. "Shit, that was my favorite shirt."

"I can take care of that for you. Take this fabric of old, make it stretch and unfold. Never to tear or break, even when the beast is awake."

With her spell, his shirt and pants repaired themselves as if he had never turned into the Minotaur. "I don't believe it," he said in disbelief. "It's even better than before."

She smiled and took a step back, watching the amazement in his eyes. "Now it will stretch when you turn."

Scooter stirred, sitting up, confused. "What happened to you guys?"

Storm chuckled. "You missed the fun part. I had to carry your ass. For a lanky guy, you're not light, buddy."

"We should find a place to camp," Johara suggested. "There's a clearing not far in Nothingness Forest where we can rest."

"Let me guess. We must cross that creepy stone bridge to get there," Scooter said, trembling.

"I'm not carrying your ass across. You're on your own." He held out his hand to pull Scooter to his feet. "You'll be fine. Just don't look down."

Talia leaned over to Storm to say, "Now that you said it out loud, he's going to look down and pass out."

"Don't worry, Maverick. It's a reflex to catch him."

The four of them made their way toward the narrow stone bridge. The darkness seemed to seep up from its depths, a constant reminder of the danger that lurked beneath. The only thing keeping the stones in place was magic, their only lifeline and protection against tumbling into the abyss below. With no visible handholds or supports, they knew one wrong step could send them plummeting into the valley below.

Scooter gulped as he looked down. He started to shake and his eye twitched. She whispered reassuringly, "You can do this, Scooter. Take my hand and focus your eyes on me." Talia took a step back as she led Scooter across the bridge. "What's your favorite thing about the Eternal Flame?"

"I like that no matter how cold it is outside, it's always warm. It's like getting a hug from Empress Ki every time I step on the tiles."

"I want you to imagine that we are in Middle Park, and we are about to step on the tile. Your goddess has her arms out waiting for you. Empress Ki wants to give the warmest hug you've ever had. Tell me about her."

As Scooter spoke animatedly about his beloved goddess, she walked beside him, taking in every detail of his passionate expression. She smiled as she watched the way he gestured with his hands and leaned in closer to emphasize his words. His enthusiasm was infectious.

When they finally reached the other side, she beamed at him. "Scooter, you made it."

Storm gave him a playful slap on the shoulder. "You didn't faint. Good job, buddy."

"You know, Scooter, Empress Ki visits from the Afterlife." Johara said, draping her arm around his and walking toward Nothing Forest. "I can tell you all about her."

"That was a sweet thing you did for him. He never would have walked across that bridge on his own."

"He just needed someone to distract him to quiet his mind. That is something I'm learning about. I haven't been able to hear Olivia in my head."

"We'll get her back and she will be saying all kinds of crazy things again."

As they ventured farther into the mystical Nothingness Forest, the captivating beauty of their surroundings enveloped them. The slender willow trees arched gracefully overhead, their branches draped in cascading tendrils of leaves that shimmered with a fascinating blend of celestial blue and light purple. The soft glow emitted by the foliage bathed the entire clearing in a magical luminescence, casting enchanting shadows that danced playfully around the explorers.

A soothing breeze rustled through the forest, carrying with it a hint of fragrant blossoms. The coolness on Talia's skin was invigorating yet pleasant, as if Circe herself was embracing her presence within this sanctuary. The more she delved into this enchanting realm, the more pronounced became the distant melody of a flowing waterfall—a soothing chorus that beckoned them closer.

The path they trod upon widened as they approached the source of the melodious rush. Sparkling droplets hung suspended in midair, creating a misty veil around them. Rays of sunlight filtered through the leafy canopy above, dappling the ground with patches of warm golden hues. The interplay between light and shadow enhanced their journey, adding a touch of drama to their exploration.

In this serene haven, time seemed to stand motionless for her. She reveled in the sheer magnificence surrounding her. The forest embraced them with its tranquility and serenity, a refuge from worldly worries and cares. It was as if every whispering leaf and gentle rustle carried fleeting giggles, drawing the adventurers deeper into the allure of the Nothingness Forest, reminding her of Olivia's carefree laugh.

"Olivia!" Talia said. She stopped walking, causing Storm to almost run into her. "I can sense her again. Something has happened."

"Is it a good or bad?" Storm asked.

"I can't tell. I can't talk to her telepathically, but I am feeling a huge rush of emotions. Then sudden confusion. There is so much going on with her. There is so much turmoil," Talia said, trying to sort through all the thoughts that were rushing to her head.

"Is she hurt?" Storm asked.

"Now she is feeling anger, loathing, and arousal. Oh, my word. Damn," she said, feeling her cheeks getting hot as she was feeling her sister's hormones racing. She tried to keep the embarrassment from her face, but she couldn't resist the heat rushing through her body, making her squirm under the intensity of it all. She rubbed the back of her neck and prevented a moan from escaping. "That's what it feels like to have real Nibmarks."

"I can think of one man who could do that to a woman like Olivia." Storm chuckled. "Shit, Jitatma is going to have a hard time commanding her."

"He's trying to bring her soul back to life by evoking an emotional response. Her response to him is strong, but she doesn't seem hurt or afraid. She is really turned on."

"That sounds like something Jitatma would do. From what I know of him, he is aggressive with women, but not harmful." He stopped walking and grabbed her arm. "As long as he doesn't turn her over to Hunter, Olivia should be fine for the moment."

"Will he? Will he turn her over to Hunter?"

"I can't answer that for sure. Jitatma is unpredictable." His calloused hands grazed her arms as he spoke. "He attacked me. I may never understand his reason, but he believed it was to save me. Looking back, in some weird, twisted way, he did. I wouldn't be standing here with you on this great adventure. As painful as this scar is to bear, it gave me you."

She tilted her head, a coy grin spreading across her face. "Well, I don't know if that makes me lucky or cursed. I think both. I'm lucky to have Storm but cursed with the Pirate."

He let out a chuckle, a low rumble in his throat. "If that's what you think, that makes me lucky to have the goddess but cursed with the Maverick."

She could sense his restraint as his thumb traced slow, languid circles on her arm, the casual gesture stoking the fire within her. As he leaned closer, she could distinguish his scent that was something uniquely him—raw masculinity tinged with mystery. It was all too tempting, the proximity, the heat radiating from him, the forest humming around them. It was nigh impossible to stay untouched, unaroused.

Storm, with his smoldering gaze and seductive words, was the trigger; Talia, avid for the sensations he lit in her, was the explosive waiting to go off. Heat pooled between her legs, an insistent throbbing beating a tantalizing melody far too alluring to ignore.

He is so damn tempting.

"Maverick makes you a gentleman and keeps you in check."

"Pirate makes you want to lose control and gets you hot." He wrapped his strong arm around her waist and pulled her forcefully against his hard chest. His rough fingers traced the line of her jaw, down to the delicate curve of her neck. She gasped as he brushed the side of her breast. Her nipples tightened against the fabric of her bodice, aching for his touch. Every nerve in her body yearned for his attention, a wild desire that threatened to consume her.

"I'm the one who gets you wet. The beast had his taste of you, and he torments me with all these images of your treasure. Your scent is driving me mad. I've been trying not to kiss you because I am afraid to lose control. I always want to have you near me, and I never want you out of my sight. You have my attention, Maverick."

Don't give in.

He loosened his hold around her waist and leaned to whisper, "You have me. All of me. Man, beast, and heart. No other woman can say that. Only you, Maverick."

I surrender, Pirate.

CHAPTER TWENTY-SEVEN

TALIA

"Oh, look, what is that?" Scooter exclaimed, pointing to one of the softly glowing fairy-like creatures. "They are friendly creatures."

"Welcome to the magic Nothingness Forest, Scooter. Those are Mixies," Johara announced. "We should rest for a little while and make camp."

As they continued their journey, the glimmering creature known as a Mixie caught Talia's eyes. Its ethereal form radiated warmth, resembling a miniature living sun. Talia instinctively reached out to touch it, and as her fingers made contact, she felt a pulse of life flowing through its delicate body. The creature's huge, glowing eyes met hers, and a sense of peace and contentment took over her.

The Mixie was not alone in its curiosity. A few more of these enchanting beings fluttered around them, their presence both curious and playful. Landing on Storm's hair, they giggled mischievously, causing a blush to creep across his cheeks as he gently brushed them away. One little Mixie even dared to land delicately on Talia's lips, leaving behind a taste of sweet nectar that brought forth a spark of joy. These whimsical interactions only deepened their connection with the mystical creatures and with each other.

Talia pulled at Storm's arm and whispered, "Follow me, Pirate."

He nodded eagerly, happily following her down a path that seemed to wind deeper into the forest. The Mixies followed them, their curiosity piqued by the presence of these intruders. They flitted about them, their wings rustling against leaves and branches. She found herself growing increasingly aroused by their presence, sensing their magic. The path opened into a small clearing filled with the glowing creatures. They began to dance around them, their delicate feet not making a sound on the soft ground. She sighed deeply, breathing in their sweet scent. It was intoxicating, reminding her of flowers and honey and sunshine.

He pulled her closer into his strong, protective embrace. Their bodies molded together as their lips met in a fiery, passionate kiss that she had been waiting for since arriving in this place. The taste of him, a blend of sweet and masculine, ignited her senses and fueled her longing for more.

With a skillful touch, Storm's hands explored the contours of her body, his fingertips leaving a trail of electrifying sensations in their wake. Each caress was deliberate and purposeful, awakening a hunger deep within her that only he could satisfy.

As their bodies danced to the rhythm of their desires, she couldn't ignore the watchful gaze of the Mixies upon her. Their delicate glow seemed to intensify, enveloping her in a warm aura that accentuated every pleasurable sensation surging through her body. The tiny creatures fluttered around them, their delicate wings creating an enchanting symphony of whispers and rustling leaves.

The forest itself seemed to hum with anticipation, aware of the profound connection being forged by this couple. Every rustle and every whisper carried an air of encouragement, as if nature itself conspired to heighten their shared ecstasy. The soft glow emitted by the Mixies bathed their entwined bodies in a luminous embrace, casting playful shadows that mirrored their desires.

She gasped and moaned, her voice a harmony to the symphony of nature surrounding them. His touch set a fire within her that burned hotter with each passing moment. The gentle warmth emanating from the Mixies seemed to merge with her own passion, amplifying every sensation until she felt as if she were floating in a sea of pleasure.

Lost in their shared intimacy, she knew the Mixies bore witness to their connection. Their presence magnified her arousal, intensifying the pleasure streaming through her body. With each breathless gasp and arch of her body, she offered herself to him completely, allowing him and the mystical creatures to witness the unfiltered expression of her love and desire.

She pulled away, feeling nervous.

"Please, Maverick, don't tease me," he whispered in a smooth but desperate voice. "I can't take it anymore."

"No more teasing, but I need you to know something." She bit her lip, unable to speak the truth about her inexperience, feeling uneasy. "I don't... I mean, I've never..."

She lowered her eyes, trying to find the words.

"Never what?" he asked, his brow furrowed in concern.

"Been with a man," she confessed, her voice barely a whisper. She felt her face heat up, wishing the ground would open and swallow her whole. "Any man, Anunnakian or Sumerian."

I can't believe I told him.

His eyes widened, surprise and excitement flashing across his features. "You're a virgin?" he asked, his voice hushed but filled with awe. He pulled her closer, kissing her again, their bodies pressing together. "This is perfect," he whispered against her lips. "I've never been someone's first before."

She shivered, her heart pounding as his tongue danced with hers. She felt his hardness pressing against her belly, reminding her of what was to come. He tilted his head, looking down at her with newly lustful eyes. He traced the line of her jaw to her collarbone. She gasped, arching into his touch as heat spread through her body.

"So beautiful." His voice was raw with desire. "I want you so badly," he murmured between kisses. He paused, looking into her eyes. He laid her back onto the soft grass, his weight pressing her into the ground. His hand trailed down to her stomach, making it flutter. She squirmed under his touch, her body begging for more. "You're so sensitive," he whispered, his breath hot against her skin. He traced her sides and down to the hem of her shirt, tracing each curve before pulling it from her pants.

Her heart raced as he undid the first button on her shirt, taking in the sight of her body with each button he opened. After a few more buttons, he exposed her white lace bra, framing her abundant breasts underneath. She allowed her shirt to slide off her arms. Kissing her shoulder, he slid the bra strap off. With a talented snap of his fingers over the clasp in the back, he removed the obstacle.

"How did you do that?" she asked.

"Removing bras is my magical power." He grinned.

He leaned in, kissing her neck, his lips trailing down to her collarbone. He nibbled softly, making her gasp. His hands roamed her body, exploring every inch of her skin. She moaned as he brushed over her hardened nipples, tracing circles around them. She felt his desire for her, the way his cock throbbed against her thigh.

"You're beautiful," he murmured, his voice rough, before taking her nipple into his mouth. She moaned softly as he teased her nipples, scraping them with his teeth and tonguing them gently. She couldn't believe how good it felt.

"Please," she whimpered. "Oh, Pirate."

He chuckled. "I like the way that rolls off those sweet lips, Maverick." He groaned, his eyes closed in enjoyment. He slid his hand between their bodies, smoothly removing her pants and panties with practiced ease. "I've been waiting for you, Maverick."

His hand, meek and unhurried, traced a path up her inner thigh. As his fingers reached her core, they grazed over her folds to find her wetness. His fingers were talented and gentle, yet firm, as they swirled and circled around her sensitive clit. With each touch, her body rippled with pleasure, her back arching off the ground as she reached for more.

"Pirate," she cried. His fingers danced and tickled her pussy, making her legs shake. She yearned for more. "That feels so..." She panted, biting her lip, allowing a loud moan to finish her thought.

He smiled against her neck, as if he were savoring her responses. His fingers traced her folds, teasing her. She felt cold wrap around her body as he pulled away to undress.

Exposed, she felt vulnerable, unsure of her own body as he removed his shirt. His perfectly chiseled chest was a reminder that she was not thin like her sister. The more he undressed, the more she felt compelled to cover herself. She sat up, pulling her knees to her chin, trying to hide her naked body. He had a delicious body, more so than she could even imagine.

He leaned in and said, "Please, Talia, don't hide that beautiful body from me." He ran his fingers down her spine, waiting for a response. "As much as I want you, are you having second thoughts?"

"You want me?" she said with a hint of doubt in her voice.

"I want all of you, not just that beautiful body of yours. I want your love. You're my everything. Let me love you." He smiled, showing off his dimples. He took her arm and pulled her back into his embrace. Staring deep into her violet eyes, he admitted, "Only you, Maverick."

He loves me.

She pressed her naked body against him. Finding his ear, she moaned, "Pirate, have your treasure."

He positioned himself in front of her, spreading her legs, revealing the way to his treasure. He gently prodded the tip of his cock at her entrance, slowly pushing inside. She gasped, her body tensing from the sudden intrusion.

He waited, letting her adjust.

"You're so fucking tight," he growled, his muscles tense. "Your body is a treasure. Tell me when it's too much," he gritted, his hips stilling.

"No," she whimpered, her eyes pleading. "Please, a little more."

With her permission, he pushed in farther. She cried out in a mix of pleasure and pain, arching her back. He groaned as he began to move, thrusting slowly, softly. She could only accommodate half his cock, tightly wrapped in warmth.

She gripped the ground beneath her, her nails digging into the soft grass. The sensation of being taken was unlike anything she'd ever felt before, and she never wanted it to stop. She wanted more. She wrapped her legs around him, encouraging him to go faster, deeper.

"Fuck, Maverick," he grunted, pushing harder. Her body conformed to his, loving every inch of him as he pounded into her. Her moans mixed with his growls, filling the forest with their passion. He moved faster, harder, and she met him thrust for thrust, her body rising to the occasion.

"Pirate! More!" she screamed.

Their passion reached its peak, and he transformed into the Minotaur, his body growing larger, his cock stretching her even further. She cried out again, but this time, it was more of a scream than a moan. It was as if she were being filled her to the breaking point taking him all in. She felt her pussy tighten around his cock as waves of moans came from her mouth.

He growled from deep in his throat like he was singing her song. He grabbed her hips, holding her still as he pumped his hips harder into her. When his hot seed filled her, he roared in ecstasy and her body shook violently. The sounds of their lovemaking had echoed through the forest. He collapsed on top of her, their heavy breaths mixing in the cool air. He kissed her softly on her forehead before rolling off her.

"I'll always protect you, Maverick," he whispered, his voice rough after their intense lovemaking. She smiled, running her fingers through his fur, still in awe of what had just happened.

"My sweet Minotaur, as much I love seeing your face, I need my Pirate. Can I have him back?" She leaned in to softly kiss his lips. As the fur on his face receded back into his skin, she felt him press closer, deepening their kiss.

"I knew you wanted a narcissistic, skirt-chasing, self-centered pirate. You have no idea how happy this makes me."

"Please, forgive this tree-hugging, know-it-all maverick for being wrong."

"You were right, and you kicked my ass."

"I am dying to know something now. I asked you a question, but you never gave me a straight answer," she said. "How much longer did you have before your Quickening cycle started over?"

With a deep rumble of laughter, he pinned her down against the soft grass. His eyes swept up and down her bare form. "Today was day six. I had a few hours left. As much shit as I went through, spending my Quickening with you was worth the wait. Now I want you again, Maverick."

"Again? Now?" She squirmed, still recovering.

"I could go like five more rounds with you. I could never get enough of your beautiful naked body, Maverick. I've never had to work so hard." He bent to kiss her lips. "I'm sure you need some time, so I will let you rest. The Minotaur wants me to tell you something important." He took her hand and placed it on the center of his chest. "I may not be able to control when the Minotaur comes out, but you do. If you ever need him, call to him and he will hear you."

"Storm, I have been trying all this time to separate the man from the beast, but now I don't need to. I love the man and the beast. All of you and only you, Pirate."

"Only you, Maverick."

"I better put my clothes back on before there are five more rounds."

"We should get back and help Johara and Scooter set up camp for the night."

They navigated their way back through the dense forest, their feet crunching on fallen leaves and twigs as they went. He couldn't resist teasing Talia, playfully pulling at her and eliciting a joyful giggle that echoed through the woods. It was as if the whole forest were alive with their laughter.

When the couple finally emerged into the clearing, Talia's jaw dropped as she took in the majestic scenery before her, completely awestruck by its beauty. A campsite had been meticulously set up, with four spacious tents standing tall and inviting in a semi-circle around a fire. Scooter and Johara lounged in sturdy wooden chairs by the fire, their faces illuminated by the warm glow and smiles of welcome. The scent of pine and wood smoke filled the air.

"How long were we gone?"

"Johara conjured all of this," Scooter said as he popped a berry in his mouth and leaned back in his chair. "It only took a few minutes, so we've been waiting for you guys ever since. I like this kind of camping."

Storm eagerly slid into the chair next to Scooter, motioning for Talia to join him. With a playful tug on her arm, he invited her to sit on his lap instead. She effortlessly maneuvered herself onto the chair and settled against his chest, feeling the warmth of his body and the steady beat of his heart beneath her back.

Scooter slapped his friend's arm. "You're happy again, Storm. I am so glad to see you more like yourself. I didn't like crabby Storm." Scooter looked at Talia. "I don't know what you did to this guy, but thank you."

A low, rumbling laugh escaped Storm's lips as he leaned over and playfully ruffled Scooter's hair.

Johara smiled. "The Mixies will have that effect on you."

Scooter's face lit up with curiosity. "What effect?"

Talia looked at Storm. "He really doesn't know?"

"He's an Enochian. He has no idea, but watch this." Storm leaned in close, his hand resting on Scooter's shoulder. He whispered something that made Scooter's cheeks flush a deep shade of crimson. Flustered and bewildered, he turned to stare at Storm with wide eyes and then at Talia.

"In the forest?"

"Yes, buddy. That's how it works. Sometimes your innocence amazes me."

"I will have to make an adjustment to our camp," Johara said, pulling out her wand.

Scooter exclaimed with enthusiasm, "You all need to see this. It's absolutely incredible."

Johara stood and raised her arm to point toward two tents behind them. The fabric of the tents fluttered gently in the wind as she waved her hand, signaling for them to be joined together to make one large tent. The tents began to shift and meld, their once distinct shapes now merging into one expansive structure that seemed to grow before their eyes. They seamlessly fused together and stretched under Johara's magical influence. Talia leaned into Storm's side, her gaze filled with awe and appreciation for Johara's skill and artistry.

"You make it seem so easy."

"That's years of practice. You'll get there too, Talia."

CHAPTER TWENTY-EIGHT

TALIA

"That was the best night sleep I've had in a long time," Talia said as she stretched and uncurled herself from the warmth of Storm's body. She shivered in her thin shirt and underwear, the coldness seeping into her bones. She reached for the fur blanket and pulled it up to her neck, seeking warmth and comfort.

"Where do you think you're going, Maverick?" he grunted. She felt his arm find its way around her waist and pulled her back. "Now that I've had you once, I want you all the time."

"Is that how this works, Pirate?"

"That's how I would like this to work."

"After we save my sister, you can have me all you want." She smiled.

"Uh, Storm," Scooter's voice came through the thin fabric of the tent, "Johara says if you two don't come out soon, she's going to send me in there to get you. I really hope you are dressed."

"Okay, Scooter. Give me five minutes."

"You have three," Johara called.

"We shouldn't make the princess mad. We can't do anything in three minutes." Talia stood from the bed, reaching down to retrieve her scattered clothing. As she bent down, she felt the sharp slap of his hand through her panties.

"Wanna bet, Maverick? She gave me three minutes of watching you get dressed."

Talia and Storm, their bodies still glowing from the magical embrace, could not contain their laughter. Their eyes met in a playful exchange, flirting as they came out of their tent. He grabbed her, and they fell into each other's arms, forgetting for a moment the mission at hand.

"Ah, there you are," said Johara. "You two look like you had fun."

"Good morning," Talia said with a lingering giggle.

"We have a half a day journey ahead of us to get to my tribe," Johara said. "The Woobles are expecting us."

As the group ventured deeper into the dense forest, Talia marveled at the vibrant foliage surrounding them. The sweet scent of blooming flowers filled her nostrils, while the sound of rustling leaves created a soothing melody. She noticed the path they were following seemed almost hidden.

After what felt like hours of walking through the dense forest, they finally arrived at the enchanting Wooble village. Pulling out her wand, Princess Johara gracefully removed the protective field that had concealed the village from view.

"Wow," Storm muttered, echoing Talia's thoughts. "I've never seen anything like this."

Talia's breath caught in her throat as she took in the awe-inspiring sight before her. The towering trees nestled the hidden paradise village. Sturdy branches suspended colorful houses adorned with vibrant flowers and intricately carved wooden details, creating a whimsical and captivating scene. These houses seemed to blend with the natural surroundings, as if they were an integral part of the forest itself.

Crisscrossing bridges, adorned with delicate vines and blossoming flowers, connected the treetops, a network of pathways that appeared to defy gravity. These bridges, constructed with such precision and care, added to the enchantment of the village. Each step taken upon them elicited a soft creaking sound, harmonizing with the rustling leaves and creating a symphony of nature's music.

"How do we get up there?" Scooter asked.

Johara pulled on a low branch. A secret door opened in a nearby tree to reveal an elevator. They followed her onto the elevator, which smoothly ascended through the treetops. After a few minutes, they reached their destination—a large platform situated high above the treetops. Tall trees seemed to guard it.

"Welcome to my home," Johara said proudly, gesturing toward the platform.

As Talia stepped onto one of these bridges, she felt a sense of wonder surge through her. The air carried a scent of sweet blossoms mingled with the fragrance of moss-covered tree trunks. Sunlight filtered through the lush canopy above, casting dappled shadows on their path. The gentle sway of the bridge beneath their feet added an element of adventure and playfulness to their journey.

The craftsmanship that had gone into constructing this breathtaking sanctuary was evident in every detail. Intricate carvings adorned each house, depicting scenes from ancient legends and tales of mythical creatures. Lanterns hung from branches, illuminating the village with a warm, inviting glow as dusk began to settle over the forest.

She experienced a sense of wonder as she marveled at the Wooble village. It was a testament to the magic that existed in the world, serving as a tangible reminder of the beauty nature could achieve when coexisting in harmony. As they continued their journey through this enchanting realm, she couldn't wait to explore every nook and cranny, to immerse herself in the rich tapestry of stories that awaited her within these suspended houses and winding bridges.

"Johara, how did you find this place?" Talia asked, her eyes wide with amazement.

"When I was forced to leave the castle, the Woobles were kind enough to take me in," she replied, her voice filled with warmth. "They became my family. We should find the Chief."

"Scooter, you don't look so good. Are you okay?" Talia asked.

I don't know why I even ask. Wait for it...

"We are so high up," he said with a trembling voice. He began twitching, first just his hand, then his eye, and soon his whole body. Looking down at the ground, his eyes rolled back into his head. Storm rushed to catch his falling friend.

Scooter is such a damsel in distress. Storm's going to spend the entire time catching him.

"How about a safety net?" Princess Johara asked. "Would that put you at ease?" She pulled out her wand. "I placed a protection spell on this village so Hunter's soldiers would not find it."

"Much like the protection spell on our house," Talia said. "You can't see it, but it's there."

"I will make it visible for you, Scooter."

The surrounding air shimmered with enchantment, and an iridescent net materialized before their eyes below. It was a masterpiece of magical craftsmanship, woven from strands of ethereal light that sparkled with a myriad of colors. The net seemed to float effortlessly in mid-air, as if suspended by invisible threads from the surrounding trees.

The intricate patterns woven within the net were reminiscent of delicate lacework. Dazzling hues of blues, greens, and purples intertwined with each other in an intricate dance, forming captivating swirls and elegant curves. The colors shifted and changed as if alive. If the Wooble village held even a fraction of the magic they had already experienced, their journey was bound to be an unforgettable one.

As they traversed the brightly colored bridges, a figure emerged from one house, walking to meet them. Chief Wooble, the three-foot-tall bear creature, exuded an aura of wisdom and experience. His once resplendent fur, a rich dark brown now streaked with silvers and whites, bore the indelible marks of countless battles fought in defense of his beloved Wooble kin. The scars told stories of resilience and courage, each mark representing a hard-won victory against King Hunter's soldiers. His umber eyes twinkling with warmth and authority.

Though he carried himself with an air of wisdom, both physical and emotional burdens weighed Chief Wooble's steps. His movements were deliberate yet graceful, an embodiment of his role as a guide for his tribe.

"Welcome home, princess," Chief Wooble greeted her and smiled kindly, embracing her in a warm hug.

"Chief," Johara nodded respectfully, "I've brought some friends who have come to aid us in our fight against Hunter."

"Ah, yes," Chief said, studying Talia, Storm, and Scooter intently. "We are grateful for your assistance in our rebellion." His attention landed on Talia and he moved closer to her. "You must be Talia, the human warrior. Our champion is here."

Champion. Who, me? Yes, that would be me.

"Yes, Chief Wooble."

"I understand that Hunter has your sister, so I've sent word to the castle to find out her condition and where Hunter is keeping her."

With possible news of Olivia, her heart caught in her throat. "Have you heard anything?"

Talia only had one fleeting moment of connection with Olivia since Jitatma took her through the portal. The absence of Olivia's voice left a hollow feeling in her mind, like shouting into an empty valley and hearing her own thoughts echo back. She would give anything to hear an outrageous or ungrateful comment. She longed for just one more moment of closeness with her sister, to hear her laugh or see her smile again.

"We have a meeting this evening. We should hear news soon."

Johara placed her hand on Talia's shoulder. "Don't worry. Chief Wooble and I have spies in the castle. Not everyone is loyal to Hunter."

"Do you trust the information you are getting from these spies?" Storm asked.

"It's all we have to go on right now. I need to get my sister back, so I'll take anything. I want to go to meet this spy. I want to hear the news for myself," Talia said. Johara and Chief Wooble exchanged uneasy glances. "Johara, What's the problem?"

"It's too dangerous. We can't risk exposing him. He's too valuable to our rebellion."

"Hunter has Olivia. I'm going to find out how to get her back. You can't change my mind." She planted her feet and squared her shoulders. "Either you let me go or I will track down this spy myself. Johara, you know I'll eventually figure it out."

Johara's gaze shifted to Chief Wooble. "I trained her in the art of tracking, so she will inevitably discover the truth. We should let her go."

"Fine." The chief pointed to Storm. "Take the big guy with you. I can't risk the life of our champion just before the big battle, even if she is as stubborn as Circe."

"That she is," he agreed.

"Please, let me introduce you to our weapon developer, Papa, and his assistant, Cody," Chief said as he gestured toward an older Wooble with a gentle expression and wise eyes.

Papa Wooble, despite being a bear of shorter stature than others in the tribe, had a confidence about him that seemed to grow with every stride he took. His fur was not as it used to be in his youth, now mostly gray with a few brown strands scattered unevenly. His green eyes peered through tinted glasses. A large green cape, worn and weathered yet regal, draped over his shoulders and dragged behind him. Papa Wooble leaned on a sturdy wooden staff that pounded on the bridge like a drum, supporting his aged body and a symbol of his experience. His young assistant followed, carrying a bundle of weapons in his arms.

"Queen Circe." Papa Wooble mistook Talia.

"I am not the queen," Talia said, shaking her head.

"The prophecy is true. You look just like her," Papa said, adjusting his glasses.

"I've been told as much." She smiled.

"Welcome, brave warriors," Papa greeted them. "I have prepared something special for each of you." He carefully presented Talia, Storm, and Scooter with a unique bracelet that contained a shield. "This special bracelet will provide you with protection and aid in your battle against King Hunter's forces."

Talia held the bracelet delicately in her hand, its smooth surface cool against her skin. As she examined it closely, she marveled at the vibrant colors that adorned its intricate design. The swirling patterns etched into the metal seemed to come alive with a mesmerizing play of hues, emerald greens, fiery reds, regal purples, and deep ocean blues.

Papa Wooble carefully crafted each button on the side of the bracelet to match its corresponding color. The green button, like a flourishing leaf, represented the power of invisibility. With a simple press, she knew she could activate the shield and disappear, becoming one with the surroundings just like the hidden village itself.

Beside it, the red button glowed warmly, symbolizing deactivation. She imagined that with a simple touch, she could release herself from the shroud of invisibility and reveal her presence once more.

The purple button stood out with its majestic shade, representing the mirroring feature of the bracelet. She envisioned herself blending effortlessly into any environment by activating this remarkable ability. It would allow her to take on the appearance and characteristics of her surroundings, making it nearly impossible for anyone to detect her presence.

Last, there was the blue button, resembling a miniature shield itself. Its serene hue brought a sense of calm and protection. She knew pressing this button would transform the bracelet into a solid shield, reinforcing her defense against King Hunter's forces. It would act as a barrier between danger and herself, providing an extra layer of safety during their impending battles.

As Papa explained each function of the buttons with splendid care, she felt a surge of gratitude for the Woobles' meticulous craftsmanship. Their attention to detail and understanding of their allies' needs were evident in every aspect of this extraordinary creation.

"Amazing," Talia whispered in awe.

As Papa handed Scooter the sleek crossbow, he nearly dropped it, but managed to recover the weapon quickly. Talia noticed the weapon shimmered, casting a soft azure light that danced along its polished surface. It was a true masterpiece of craftsmanship, a testament to the Woobles' ingenuity and dedication to their cause.

The crossbow had an elegantly streamlined design that perfectly balanced form and function. The smooth contours seemed to fit snugly in Scooter's hands, as if it were an extension of his arm. Supple leather wrapped the grip, providing both comfort and stability, while intricate engravings adorned the body of the weapon, depicting ancient symbols of power and protection.

But it was the bolts that truly set this crossbow apart. Each bolt glowed with a faint blue luminescence, giving off a beautiful aura. These laser bolts were no ordinary projectiles; they possessed a magical quality that made them unparalleled in accuracy and reloading speed. With a simple pull of the trigger, the crossbow would automatically load another bolt, ready to hit its target with deadly precision.

He'd better be careful with that weapon or I'm going to end up with an arrow in my ass.

Turning her attention to Storm, Talia was awestruck by the formidable weapon Papa presented to him. The seven-foot double-bladed axe exuded raw power and unyielding strength. Its imposing size alone would intimidate any opponent who dared stand in Storm's way.

She thought it was the details that made this weapon truly extraordinary. The blades themselves gleamed with a razor-sharp edge, reflecting the light around them with a terrorizing glint. Engravings etched into the surface depicted scenes of ancient mythical creatures, showcasing the rich history and heritage of the Woobles' warrior lineage.

As Storm hefted the axe in his massive hands, the balance and movement of the weapon looked natural, as if it were an extension of his own immense power. He swung it experimentally, the air parting with a satisfying whoosh as the axe cleaved effortlessly through imaginary adversaries.

Talia wondered if the time he was on Prison Island was spent swinging an axe, but she didn't dare bring up the subject. The double-bladed axe seemed to awaken a primitive ferocity within him, igniting a fire that burned brightly. She imagined Storm charging into battle as the Minotaur, twirling the mighty axe with lethal precision, striking fear into the hearts of King Hunter's soldiers.

"Thank you, Papa," Talia, Storm, and Scooter said in unison, their hearts filled with gratitude. Talia knew these powerful weapons would be invaluable in their fight against King Hunter.

"Use them wisely," Papa advised sagely, "and remember the true strength of a warrior lies not in their weapons, but in their heart."

"Thank you for your wisdom, Papa," Talia said sincerely, clutching the bracelet tightly in her hand. "We promise to use these weapons wisely and to fight with all our heart and spirit."

Storm added, gripping his axe with pride, "We will not let you down."

Talia's gaze followed Scooter's every move as he carefully examined his new crossbow. He turned it over and over in his hands, looking at every inch as if trying to figure it out. He pressed a button on the side. The weapon was loaded, and his finger twitched dangerously close to the trigger, the bolt pointed near his face.

In a split second, she reacted and knocked his arm out of the way just as a rogue laser bolt shot out from the crossbow. The bolt hit little Cody in the leg with a sharp crack, causing him to cry out in pain. She thanked her quick reflexes for preventing a potential disaster.

"For the love of Ki, Scooter! Were you not listening? Papa just said to use it wisely," she scolded as she grabbed the stock of the crossbow and snatched the weapon from his grasp before he could reload. Drawing on her training, she sharply stated, "Respect the weapon and it'll never fail." She shoved the bow in Johara's hands. "Train him how to use this. I don't want a bolt in my ass. He doesn't touch any weapon until he knows exactly what it does."

Johara nodded.

As Talia cautiously approached Cody, her heart ached at the sight of his injured form. The pungent stench of burned fur filled her nostrils, and she fought back a wave of nausea. With gentle hands, she kneeled and carefully removed the dart-like projectile from his leg. As her fingers closed around it, an intense heat seared through her palm, causing her to gasp in pain. She quickly dropped the bolt and inspected her hand.

She called upon her healing abilities, rubbing her hands together to activate them. With a wave of her hand, she focused on Cody's injured leg, using her powers to cauterize the wound and mend his fur. She helped the little bear to his feet.

Cody's furry face was lit up with pure joy as he spoke, his small voice filled with excitement. "That was incredible! It felt like a warm hug from Queen Circe herself." His beady black eyes were fixed on her, and he couldn't resist reaching out his paws toward her. He gently planted them on her face, rubbing her skin. "You are so pretty. You have purple eyes." He squeezed her cheeks and planted a kiss on her nose. "They're kind of like Circe's. Your skin is so soft, like my paws."

"You have soft paws and you're adorable, kind sir."

"Thank you, pretty lady."

Talia patted the little bear's head before standing. She then turned around to find Storm standing there with his usual playful grin. "He's a little heartbreaker. Looks like I have some competition."

She rose on her tiptoes and pressed her lips against his, whispering, "I prefer the rough fur of the Minotaur, but it wouldn't hurt for you to remind him to groom himself."

CHAPTER TWENTY-NINE

TALIA

T alia and Storm trailed behind Chef Wooble as they ventured away from the protective canopy of the Wooble village. The thick foliage rustled, drowning out the sounds of their footsteps on the forest floor. They finally reached a small stream. Its clear waters bubbling over rocks and pebbles as it twisted through the underbrush, carrying with it the scent of fresh water, mixed with the slightly pungent odor of decaying plant matter.

Remaining vigilant, she scanned their surroundings and listened intently for any unusual disruptions among the usual sounds of the forest. The dense brush provided ample cover as they waited, blending seamlessly into their surroundings. Crouching low on one knee, her hand rested on her belt just above her Chakram, waiting.

As the gentle trickling of water filled her ears, Talia's keen senses picked up the faint snap of a twig breaking nearby. Before she could even turn to face the source of the noise, the unmistakable sound of Storm's grunting reached her ears from behind. With powerful hooves pounding against the ground, the Minotaur charged past her with intimidating speed and strength. She felt a surge of admiration for the creature's ferocious grace as it continued on its path without so much as a glance in her direction.

Just as the Minotaur crossed the stream, a man in a red cape emerged from the brush. Storm, his muscles rippling with adrenaline and anger, threw a powerful punch toward the man. The impact sent the man sprawling back onto the ground. She rushed over, and Chief Wooble followed close behind. With his fist still raised, Storm stood over Jitatma, his body tense and poised for another strike.

He placed his hoof on Jitatma's chest. "Move so I can crush you. I know your smell anywhere."

"Jitatma is your guy!" Talia threw up her arms at Chief. "He's your spy."

"Permission, Maverick, to crush this asshole."

"Permission granted, my beast."

"You can at least give me a chance to explain," Jitatma said. "You owe me that, Storm. I saved your life once."

"You took my sister. I should let the Minotaur stomp your heart into your spine for that alone," she said. "Then he can take the rest of his aggression out on your Nibmarks like you did to him."

Jitatma turned his head to Talia. "Call off your pet. I'm trying to help Olivia. Hunter wiped her memory with water from the River of Forgetfulness. She's starting to remember you."

"That's why I felt her for a moment yesterday and her emotions were scattered."

"I'm trying to remind her that she is an empath and stirring up every emotion I can think of. She's been scared, angry, and sad."

Touching his arm, Talia commanded, "Stand down, Storm." She started pacing, shaking her head. There was only one emotion that could spark a response in Olivia so powerful that it would bring back her memory. It was the only thing that Olivia yearned for. It was a longing that could never be fulfilled, no matter how much Olivia desired it. "Jitatma, are you full-blooded Sumerian?"

As soon as Storm removed his hoof, Jitatma stood to brush himself off. "Yes, I am. Why do you ask?"

I can't believe I'm about to use these words out loud.

As if responding to an unspoken command, Storm's Minotaur form melted away, and he returned to his true Sumerian form. She flinched, secretly wishing he had remained in his beastly state for what she was about to say next.

"I'm going to regret telling you this, but I know how to get Olivia's memory back." She stopped to turn to Jitatma and Storm. "She needs to be backed against a wall, her pussy railed, her ass spanked, and called a good girl. Her deepest desire is to have possessive, rough sex. She wants to be dominated by a Sumerian man."

Talia watched Storm and Jitatma's expressions closely. Their eyes widened in shock, causing Storm to stumble back a step and Jitatma to shift his footing. After a moment of hesitation, Jitatma regained his composure and stood firm again.

"Well, that's some news." Storm let out a nervous chuckle. "I never expected you to say words like that."

"Those are Olivia's words, not mine," she clarified. She stepped closer to Jitatma and pointed at his chest. "I swear if you harm her, I will fry your dick."

"Easy, Talia. I know my limits with women. I can be rough, but not stupid," Jitatma said, putting his arms up. He relaxed, and a smile spread across his face, similar to the one Storm always wore. "I don't suppose you know what your sister's limits are."

Talia lowered her head and shook it in disbelief. "Oh, Lord Gorgon, do all Sumerian men have the same shit-eating grin?"

I can't believe I'm having this conversation in front of the Chief. Thank Anu, Olivia can't hear me now, but maybe she will thank me later.

"Olivia isn't a typical Anunnakian woman. She may look sweet, but she'll be able to handle you. You'll know when she's at her limit when she uses the defensives moves I taught her. That'll be her safe word."

"Which moves, Maverick? Would that be your lean?"

"I'm not saying. I'll let Jitatma experience them for himself."

"Talia, I know you have no reason to trust me, but everything I do is for a good reason," Jitatma said. "I begged Hunter to allow Olivia to remain in my care so I could protect her. Someday you and Storm will know the truth that everything that is happening is bigger than you realize."

"What side are you on?" Storm asked. "What truth?"

"I'm on the side of this kingdom."

"We have to get back to the village," Chief Wooble said.

As the sun dipped below the horizon, painting the sky in hues of fiery orange and dusky pink, Talia led her companions to the platform where the Woobles had arranged an impressive celebration feast. The air was thick with the mouthwatering aroma of roasted roots and spiced berries, a testament to the Woobles' culinary prowess. Scooter's eyes shone with childlike wonder, reflecting the flickering torchlight that encircled the banquet area. Princess Johara glided beside them, her grace undiminished even in these most rustic of settings.

"Look at this spread!" Storm exclaimed, his gaze darting from one dish to another.

The Woobles had outdone themselves by piling platters high with succulent roasted roots glazed in honey and sprinkled with fragrant herbs. Bowls overflowed with a medley of spiced berries, their deep reds and purples glistening invitingly under the torchlight. The Woobles, round and rosy from the glow of the feast, welcomed them with open arms and merry cheers.

A smile tugged at the corner of his mouth as Storm settled next to Talia. Princess Johara gracefully seated herself next to Scooter across the table.

Scooter was just about to bite into a skewer of honey-glazed root vegetables when a small figure emerged from under the table. Talia recognized the tuft of fur that stood upright like a blade of grass. With his eyes wide with curiosity, Cody waddled over to Scooter and clambered onto his lap without invitation.

"What are you eating? Is it sweet? Can I have some? What's your name?" Cody bombarded Scooter with an endless stream of inquiries.

"Hey, now, little guy." Scooter chuckled, trying to balance his plate while Cody fidgeted restlessly. "I'm Scooter, and sure, it's sweet. Maybe you should grab a plate and join us?"

Cody seemed to only have eyes for Scooter, treating him like a fascinating new playground. He poked at Scooter's pockets, tugged at his sleeve, and chattered away, continuing his line of endless questions. Talia giggled at the way Cody seemed to want to know everything about Scooter.

"Cody is our little beacon of curiosity," Johara explained to her, watching the scene with a fond chuckle. "He's got a heart bigger than himself, which means he can be a bit overwhelming."

"He's like a short, furry version of Scooter," she observed, amused by the interaction.

"Maybe little Cody can show Scooter what it's like to want personal space," Storm added, the corners of his eyes crinkling in genuine amusement.

Cody showed no signs of slowing down, peppering Scooter with more questions. His boundless energy was infectious. Laughter bubbled up around the table as Cody got close to Scooter, making amusing faces at him. Scooter grinned at the little Wooble's enthusiasm.

"Looks like you've got yourself a sidekick," Johara teased.

Scooter, who by now had surrendered to Cody's antics, was sharing bits of his meal with the energetic little Wooble. "Every hero needs one, right?"

The warmth of the fire danced in Talia's eyes as she watched the Woobles gather on the broad platform erected at the heart of their village. The flickering flames cast long, undulating shadows across the faces of the assembled crowd, their expressions a mixture of excitement and solemnity. A deep, rhythmic drumming began to resonate, grounding the gathering in an ancient cadence.

The Woobles moved gracefully, their feet thumping against the wood in synchronization. Muscles flexed and relaxed under fur-covered skin as they wove around each other in intricate patterns, orbiting the fire like celestial bodies drawn by its gravitational pull. Their battle chant rose into the night, a haunting melody that seemed to call to the very stars above.

As the dance reached its crescendo, Chief Wooble stepped forward. He was an imposing figure, his fur more silver than black, each strand telling tales of battles past and wisdom hard-earned. He raised his arms, and the platform fell silent, save for the sound of the fire.

"Tonight, we feast and dance not just for victory, but for our ancestors who watch over us," Chief Wooble boomed, his voice rich and powerful. "We honor their strength, their courage, and their spirit, which lives on in each of us. Let the fire's glow remind you of the flame within your hearts—a flame no darkness can extinguish."

Talia felt a shiver run down her spine, inspired by the chief's words. She glanced at Storm to see him staring intently at the chief, the firelight reflecting in his eyes. Bringing her attention back to the show, Chief Wooble presented the crowd with a long piece of fabric. He held it up over his head, and they all seemed to know what it meant. Two Mixies flew over to Chief Wooble, taking the fabric from him.

"The Mixies have called for the Claiming Ritual before battle tomorrow," Chief Wooble announced. There was cheering from the crowd.

Talia leaned over to Johara to ask, "What's the Claiming Ritual?"

"I probably should have warned you before the Mixies took you and Storm away earlier," she said. "It's an honor to be chosen. If the Mixies witness a mating in Nothingness Forest, one must claim the other before battle. It ensures the warrior will return home to their lover."

"For the first time, the chosen are both warriors. We have a dual claim. This means if they accept the claim, we will be victorious on the battlefield," Chief Wooble said.

"Do you mean marriage?" Talia asked. "I am not ready for that."

"Yes, it's a marriage bond," she confirmed.

"The Mixies have chosen Talia and Storm," Chief Wooble added.

Oh, shit!

"That's us, Maverick," Storm said, thrilled.

"Do you know what the Claiming Ritual means?" she asked.

"No, but we won," Storm said, grabbing her hand and pulling her out of her seat.

As the Mixies gracefully descended toward Storm and Talia with the shimmering fabric in their delicate grip, the air crackled with a sense of anticipation. Chief Wooble's imposing figure approached the couple, his silver fur glinting in the firelight as he solemnly wrapped the intricately woven cloth around their clasped hands. The assembled crowd erupted into cheers and applause, their voices blending into a joyous cacophony that reverberated through the night.

Talia's heart pounded in her chest as she felt the weight of Chief Wooble's actions settle upon her. The realization of what the Claiming Ritual truly meant dawned upon her. She turned to Storm, her eyes wide with nervous laughter, trying to mask the growing panic within her.

Storm leaned in close to her his voice barely above a whisper. "Is there something wrong?"

Talia hesitated for a moment before summoning the courage to confide in Storm. "The Claiming Ritual is a wedding," she revealed quietly, the words hanging heavily between them. "We were chosen because we had sex in the forest," she admitted, her cheeks flushing with embarrassment. "We have to accept."

As Storm processed her words, the color drained from his face and his features contorted in disbelief. The implications of their actions echoed through the sacred ceremony in which they now found themselves entwined. The weight of tradition and destiny bore down on her like a heavy cloak, binding them together in a way neither of them could have foreseen.

The flames leaped higher in the fire pit, casting flickering shadows across their faces as the night sky glittered with stars. The rhythmic beat of drums underscored the gravity of the moment, infusing the air with a sense of solemnity that resonated within her heart.

The Chief Wooble stepped back, allowing the couple a moment of quiet. With the celebration raging around them, Storm turned to Talia with a reassuring smile. In that fleeting instant, they shared an unspoken promise to stand together against whatever trials awaited them on this unexpected journey they were now bound to embark, as partners not just in battle, but in life.

"Talia Trismegist, do you accept the claim of Storm Smoke?" Chief Wooble asked.

"I claim Storm Smoke," she said, looking up at him.

"Storm Smoke, do you accept the claim of Talia Trismegist?"

"I claim Talia Trismegist," he said as he squeezed her hand from under the fabric.

"I will take them to finish the ritual in private," Johara offered.

Johara motioned for the couple to follow her to a guest house across the bridge, away from the crowd, in the highest tree of the village. Intricate carvings adorned the doorframe, welcoming them in. Plush cushions embroidered with shimmering threads furnished the room, offering a comfortable respite from the intensity of the ceremony outside. Johara bid them goodnight, closing the door behind her.

"I finally have you to myself," he said excitedly.

"Just so you know, I am not changing my last name." She giggled.

With the door securely shut behind them, Storm slipped his hand under her chin and gently lifted her face toward him. "I wasn't planning on changing mine either," he murmured huskily, his voice vibrating through her.

Their lips met in a devastating kiss, tongues connecting and exploring each other. Her hands roamed over his body, tracing the definition of his muscular back, pulling him closer to her. A sly smile played on her lips; he made no attempt to hide how much he wanted her.

She began to trace a tantalizing path along his powerful abs. He reached out, pulling her into another frenzied kiss while nudging her toward the bed. Their bodies fell in a tangled heap amongst the plush cushions, their lips never breaking contact as they eagerly explored one another.

On instinct, her legs wrapped around his waist, drawing him closer. Her back arched, pressing her breasts against his firm chest, eliciting a strangled moan from him. She felt his cock pressed against her core through the layers of fabric separating them.

"I will be gentle with you again," he said softly.

"No way. It's my turn." She pushed him down to the cushions on his back. Her boldness surprised him. "I claim you, Pirate."

With slow, deliberate movement, he reached out to tug at the intricate laces that held her bodice together. She leaned back, wanting him to have a good view of her body. She bit her lip as she unbuttoned her shirt with a seductive smile. In his presence, she felt desired and beautiful, and she wanted him to appreciate every inch of her skin.

"How did I get so lucky?" he groaned as she completely unfastened her shirt, her nipples hard through her bra. He drew her in, pressing her body against his. "Only you, Maverick."

With her shirt now fully undone and falling off one shoulder, she deftly unhooked her bra, allowing it to slip to the floor. He pulled at her pants. Her fingers wasted no time undoing his belt buckle, releasing the pent-up heat he held within his pants. As he removed his shirt, his chiseled jaw tightened, his hands clenched around the fabric of his discarded shirt, veins pulsating with pure, animalistic need.

"Only you, Pirate." Her words, delivered in a seductive tone.

Tracing the broad expanse of Storm's muscular chest, she savored the sight of his chiseled physique. Her finger mapped out every inch of his hard body, leaving a tantalizing trail of goosebumps in her wake. She adjusted herself to allow him the opportunity to remove his pants.

This man, so tempting. I am going to fuck him so good.

With a devilish glint in her eyes, she pressed her warm palm against the tight skin, feeling the steady drumming of his heartbeat beneath. His masculine scent filled her senses with an intoxicating blend of sweat and raw desire, prompting her to push him back slightly. She guided him onto the plush cushions below, swinging her leg around him. She relished the feel of his taut muscles beneath her. He was hers to control, and she knew it.

Nestled between her thighs, she felt the wetness seeping onto his rock-hard shaft. She lowered herself onto him, delighting in every inch that entered her body. He gripped her hips tightly, matching her movements. She felt him deep inside her, pulsing and pounding against her walls as she rode him with carnal abandon.

He heaved himself forward to take one of her breasts into his mouth. With the dual assault of sensation, she cried out in pleasure, arching her back to offer him more. She moved faster, swaying her hips to feel his cock easily slide through her wetness. She clenched her walls around him in an inviting symphony of pleasure.

He passionately trailed kisses along her collarbone before moving up to claim her mouth. Their tongues tangled fervently, matching the rhythm of their bodies locked together. His fingers dug deeper into her hipbones as she lost herself with his cock inside her body, craving that sweet release that was about to come.

As she tightened around him once again, he groaned loudly as the waves of her orgasm washed over her. A few thrusts later, he followed suit, letting out a loud grunt as he emptied himself inside her.

"I am claimed, Maverick."

In the aftermath of the Claiming Ritual, Talia stood at the window of the guest house, wrapped only in a blanket. The sounds of the celebration below became a distant melody. The flickering fire illuminated the huts and pathways, creating a warm, inviting atmosphere. The wind carried the scent of burning wood and the distant aroma of the feast to their elevated perch. She watched as the celebrations below began to wind down, and the Woobles started making their way back to their homes.

In the moonlight, Hunter's castle stood like a sentinel against the backdrop of the Enlightenment Mountain. The lavish structure was complete with a walled courtyard, a garden, and towers. The castle's grandeur was undeniable, its spires and towers reminiscent of a fairy tale illustration, but to Talia, there was an unmistakable chill that settled in her bones at its sight. The elongated shadows cast by its turrets and spires seemed to stretch over the valley below, as if warning all who approached to tread carefully.

Olivia was so close. She could feel it.

"Tell me, Pirate. Do you think we are ready?" she asked, breaking the silence.

"I think so. I feel good about my axe." Storm joined her at the window and wrapped his strong arms around her. She leaned into his embrace, seeking comfort and safety. Closing her eyes, she took a deep breath in an attempt to calm her racing nerves.

"There is something about this place. Do you feel it?" She turned to look at him. "It's like one big energy charging my powers and it feels comfortable."

"I know what you mean." His face was serious, looking over the landscape of the Far Viscera, toward Punishment Valley. "It's this place."

"Did you hear that?" Talia asked, standing straight to pay attention to the sound of faint rustling leaves and chatter. "It's Hunter's soldiers."

CHAPTER THIRTY

TALIA

F ear clouded Talia's mind as she stood in the hidden clearing, her Chakram gripped tightly in her hand. She knew what they were about to do was treasonous, but it was necessary. Princess Johara, a pillar of strength next to her, had her wand at the ready. Storm, in his Minotaur form, paced, double-edged axe in hand. She looked up to check on Scooter. He perched high in a tree, crossbow ready, bristling with anxiety.

I hope he doesn't fall. Storm will be too busy.

The sound of King Hunter's soldiers grew louder with each passing second. Their heavy footsteps and clanking armor echoed through the woods. The air was tense, electric with anticipation and dread. Perspiration trickled down her spine, and she could taste the adrenaline on her tongue. The crunch of twigs underfoot grew louder, signifying their imminent arrival. She took a deep breath and focused.

She scanned the area with her hands trembling slightly, taking in all the detail. Her lips moved in a silent prayer. The rustling of leaves and snapping of twigs filled the clearing as the soldiers grew closer. A low growl rumbled from Storm's throat, as if warning the enemy away from his territory.

The first soldier rounded the corner, his sword drawn and ready for battle. He stopped in his tracks upon seeing Storm, eyes widening in surprise. Before he could utter a word, a bolt zipped, embedding itself in his shoulder from Scooter's perch high in the trees. He yelped in pain, cursing the traitors who dared attack.

More soldiers followed, unaware of the ambush. The Wooble archers, hidden among the tops of the trees, took their commands from Scooter. As he signaled for the attack, arrows flew like deadly rain, each one finding its mark. Screams pierced the silence as soldiers fell to the ground, writhing in agony.

Talia smiled grimly, her invisibility shield holding strong, ensuring she remained hidden from the soldiers' sight. The shimmering effect engulfed them all, making them seem like ghosts floating through the clearing. She signaled for the ground force Woobles to stay hidden in the tree line, to be ready to join the fight when needed.

In this continuation of their daring mission, she surprised the unsuspecting enemy soldiers when she summoned sparks of crackling lightning from her fingertips. As electricity shot forth, the ground shattered beneath their feet, causing their formation to crumble in confusion. She unleashed a frenzy of blue and purple thunderbolts.

Seizing the opportunity, she swiftly reached for her Chakram. With remarkable precision, she released the weapon, watching as it whirled, blending the three swirls as one and struck two soldiers across the chest. The metallic ring of impact echoed through the clearing, a testament to her skill.

Not to be outdone, Princess Johara twirled her wand above her head. As if in response to her command, a gust of wind rose from the forest floor. Leaves danced and swirled around the bewildered soldiers, knocking them off balance with an unexpected force.

Storm's muscles rippled with tension as he sprang into action, his massive axe slicing through the soldiers. The clash of metal on metal reverberated throughout the clearing, creating a symphony of chaos that drowned out the shouts and cries of their foes. The weight of his strikes sent shockwaves through the soldiers' armor, leaving them stunned and disoriented.

As the dust settled and silence slowly reclaimed the once tumultuous clearing, Talia let out a slow breath. Her body trembled, every muscle aching from the tension and power building in her body. The invisibility shield that had kept them concealed shimmered and faded away, revealing her and her allies.

The scene that met their eyes was both haunting and triumphant. Fallen soldiers lay scattered across the blood-soaked ground. Some lay motionless, forever silenced by the brutality of the fight, while others clung to the remnants of their shattered pride, begging for mercy through gasps and pleas.

Storm's voice rasped from the strain of combat as he spoke, scanning the aftermath of their victory. "Never mess with my Maverick," he stated, his deep voice carrying a mixture of exhaustion and pride. Talia's gaze shifted downward, falling upon her Chakram. It bore the marks of battle, smeared with blood and dirt, evidence of the carnage she had unleashed upon their enemies. A strange sense of satisfaction came over her, mingling with the weariness in her bones.

They quickly set about collecting what they could salvage from the defeated soldiers. They methodically searched for any valuable information that might aid them in their ongoing fight against their sworn enemy.

Satisfied with their findings, she looked at her comrades, a silent agreement passing between them. They disappeared into the shadows once more, leaving behind the stark evidence of their victory. With each step deeper into the forest, they retreated to a hidden location where they would regroup and plan their next move.

The night air was cool on her skin, her heartbeat slowly returning to normal, waiting for the next wave of the enemy. She glanced at Storm, his eyes fixed on the path, admiring his Minotaur form. He towered over her, axe at the ready, protecting her. She wanted to tell him how she felt, but that would mean there would be a possibility they would not survive this battle. Instead, she grabbed his large arm.

The sound of steps echoed through the trees, soldiers approaching fast. They couldn't have seen them, hidden away as they were, but they knew they were there. Talia took up a defensive position, lightning dancing around her fingertips, ready to strike.

With a burst of energy, she charged forward. Lightning crackled around her, hiding behind her shield. Her sudden appearance took the soldiers aback, their faces showing confusion. She struck one with a lightning bolt that sent him flying back into his comrades, knocking them down like dominos. They scrambled to their feet, unsure how to defend against an unseen enemy. Thunder roared in the distance, adding to the chaos.

She weaved between them, her agility on full display as she dodged their attacks. Every time she landed a blow, lightning bolts struck, causing chaos and disarray. The soldiers' panic set in when she threw her Chakram and cut several soldiers across the neck and face, finishing each off with a lightning bolt.

Blood and ash mixed in the air, filling the night with a metallic tang. A soldier stumbled toward her, his sword raised high. She stepped aside at the last moment, letting the blade slice through empty air, then attacked him from behind, cutting him from hip to shoulder. His organs spilled out, steaming in the cold night air. Another soldier attempted to run away, but a bolt of lightning struck him down, propelling him into a tree and causing his body to go limp.

As more soldiers came at her, she summoned a ball of lightning in her left hand and hurled it at them, engulfing them in a blinding blue-white flash. She heard the burst of electricity and smelled burning flesh as they fell back, screaming.

Storm roared, sending a gust of wind that knocked them off their feet. They tried to get up, only to be met with a wave of wind that sent them tumbling again from Princess Johara's wand. Their cries for help echoed through the forest, but it was too late. The group was unstoppable as they mowed down their attackers with ease.

The remaining soldiers scattered and fled into the darkness, leaving behind their injured and dead comrades. Talia stood tall, breathing heavily from exertion. She tasted blood on her lips. The forest was alive with the smell of death.

Storm grinned at her. His eyes were alight with pride. "Well done, Maverick," he said as he pulled her into a tight embrace. She smiled and leaned against him as they caught their breath.

"You are not so bad yourself, Pirate."

But the battle wasn't over yet. Suddenly, they heard hundreds of footsteps approaching from behind. They whirled around and saw an army of soldiers charging toward them, led by Lieutenant Malta. They drew their weapons and looked determined to take them down. There was no escape. Talia closed her eyes as she prepared for the inevitable.

Just as the soldiers raised their swords to strike, she heard the Woobles dart out from behind the trees and bushes. These small creatures fought with speed and agility as they weaved through the enemy. They leaped onto the soldiers' shoulders, which caused them to stumble and fall. One soldier tripped over a tree root that sent him flying face-first into the dirt. Arrows flew from the trees to help hold the soldiers back.

Malta roared in frustration, indignant at being thwarted by these pint-sized troublemakers. He raised his sword, aiming a deadly strike at a Wooble. Talia and Storm rushed to intervene, pushing the creature out of harm's way just in time. Talia turned to face the lieutenant, ready for battle once more.

From the towering tree above her, Scooter's voice boomed, "Holy Anu!" She instinctively crouched as a blazing bolt of laser shot past her cheek, singeing a few strands of hair. Feeling the sudden heat, her eyes followed the path of the laser bolt, watching as it struck Malta square in the backside. His startled yelp echoed through the forest as he leaped forward, nearly stumbling over his own feet in surprise.

"Scooter!"

"Sorry, Talia," he yelled back.

"Nice shot, but that was too close to my face."

"Someone get that spaz out of the tree," Malta ordered as he limped away behind the protection of his soldiers.

The soldiers felt confusion as they faced a sudden attack from all sides. The ground trembled nearby, sending chunks of debris flying. One soldier tried to shield himself, but it was not enough. Another dove for cover under a nearby tree, only to be struck down by a fallen branch. Panic set in; they didn't know where the attacks were coming from or how to defend themselves against an unseen enemy. Talia smiled at Johara for causing such confusion.

She took advantage of the disarray, using her agility to dodge attacks and strike with precision. Her Chakram flew with deadly accuracy, cutting several soldiers across the neck and face before finishing each off with a lightning bolt. She disappeared and reappeared, dancing between them like a whirlwind of death. A soldier charged toward her, only to be stopped short by Storm's axe.

The soldiers' fear grew as they realized they were no match for these supernatural beings. Their attempts to defend themselves became more desperate. The odds overwhelmed them. Soon, only moans and cries filled the air as wounded soldiers tried to crawl away.

Believing they could taste victory, she pushed forward.

King Hunter's sword-wielding soldiers managed to rally. They closed ranks, their eyes ablaze. "We will not fail!" they yelled in unison as they pushed harder against the advancing team. The air was thick with the taste of adrenaline and sweat. The Woobles bravely charged forward, but this time, they encountered a resistance that even their stamina couldn't overcome.

Storm swung his axe with all his might. As he cleaved through one soldier after another, he left a trail of gore in his wake. He grunted with effort, losing count of how many enemies he had taken down.

The battle intensified. Swords clashed against swords, axes against shields, and the ground shook under their feet. King Hunter's troops regained their footing and pushed back the Woobles. She knew they were losing their ground when she saw a soldier lunge at Storm, but he ducked under the blade and kicked him in the chest, sending him flying. Another tried to strike from behind, only to be parried by her Chakram, which she caught mid-air and hurled back at him. With a sickening thud, the soldier crumpled to the ground.

Her lightning bolts became more powerful now, zapping soldiers left and right. Her eyes glowed bright purple as she focused on her targets, never missing a beat. She dodged as a sword swing and lunged forward. Her fist connected with a solid punch to the jaw of another soldier. She tasted blood on her lips as she landed back on the ground after another daring leap over falling debris.

The wind picked up suddenly. It whipped around Talia, turning dust into stinging sandstorms. One Wooble looked up at her worriedly. She nodded encouragingly and sent another bolt of lightning toward the sky. The bolts danced around her fingers like fireflies before shooting forth toward their attackers. They struck true this time, frying several soldiers at once.

"Talia!" Scooter yelled as a soldier lunged toward him, then quickly climbed higher into the tree. The man's hands grasped at the empty air where he was moments ago. She sent the Woobles to his aid, biting and scratching at the man's ankles until he fell to the ground. They celebrated their small victory with shrill shrieks and cheers, their triumphant laughter filling the air.

Talia watched as Storm took on three soldiers at once, his axe a blur of silver as it cut through the shadows. She saw the gleam in his eyes. "Get off!" he shouted as he parried a strike from one soldier while he kicked another away.

The third soldier managed to cut him deeply on the side, making him stumble back. Blood seeped from the wound and stained his shirt. "Storm!" she cried as she ran toward him.

As she reached Storm's side, she saw the exhaustion etched on his face. His body trembled with the effort to remain standing, his grip on the bloodied axe weakened. Concern flooded her heart, and she knew that she must protect him at all costs.

In her worry, a soldier charged at her from behind, sword raised high. Her instincts kicked in, and without hesitation, she swiftly pivoted on her heel and unleashed a powerful lightning bolt straight into the soldier's chest. The electricity ran through him, causing him to convulse and release a guttural scream. He collided with a tree trunk with a resounding thwack. A momentary satisfaction filled Talia's being, but there was no time to savor the victory.

She quickly refocused her attention on Storm, who appeared weakened and vulnerable. The onslaught of soldiers continued unabated as they pressed forward, their injuries forgotten in their relentless pursuit. She took a deep breath, her gaze focused inward as she tapped into her healing power with one hand and fought off the approaching enemy with the other.

As she drew upon her connection to the elemental forces that fueled her abilities, she summoned another lightning bolt. This one contained even more raw energy than before. Its brilliance illuminated the surrounding chaos. With an elegant wave of her hand, the bolt arced forth from her fingertips and crashed into the tightly clustered group of soldiers.

The impact was devastating. The crackling electricity engulfed them in a blinding display of power that sent them hurtling in all directions like rag dolls. The metallic clang of armor colliding against armor echoed, intermingling with the sickening sound of trees snapping under the force of the bodies crashing into them.

Amid this momentary reprieve, new adversaries emerged from the shadows. Fresh soldiers, undeterred by the fate of their fallen comrades and driven by their unyielding loyalty to King Hunter, surged forward. Their weapons gleamed menacingly in the dim light, and their eyes blazed with fanatical fervor.

Her heart raced as she assessed the situation. Storm needed her protection, and she could not allow these soldiers to reach him. With each lightning bolt she unleashed, her power grew more potent. The sizzling tendrils of electricity weaved, illuminating the battlefield with their dazzling display. The sheer force of her elemental assault threw soldiers off balance knocking them to the ground. The metallic tang of ozone permeated the air as it mingled with the scent of sweat and blood.

In this harrowing dance of life and death, her lightning bolts became more powerful and precise. They arced through the air with blinding speed, finding their targets with unerring accuracy. Soldiers crumpled under the onslaught, their bodies convulsing in spasms before succumbing to stillness.

The Woobles darted in and out of the skirmish with fleeting swiftness, exploiting their diminutive size to pierce through enemy defenses. Their relentless bites and scratches created openings for Talia to exploit, further tipping the scales in their favor. She had a few precious seconds to focus her healing power on Storm, but his wound was deep, much deeper than she expected.

Despite their courage and resourcefulness, they faced over-whelming odds. The soldiers were halted momentarily by the raw power unleashed by her lightning bolts, but they continued to pour forth like an unstoppable tide driven by their loyalty to King Hunter.

The soldiers screamed in agony as searing arcs of electricity engulfed them before they surrendered to unconsciousness. Or worse. The smell of burned flesh and ozone mingled as the bat-tlefield became a chaotic tableau of writhing bodies and flickering blue-white light.

She was losing him.

She watched helplessly as his eyes fluttered closed. With exhaustion taking over her body, she could not split her powers anymore. She had to decide.

Her life or his.

CHAPTER THIRTY-ONE

TALIA

Talia stood strong and tall, and her battle cry echoing throughout the kingdom. As she raised her head high and parted her lips, a brilliant flash of light encircled her entire form. Time seemed to stand still as she transformed into a living embodiment of electricity itself. A torrent of raw power surged through her.

The sheer force of her power sent shockwaves rippling across the battlefield, toppling every soldier in its path. A symphony of cries echoed in response to this assault. The ground itself seemed to shudder, as if it could not contain the magnitude of Talia's unleashed might.

Her heart raced as she kneeled beside the fallen Storm, her hands trembling over the deep gash on his side. The scent of iron filled the air, and the sticky warmth of his blood soaked into the ground beneath them. With a deep breath, she focused her energy, and her hands began to emit a soft, golden glow.

"Come on, come on," she whispered, her voice barely audible above the chaos that surrounded them. The wound was healing, but it was a slow process, and time was not on their side.

Sensing the urgency of the situation, she watched his body convulse as he transformed back into his Sumerian form, his once magnificent beast dissipating into thin air. The pain was too much for him to bear, and with a weak groan, he passed out.

"Storm!" Talia cried as her heart clenched with fear. Her hands continued to work their magic, but the reality of their situation was sinking in, and panic threatened to overwhelm her. She lifted his head, wrapping her arms around his neck.

"Everyone, retreat!" she called, her voice laced with desperation. "We need to fall back now!"

The Woobles, loyal creatures that they were, obeyed without question. They scrambled to gather their wounded comrades, retreating from the battlefield as swiftly as they could. In the chaos, her mind raced with thoughts of what had led to this moment, and how her love for him had bound their fates together.

"Please, don't die on me," she murmured, her vision blurred by tears. The wound was healing, but not fast enough. She knew they couldn't stay here, exposed and vulnerable to King Hunter's forces.

As if summoned by her thoughts, the sounds of approaching footsteps reached her ears. Her heart pounding, she lowered Storm's head to the ground and rose, preparing to face whatever was coming their way.

"Stay strong, my pirate," she whispered, giving Storm one last glance as she turned to confront the approaching danger.

King Hunter's soldiers emerged from the shadows. She swallowed her fear and stood her ground, ready to protect Storm at all costs.

A commanding voice rang out. "Stand down!" Malta approached, his stern gaze fixed on her, clearly still limping. "Put your hands up and step away from him."

She complied, but reluctantly. As soon as she stepped back, the soldiers moved in swiftly, overpowering her before she could react. They clamped cuffs around her wrists, designed to suppress her magical abilities. She gritted her teeth, feeling a chill run down her spine as they snuffed out the magic within her.

"Johara! Scooter!" Talia cried, her heart sinking as she saw her friends captured and cuffed as well. The soldiers showed no mercy, stripping them of their weapons and binding them securely.

"Take them back to the castle," Malta ordered, his voice devoid of emotion. His eyes met Talia's for a moment, and she sensed a flicker of uncertainty behind his steely facade. But it was gone as quickly as it had appeared, and he turned his attention back to the task at hand.

"Move!" one soldier barked, shoving Talia forward. With heavy hearts and the weight of defeat bearing down upon them, Hunter's soldiers led Talia, Johara, and Scooter away from the battlefield.

"Storm..." Talia whispered, and her voice broke as she looked at her unconscious love. Despite partially healing his wound, he still showed pain on his face. She wanted to reach out and comfort him, but a soldier dragged her away. She watched as the soldiers loaded his nearly unconscious body onto a cart to be transported.

"Stay strong," Johara murmured, her eyes glistening with un-shed tears. "We will find a way out of this."

Exhausted from battle, those words seemed to echo in the early morning light as they made the long walk back to the castle. The three friends huddled together for warmth and support, trying to hold on to the flickering flame of hope in the suffocating shadows of their captivity. She could hear the cart behind her. Talia turned to check on Storm, but a soldier pushed her to keep walking.

"Talia," Scooter whispered, "did you heal Storm?"

"I don't know. I wasn't able to close the wound completely before we were captured. I can't let him be taken to the empty void."

Talia, I feel your pain. Storm is still breathing, but he is not doing well. I am going to send him my strength to keep him alive because your protection spell was broken.

Tears filled Talia's eyes when she heard her sister's familiar voice in her head.

Olivia, we've been captured. I failed you.

Don't worry. I'm here now.

It's so good to hear you in my head again. It's been so lonely. I missed you, sis.

She whispered, "I can hear her voice."

"I am praying to Emperor Anu to save him. We can't lose Storm."

After walking for what seemed like hours, the trees finally gave way to the sight of King Hunter's fortified castle. Soldiers guarded the strong, tall walls against any invading enemy, but King Hunter did not provide defense to the village just outside the castle. The soldiers led the prisoners through the village like a parade of their king's power. The villagers scrambled to get out of the way, staring at the prisoners with curiosity. The soldiers lowered the draw-bridge to welcome them back from the battle.

"Separate them," Lieutenant Malta ordered, grabbing Talia by the arm. "Take the rest of them to the dungeon."

Malta dragged her away from her friends as they were led toward the dungeons. Her heart raced with fear and uncertainty, but she knew she had to remain strong for their sake.

As they entered the castle, she noted its grandeur and opulence. Tapestries depicting scenes of past victories adorned the walls, while the marble floors echoed the footsteps of everyone who walked through the vast halls. It was a stark contrast to the lifeless village outside.

"Keep moving," he growled, tightening his grip on her arm.

They arrived at the judgment chambers, where Hunter awaited them. The room was dimly lit, with only the flickering light of torches casting eerie shadows on the cold stone walls. King Hunter sat on his massive throne at the end of the room, with Jitatma standing guard next to him. His eyes narrowed as he studied Talia's face, captivated by her resemblance to his late queen.

"Leave us," Hunter commanded, his voice resonating throughout the chamber.

Glancing over at Jitatma, Malta hesitated before reluctantly obeying the order, leaving the chamber and closing the heavy red door behind him.

"Talia, your resemblance to my beloved Circe is uncanny," he said, leaning forward on his throne. "But your eyes betray you. You do not possess her gentle spirit. I will have to change that."

She clenched her fists, feeling both insulted and frightened by his words. Curiosity piqued, she listened as Hunter revealed his twisted desires. He planned to bring Queen Circe back by placing Olivia's spirit into Talia's body, forcing her to become the vessel for his lost love.

"Are you insane?" Talia snapped, horrified by his intentions. "You cannot possibly think I would agree!"

"Your cooperation is irrelevant," Hunter said coldly. "You will do as I command, or your friends will suffer the consequences."

"And if I comply, then what?" she asked.

"Then your friends will live."

"Somehow you don't strike me as a man who keeps his word," she snarled.

"I can promise you, Talia, I will have my wife back, even if I have to take her back," he growled, his patience wearing thin. "Commander Jitatma, bring Olivia to my judgment chambers."

CHAPTER THIRTY-TWO

HUNTER

Hunter's strong, calloused hands gripped Talia's arm tightly as he dragged her toward his private chambers. Her wrists were bound in steel cuffs, making it difficult for her to resist. He slammed the heavy wooden door shut behind them, the sound reverberating throughout the room.

The large white marble fireplace was the centerpiece of the room, with a fire already burning to light the room. His bed was waiting. His bed, draped in rich fabrics and adorned with intricate carvings, beckoned to him from the far side of the room.

He finally had her alone, and he was going to enjoy it.

With a predatory gaze, his eyes bored into her. She stood with her feet planted, her shoulders square, which turned him on with her defiance. Her nose turned up like she was better than him. It wouldn't be long for that face to turn to fear.

His grip on her arm was strong as he pulled her closer, knocking her off her strong stance. The scent of wildflowers mixed with her sweat filled his nostrils. She glared at him with disgust, trying to pull away from his grasp.

"Don't touch me!" she hissed.

"Good. I was hoping you would fight. It will make this interesting."

His expression darkened, his eyes narrowing at her resistance. With a snarl, he grabbed her by the waist and threw her onto the bed. The softness of the silk sheets beneath her did little to ease the impact. Frantically, she scrambled to get off the bed, but he was quicker. He reached across the mattress, grabbing her by the hair and yanking her back. She gasped in pain as he leaned in close to her ear.

"Let me make myself clear," he whispered, his voice laced with venom. "You will submit to me, or you will suffer the consequences, Talia."

He felt her whole body shudder, seeing the tears pricking at the corners of her eyes. That was the frightened expression he had hoped to evoke on her face. He relished breaking her willpower. He distracted himself with her beauty in his bed.

Seizing the opportunity, she swung her metal-cuffed wrists at his face, connecting with a resounding blow. The king reeled back, momentarily stunned by her unexpected move. She scrambled off the bed and sprinted toward the door. Just as she reached for the handle, he leaped off the bed and cut her off. His threatening tone and vulgar language filled the air, making it clear he wouldn't tolerate any further acts of rebellion.

"Think you can defy me, bitch?" he spat. "You're nothing but a toy for my amusement, and you'll learn your place."

With a swift motion, he punched her in the face, his fist connecting with her cheekbone. The force of the blow sent her careening backward. As she struggled to regain her footing, he felt the power dynamics at play, his authority and her resistance.

He advanced on her once more, dragging her back to the bed by her hair. She fought him, but his grip was like iron. This time, he used a magnetic restraint on the headboard to secure her cuffed wrists, leaving her immobilized.

"That's enough foreplay."

"Let me go!" she screamed. Tears streamed down her cheeks as she continued to struggle.

"Silence!" he barked, his face inches from hers. "No one can save you now. You belong to me."

He removed his cape and shirt, revealing his muscular chest and powerful frame. He prowled onto the bed, his eyes ablaze with desire, every inch of him screaming dominance. He loomed over Talia, his presence overwhelming, like a predator eyeing its prey, hungry and relentless. With the precision of a man used to getting what he wanted, he stripped Talia of her clothes — no frills or hesitations, leaving her exposed and vulnerable. Just the way he wanted her.

"Remarkable," he mused, his eyes roving over her naked body. "You look exactly like my wife." The perverse satisfaction in his voice made Talia's twisted in a look of disgust.

"Please, don't do this," she whispered, her voice shaking.

"Your pleas mean nothing to me," he replied coldly. "I will have what I want."

Talia lay naked on the bed, still trying to struggle against the magnetic restraints that held her wrists firmly in place. Her efforts were futile, and he knew it. She was right where he wanted her.

He took his time aggressively touching her body, reveling in the power he had. He watched her fight, kicking and squirming beneath him, her hands pulling against the bonds.

"Stop it!" she cried, her voice sounding strained under the weight of her fear and despair. "Please, just stop!"

Her words fell on deaf ears. He continued his assault. His hands roamed her body as if he owned her. Unable to endure the torment any longer, she screamed for help at the top of her lungs. Her voice echoed through the room, a desperate cry for salvation.

At that precise moment, the doors to the chamber burst open. Jitatma entered, his eyes widening in shock as he took in the scene before him.

"Your Majesty," he stammered, bowing quickly with an apologetic expression. "I am deeply sorry for the interruption."

Hunter glared at the unwelcome intrusion, his lustful intentions momentarily thwarted. He climbed off Talia as his anger simmered beneath the surface. "This had better be important, Commander," he said venomously, emphasizing each word.

"Again, my deepest apologies, Your Majesty," Jitatma continued, his voice trembling slightly as he maintained eye contact with the furious king. "I have Olivia in the judgment chambers. We must prepare for the transfer. I have sent for Princess Johara to perform the chant to release Circe's soul."

The tension in the room was intense. Her fate hung in the balance. He hesitated, his gaze flicking between Jitatma and the vulnerable woman on the bed.

With a final, frustrated growl, he relented. "Very well," he said through gritted teeth, stepping away from the bed. "But we will continue this later." His eyes bored into her, promising retribution for the interruption.

"Shall I take Talia with us?" Jitatma asked, trying to be a gentleman and not stare at her naked body lying on the bed.

"Leave her for later, just the way she is."

CHAPTER THIRTY-THREE

TALIA

As Hunter stormed out of the room with Commander Jitatma, Talia remained bound and naked on the bed. While she was grateful for the temporary reprieve, her heart pounded in her chest with lingering fear and uncertainty. She could not shake the knowledge that he would return, his intentions clear and his anger only intensified.

In this fragile moment of solitude, she prayed for strength and courage to face whatever horrors awaited her. Deep within her soul, a flicker of hope ignited, that she might yet find a way to escape this nightmare and reclaim her freedom.

Her heart raced as she listened to the retreating footsteps of Hunter and Jitatma. Her mind was a whirlwind. She attempted to process the terrifying events that had just unfolded. The lingering scent of him filled the room, making her feel nauseated.

"Stay strong," she whispered, trying to steady her shaking hands and racing thoughts. "You have to find a way out of this."

As soon as their presence faded, she began to struggle vigorously against the magnetic restraints. She pulled, twisted, and writhed, desperate to free herself before he returned to fulfill his monstrous threat. But no matter how hard she tried, the restraints held fast, leaving her feeling more helpless than ever.

"Damn it!" she cried, tears streaming down her face as she realized the futility of her efforts.

Minotaur...

Amid her despair, she heard a faint scratching sound at the door. Her heart caught in her throat as she feared Hunter's return, but the sound was different, almost timid.

"Who's there?" she asked in a hushed voice.

The side door creaked open, and to her surprise, Scooter slipped into the room. "Holy Anu!" His eyes widened in shock at the sight of her, but he quickly composed himself.

"Please, don't make a sound," she pleaded. "King Hunter is just outside the door." Her emotions were in turmoil. She was relieved at the unexpected aid, but embarrassed and fearful that Hunter would return at any moment. "I am so glad to see you, Scooter," she said, hope flickering in her tear-filled eyes.

"Commander Jitatma gave me the access to release your cuffs," he said as he leaned on the bed. He placed his thumb on the print scanner. The light flashed green, and the cuffs released.

"Thank you," she whispered as the cuffs fell away from her wrists.

"Quickly, get dressed. Storm is in the hallway. He's awake, but he needs more healing," he urged, handing Talia her discarded clothes.

She slipped through the side door of Hunter's private chambers, Scooter clinging to her shoulder. The dimly lit servant hallway stretched out before them, its walls adorned with flickering torches casting elongated shadows on the cold stone floor. She could still feel the phantom touch of Hunter's hands on her, but pushed the memory aside as they made their escape.

Walking a few steps down the hallway, she spotted Storm leaning against the wall, holding his side. A pained smile spread across his face when he saw her, but his eyes held a hint of concern she couldn't ignore. "Talia," he breathed, relief evident in his voice.

"Storm!" Talia rushed to his side.

"It's so good to see your beautiful face," he replied, wincing as he shifted his weight. His gaze landed on the bruise forming on her cheek. "What happened to you? Did King Hunter hurt you?"

She avoided his eyes and shook her head. "I'm fine," she insisted, though the tremor in her voice betrayed her. Her fingers traced the outline of the bruise, the pain a reminder of Hunter's cruelty.

He didn't look entirely convinced, but he didn't press the matter further. Instead, he let out a slow breath and winced again at the pain in his side. "Can you heal this?" he asked, gesturing toward the wound.

"Of course," she murmured. Her hands glowed with a soft, golden light as she placed them on his side. The warmth from the healing magic seeped into his skin as it mended the torn flesh and knit broken bones back together. Within moments, the pain had subsided, and he straightened as he tested his newly healed side. "Where's Johara?"

"They took her to Hunter's judgment chambers."

Olivia, where are you?

I'm with Johara. You better get in here, sis. Hunter is trying to get the spell from Johara.

"Thank you," he said softly, his gratitude genuine. He reached out to touch Talia's arm, concern etched on his face. She flinched and recoiled. The sensation of Hunter's rough hands still haunted her skin. He furrowed his brow.

"Please, Talia, tell me what happened in there," he said gently, trying not to push her too hard.

Talia bit her lip. Her eyes welled up with unshed tears. "He tried," she whispered.

A guttural growl erupted from deep within Storm's chest, and his fists clenched at his sides. "I swear, I will make him pay for this," he vowed through gritted teeth. "Take me to him."

"We can't just go charging in there," Scooter said.

"The Minotaur says we are." He began the transformation into the Minotaur.

"*You!*" Storm bellowed. His deep voice shook the very foundations of the chamber. Talia did not have time to react as he charged toward Hunter with hooves thundering and horns lowered. "No one messes with my Maverick, not even a god!"

"Stop him!" Hunter yelled. His guards scrambled to obey as they rushed forward with their weapons drawn.

"Pirate, no!" Talia cried. Her heart raced as she watched the chaos unfold. She knew Storm's anger was justified, but she couldn't bear the thought of him being hurt in his blind rage. As much as she wanted Hunter to pay for his actions, she knew charging headfirst into battle was not the solution.

The Minotaur's wrathful assault persisted on every one of Hunter's soldiers who dared step in his path.

"Storm!" Johara called, desperation lacing her voice. "Please, listen to me! We have to find another way!"

"Pirate! Stand down," Talia yelled. Her voice trembled with fear and anger. She knew he was out for blood, and she couldn't blame him. But the thought of losing him, of seeing him hurt or worse, made her feel like she was being torn apart inside. She couldn't shake the memory of Hunter's touch, his hands trying to claim her. It made her skin crawl, and a lump formed in her throat as bile rose in her stomach.

Hunter raised his staff and waved it twice. The Minotaur stopped his charge. Four glass walls came up out from the floor and a ceiling came down on him, enclosing him in a prison. He stood, trapped in a glass cage, his massive form nearly filling the space. Scratches marred the glass where he tried to escape, leaving behind streaks of blood.

"Ah, Talia," Hunter said. "I'm glad you could join us."

"Let him go!" she demanded, her fists clenched at her sides.

"Or what?" Hunter taunted.

A sickening hiss filled the room as the air vent on the top of the glass cage closed. Storm's breaths became more labored, each breath sounding heavier than the last. His eyes locked on Talia's, desperation and pain mingled on his face.

"Please... stop..." she begged as tears streamed down her cheeks. She felt helpless and useless, unable to save the one she loved. She rushed over to the glass cage, reliving the nightmare of losing Storm once again.

"Your precious Storm should have known better than to challenge me," Hunter spat.

"Storm," she whispered, pressing her palm against the cold glass as if trying to reach him through it. "Hold on."

"Time is running out, Talia," Hunter said, as his eyes gleamed with cruel satisfaction. "How long can he last without air?"

Her mind raced, her thoughts a whirlwind of panic and desperation. Every second that passed felt like an eternity, and she felt Storm's suffering as though it were her own. The ache in her chest grew heavier, threatening to crush her under its weight. But she couldn't give up, not now, not when he needed her most.

"Fight it, Storm," she urged, her voice barely audible over the pounding of her heart.

"Enough!" Johara's voice rang out in the judgment chamber. "This torture will not continue."

Hunter smirked, his gaze flicking between Talia and the defiant princess. "And what do you propose to do, Your Highness? You are in no position to make demands."

"Let Storm go," Talia pleaded, her eyes never leaving the glass cage as beads of sweat began to form on Storm's brow. "He's done nothing wrong."

"Nothing wrong?" he scoffed. "He dared to defy me and stand in my way. That is reason enough."

Johara crossed her arms, her chin held high despite the threat looming over them all. "You seek power at any cost, but it will be your undoing, Hunter. The people will see through your lies and deceit."

"Silence!" Hunter barked, his patience wearing thin. "I grow weary of your empty threats."

"Very well," Johara said coolly. "But know this. Whatever power you think you have won't save you when your kingdom crumbles around you."

"Your words mean nothing to me," he snarled. "Now, Talia, I'll give you one last chance. Choose. Storm or Olivia. Whomever you don't choose will be lost forever."

Her heart pounded in her chest, her breathing as labored as Storm's. Her mind raced, searching for a solution that didn't involve sacrificing someone she cared about. She looked at Johara, who returned her gaze with sympathy.

"Make your choice," King Hunter demanded, his voice cold and merciless.

"Johara, can you truly perform the transfer without harming Olivia?" Talia asked, her voice wavering with fear and uncertainty.

"Without harming her? Perhaps. But there would still be consequences, and it would be irreversible," Johara admitted. "But if it can save Storm—"

"I can't," Talia interrupted, her decision made. "I'm sorry, Olivia. I'm so sorry, Storm. I love you."

CHAPTER THIRTY-FOUR

TALIA

As she stood before him, Talia felt the sweat begin to trickle down her back, despite the coolness of the surrounding air. His gaze was boring into her, searing through her skin like a branding iron, marking her as his own. Her heart thundered in her chest as she forced herself to hold his stare, praying her plan would work. "Your Majesty," she began, "I beg of you to spare Olivia and Storm. Let me take their place."

Hunter watched her with interest as amusement danced in his eyes. "And just how do you propose to do that?"

Talia swallowed hard, refusing to show any fear. "I will offer myself."

His face darkened slightly, and he leaned forward on his throne, studying her. "And why would I agree to such a proposal?"

She said, her voice quivering only slightly, "You have always wished to bend me to your will. To break me. Take me as your own. If I am at your side, you can have that power over me. You don't need to take their lives as well."

He smirked, a slow, predatory smile that sent shivers down her spine. "Interesting proposition," he mused, his voice echoing off the walls of his throne room. King Hunter waved his hand to turn on the air vent in Storm's prison.

"Talia, don't do this," Scooter whispered.

"Not now, Scooter."

Talia held up her hand to reassure Scooter she knew what she was doing and to stay back. Cautiously, she made her way around the pool of blood to Hunter.

As she approached him, he grabbed her arm, forcefully throwing her over the nearby pool of blood. One hand secured her firmly at the back of her neck while the other gripped her shoulder with brute strength. Her gaze met his intense eyes, swirling with darkness and desire.

"I will have you, my queen," he hissed in her ear. "I will make your beast watch."

Then she noticed it, a glint of black onyx on his finger, resembling her ring, cursed to be worn all this time. It was his ring, just like hers, only bigger, black onyx wrapped around a red opal.

"United as one, divided by one." She remembered the prophecy. With a quick move, she reached up and snatched it from his finger, feeling it slip on her own.

"What?" Hunter's eyes widened as he felt the protection drain from his finger.

Before he could react, Talia had fused the two rings together, creating an entirely new sort of magic. She felt the surge of power flowing through her, amplifying her own abilities and strengthening them more than ever. She saw the confusion on his face, the fear in his eyes. He didn't understand what was happening, and in that moment, she knew she had the upper hand.

With a burst of energy, she pushed him off her. The force was so intense that it sent him flying across the room. He crashed into the wall with a sickening thud, his breath knocked out of him.

"You little bitch," he hissed, his voice low and threatening as he slowly pulled himself off the ground. "You think you can just take what's mine like that?"

Talia raised her chin defiantly, her eyes burning with grit. "I'll take everything from you."

He lunged at her, his fists clenched. She knew he could kill her easily, but she was ready for it this time. Using all the power at her disposal, she pulled her arm back, landing one well-deserved punch, forcing him back. He stumbled back, surprised by her newfound strength. She took a step forward. Her body trembled as her heart pounded with adrenaline.

"You shouldn't have underestimated me," she said, her voice strong despite the shaking in her body. "No one disrespects me like that and gets away with it, you little bitch."

His eyes narrowed. "You think this is over?"

Before she could answer, he charged at her again. She braced herself, letting the magic flow through her veins as she watched him come closer. The minute he was within reach, she lashed out with a bolt of lightning so powerful it knocked him off his feet. He landed hard on the ground, his body now smoking and covered in burns. She felt invincible, like she could take down anyone who stood in her way.

"You think you can defeat me like this?" he screamed, struggling to his feet, summoning his staff. He hurled the staff, and it turned into a spear. To his surprise, she struck it with lightning, causing the spear to fly off course. Hunter's staff fell next to Talia's feet.

She smiled with a hint of evil satisfaction. She focused on the stolen ring on her finger, remembering how it had given her this power. She couldn't explain it, but it felt like it was a part of her now, a natural magic she had never known existed before. With this power, she knew she could defeat him once and for all.

He came at her again, faster this time. She met his every attack, sending waves of electricity flying. They circled each other, their bodies glowing with energy as they fought. Sparks flew and the room filled with the sound of explosions. She tasted the ozone in the air, smelled the sweat and fear emanating from both of them.

He lunged at her, but she was too quick. She dodged his strike and sent a bolt of lightning straight into his gut, causing him to stagger back. He roared in anger but refused to give up. They continued like this, their movements a blur of motion and light. Every time he attacked, she blocked it or deflected it and sent it right back at him. Her body ached from the constant exertion, but she pushed through, fueled by the rush of adrenaline and the thrill of victory.

Suddenly, she saw an opening. He dropped his guard for just a moment, and she lunged at him. Her hands crackled with electricity as she grabbed his throat. He tried to fight back, but she was too strong. With one last surge of power, she sent him flying across the room and slammed him into the far wall. He crumpled to the ground, gasping for air and clutching at his chest.

She stood over him, her eyes blazing. "Surrender to me," she demanded, feeling more powerful than ever before.

He glared up at her, defiance in his eyes. "Never," he rasped between ragged breaths.

Talia watched as he struggled to stand, his muscles straining against the pain she'd inflicted. But he was still standing, and that was all she needed to know. This man was dangerous, and she wouldn't stop until he couldn't hurt another innocent woman ever again.

She aimed another shot of lightning at his manhood, feeling the heat radiating from it as it fried his skin. This time, she didn't hold back. She wanted him to feel the full force of her wrath, to know what it felt like to be helpless and vulnerable. His screams filled the air, echoing off the walls.

After finishing, she stepped back and took a shuddering breath. He lay on the ground, twitching and whimpering, a dark stain spreading on his pants. She slowly walked over to him. She kneeled beside him and leaned down, her voice soft but cold. "Surrender," she whispered.

"I surrender."

CHAPTER THIRTY-FIVE

TALIA

T alia and Princess Johara stood at the pool of blood over King Hunter. He awaited his fate, burned and defeated.

"Just get it over with. Kill me," Hunter uttered.

"I would never give you that satisfaction," Johara said, her voice dripping with disdain. "You will never again rule this kingdom."

"What are you going to do to me?"

"Strip you of your powers. A fate worse than death," Johara announced.

Johara took a deep breath, her eyes locked on Hunter as she began to chant the ancient spell. Her voice resonated with authority and magic, instilling fear and awe in all those present. "From the darkness of this night, take this human's powerful might. Never to reign in terror again, making him a mere mortal of men."

As the words left Johara's lips, the very air in the room seemed to crackle with an unseen energy. The walls vibrated ever so slightly, as if they, too, were reacting to the force of the spell. Hunter's once-confident gaze faltered, becoming clouded with uncertainty, as if feeling the weight of his consequences bearing down upon him.

Talia stood at Johara's side, her heart pounding in her chest as she witnessed the display of power before her. She felt the heat of the magic surging through the room, mingling with the scent of blood and sweat that filled the air. In that moment, she understood the true extent of Johara's strength, and it filled her with a renewed sense of hope for the future of the kingdom.

Hunter's expression shifted rapidly from arrogance to fear as his powers were being slowly drained away. "Curse you both!" he snarled, his voice tinged with desperation. "You may take my powers, but as long you wear that ring, you can never break our bond. You will always be mine, Talia!"

She was ready to protect herself and her friends from any retaliation. She took a deep breath, steadying herself, before joining Johara in repeating the spell.

"From the darkness of this night, take this human's powerful might," Talia echoed Johara, her voice strong and unwavering. "Never to reign in terror again, making him a mere mortal of men."

As they chanted together, the energy in the room reached a crescendo, the air quivering around them. Storm's prison shattered, releasing him. Hunter's face contorted in anguish, feeling his powers slipping through his fingers like sand. He looked up at Talia and Princess Johara, his eyes pleading for mercy, but found none in their resolute expressions.

"Please," he whispered. But it was too late; the spell had done its work, leaving him weak and powerless.

"What have you done?" he stammered, his voice trembling. "You cannot do this to me! I am your king!"

"Your reign is over," Talia replied, her voice steady and unwavering. "The people of Far Viscera will no longer suffer under your tyranny."

"Please, Talia... Have mercy on me," Hunter begged, his eyes welling with tears. But there was no sympathy to be found in the eyes of the two women who had defied him. They had seen firsthand the pain and suffering he had inflicted on countless innocents. There would be no mercy for him now.

"May you live out the rest of your days reflecting on the harm you've caused," Johara declared, her voice filled with both authority and finality. "And may you never wield such power again."

As Hunter, now a mere mortal, stood trembling in the aftermath of his defeat, Talia knew his reign of terror had finally ended.

"Soldiers!" Johara called, her voice echoing throughout the chamber. "Seize Hunter and throw him into the dungeon. Ensure that he can no longer cause harm to our people."

The soldiers hesitated for a moment, glancing at one another as they absorbed the shift in power. It wasn't long before they recognized the true ruler of Far Viscera standing before them.

"Your Highness," Commander Jitatma stepped forward and bowed deeply, a sign of respect and submission, "we pledge our loyalty to you, the rightful heir to the throne. Our lives are yours to command."

"Thank you, Commander." Princess Johara nodded, acknowledging his oath. "Now you have saved my life twice. I have to admit, Commander, when you first told us about your plan to defeat Hunter, I thought you were crazy."

"Enough!" Hunter shouted, his voice strained and weak as the soldiers dragged him away. His once mighty figure now seemed small, diminished by the loss of his power.

"Thank you, Talia," Johara whispered, her voice barely audible above the hushed murmurs of the soldiers and onlookers. "For everything."

"Always, my princess," Talia replied, the bond between them stronger than ever before. "I mean, my queen."

"I knew you could do it," Storm said.

In that sweet, fleeting moment, her lover's strong arms swept her up, and she surrendered herself to the dizzying feeling of being lifted off her feet. Giddy with joy, he twirled her around as if they were dancing on a cloud made just for them. As she slid down his chest, their lips met in a passionate, tender kiss. A rush of warmth spread through her body as she lost herself completely in his loving embrace. "I'll shield you, but only you, Maverick."

"Only you, Pirate." Talia smiled, pressing her lips to his again.

Commander Jitatma signaled the soldier to offer their belongings. He took Talia's Chakram, presenting it to her. "I believe this belongs to you."

"Thank you, Commander, for everything," Talia said.

"That was absolutely brilliant." Olivia surprised Commander Jitatma. Jumping into his arms, she wrapped her legs around his waist. He tried to maintain his professional composure. She embraced him in a passionate kiss, revealing their affair. He wrapped his arms around her.

"I am going to miss you, Olivia Trismegist." Jitatma smiled.

"I will see you again someday, Commander," Olivia promised.

Scooter stepped forward with his finger in the air. "I would like the record to state that I didn't run, hide, or faint the entire battle."

Queen Johara approached him and said, "My brave knight."

When she wrapped her arms around his waist, she leaned in and kissed him. Scooter's eyes widened in shock. Storm instinctively jolted forward, ready to catch his friend if needed, but Talia reached out and grasped his arm, sensing that this time, someone else could take care of Scooter. His eyes rolled to the back of his head as Johara adjusted her hold on him, deepening their passionate kiss.

Storm looked confused. "How did that happen? When did that happen?"

"Pirate, we were so busy with each other. We left them alone most of the journey. I think it's sweet." She smiled.

Olivia giggled. "I leave you alone for a few days and look what happens, sis."

Before Olivia could say another word, Talia scooped her sister up in the tightest embrace she could give, so grateful to hear her sister's laughter again. The warmth of their reunion washed over them like a comforting blanket, wrapping them in a moment of pure joy.

Talia, what's a Claiming Ritual?

I'll explain later.

Queen Johara asked, "Are you ready to go back?"

"I am so ready," Scooter announced.

"I believe you can open the portal on your own, Talia." Queen Johara nodded. "You are definitely strong enough."

"With these words, I call forth the gateway to allow us among the living in a realm faraway. With this key, I cross now the great divide and bring us to the bridge of the other side," Talia said confidently.

The pool of blood, shimmering in an otherworldly crimson hue, seemed to respond to her command. Wisps of energy began to dance across its surface, forming intricate patterns that seemed to pulse with a life of their own. The air around Talia sizzled as she raised her hands, palms outstretched toward the pool, a faint glow emanating from her fingertips.

With a sudden surge of energy, a bolt of lightning shot forth from Talia's hands, arcing with a brilliant flash. The room was illuminated in a dazzling display of colors—shades of blue and purple swirling with streaks of gold and silver, creating a mesmerizing spectacle that seemed to defy logic and reason.

As the lightning bolt struck the surface of the pool, a ripple effect spread outward, causing the blood to churn and froth as if stirred by an unseen force. A low rumble filled the chamber, growing louder and more intense with each passing moment, until it seemed as though the very fabric of reality was being torn asunder.

And then, in the center of the pool, a shimmering portal began to take shape. It glowed with a soft, ethereal light, swirling with hues of azure and emerald, like a living painting come to life. The edges of the portal rippled and shifted like liquid glass, beckoning those brave enough to step through into the unknown.

Scooter stepped on the edge of the pool. Eager to get back, he was the first to enter. Olivia followed him. Storm held out his hand to Talia, stepping on the stone together. Talia turned back for a moment to give Princess Johara and Commander Jitatma one last nod good luck. Storm squeezed her hand as they jumped together into the gateway home.

The wind whispered through the trees surrounding the Eternal Flame, its flickering light casting dancing shadows on the ground. As Scooter, Olivia, Storm, and Talia emerged from the portal that connected the realms, a sense of tranquility settled over Middle Park. The air was cool and crisp.

The park was bathed in darkness, with only the soft glow of stars above and the distant twinkle of city lights breaking through the night. As they stood near the Eternal Flame, its flickering light casting warm hues of red and gold around them, they felt a sense of accomplishment wash over them. The journey they had embarked on was fraught with danger and uncertainty, but now they stood on familiar ground.

"Mr. Smoke and Miss Trismegist, welcome back."

"Enforcer Markson," Talia said, surprised. "We can explain."

"Don't arrest us. I can't go to jail," Scooter shrieked as he dove behind Storm.

"I'm not here to arrest you," Markson said softly. From her pocket, she retrieved an item and walked over to Storm, placing it carefully in his palm. He held up a toy that was old and worn, its once vibrant colors now dull and chipped. Talia could see the intricate detail of the dragon's scales and wings, evidence of a skilled craftsman. "I'm here to say that you owe me one."

"Little Dragon," he said, breathless. "You're the Saqqara Queen."

"I figured after seeing my shifter form, you would recognize my scent in my Sumerian form."

"I can't believe it," Storm whispered, carefully tracing the dragon's wings with his finger. "I haven't seen this toy since I was a child."

Markson's lips curled into a small smile. "I knew you would remember me."

"All this time, you've been chasing us around this park, you knew what was going on," Talia said, taking a step forward.

Markson leaned over to Talia and lowered her eyes. "Like I said, Storm Smoke is never seen with the same woman twice. You were the first. I knew it was my chance to get my flock back from Hunter." She winked. "For that, I owe you one."

"How about you keep our secret, and we'll call this even?"

"Fine, but I do ask you to be careful with your magic. It's my job to protect." Markson took a step back and asked, "Now, who wants burgers? Burger Shack is on me, and you guys can tell me how you took down that asshole."

With laughter and excitement, they prepared themselves for a well-deserved night out. As they gathered their belongings and headed out of Middle Park, Talia took one last glance at the Eternal Flame, a quiet thank you to the gateway that had brought her sister home.

Arm in arm, they ventured into the night, their spirits soaring as high as the stars above. And while the future held its share of uncertainties and challenges, they knew the strength of their love and unity would guide them through whatever lay ahead.

For now, they reveled in the joy of their victory, celebrating their unbreakable bond that transcended any magical spell or worldly threat. Together, they had triumphed over darkness and restored light to their lives—and in that moment, nothing else mattered.

CHAPTER THIRTY-SIX

HUNTER

As the door swung open, rusty hinges creaking in protest, revealing a dimly lit cell within, Gorgon peered inside. The feeble glow from distant torches barely illuminated the haggard figure chained to the damp wall, their silhouette etched against the rough stones like a shadowy painting.

Gorgon's steely gaze met Hunter's hollow eyes, a silent acknowledgement passing between them. It was a moment thick with tension, as if the weight of their shared history and animosity hung heavily in the air. The room seemed to hold its breath, awaiting the outcome of this encounter.

Gorgon stood at the entrance of the dimly lit prison, his gaze sweeping over the desolate living quarters that had become Hunter's home. As he waved the guard away, a heavy silence settled in the air, broken only by the faint sound of chains rattling against the damp walls.

Descending a few rugged and poorly built steps, Gorgon carefully traversed the worn stone floor toward Hunter. The light from the flickering torches lining the corridor played upon the rough surfaces.

To Hunter's right, a small, old table stood with a metal tray bearing untouched food, a stark reminder of his confinement. The scent of stale bread and cold broth hung in the air, mingling with the damp mustiness that permeated every corner of the cell.

On the other side of the room, an uncomfortable cot sagged under the weight of exhaustion and despair. Its thin mattress offered a slight reprieve from the unforgiving hardness of its rusted frame, providing only fleeting moments of respite during sleepless nights.

The air within the prison seemed laden with the mix of hopelessness and determination that clung to Hunter's spirit. It was an atmosphere where time crawled, each passing hour an agonizing reminder of his loss, his fading strength, and the uncertain future that loomed before him.

"Brother, you have fallen far," he said with a wicked smile. "You underestimated our little warrior princess. You allowed Talia to destroy your reign and take your kingdom. Your daughter was not your undoing. Your dead wife was."

"My wife was my everything," he said, jumping to his feet, lunging at his brother, anger set deep in his eyes. "She will never be my undoing. I will always be connected to her, and I will have her back!"

"I was hoping you would say that because I brought you something." He held out his hand to summon Hunter's staff.

"My staff is just a piece of wood without my powers."

Gorgon carefully pulled a vial from under his cloak. He examined the small vial in his hand, its contents shimmering. Hunter knew the vial contained a single drop of Emperor Anu's blood, a powerful ingredient that held the key to unlocking a concealed ability — cloaking magic. The mere thought of harnessing such magic filled Hunter with a surge of anticipation and ambition. With this remarkable gift, he could escape the confines of his prison undetected, evading the watchful eyes of Commander Jitatma and his entourage.

His initial excitement at the prospect of freedom was tempting. His eyes narrowed, his caution growing as he observed the vial. The offer seemed too good to be true, and their years of rivalry had taught him not to trust his brother's motivations blindly. As he studied Gorgon's face, he saw a glimmer of satisfaction behind his eyes, a sinful pleasure in orchestrating their meeting and manipulating the circumstances to suit his own desires.

"Cloaking magic?" he asked warily, his voice betraying his suspicion. "What's in it for you?" He knew Gorgon was not one to perform acts of kindness without ulterior motives.

A wicked smile continued to play upon Gorgon's lips as he reveled in Hunter's astute observation, his eyes glinting with a mix of intrigue and mischief. "You know me so well," he admitted with twisted amusement. "I require your assistance in acquiring the Book of the Dead. With your connection to Talia, you are uniquely positioned to retrieve it for me."

The mention of Talia's name immediately roused conflicting emotions within Hunter. The mere mention of her stirred both love and resentment deep within his heart. It seemed Gorgon was aware of Hunter's conflicting sentiments and aimed to exploit them to his advantage.

"In exchange for retrieving the book for me," Gorgon continued, his voice dripping with calculated persuasion, "I will restore your powers, dear brother." His words hung in the air, carrying the weight of promises and possibilities.

Hunter's eyes narrowed.

As the weight of Gorgon's proposition settled on him, his skepticism deepened, and he wondered if his brother's intentions were truly aligned with his own, or if this was merely another ploy to further his own agenda. Yet the tantalizing promise of regaining his lost abilities and seeking retribution against Talia tugged at Hunter's heartstrings.

"And once my powers are restored," Hunter replied, his voice tinged with a mix of skepticism and curiosity, "what guarantee do

I have that you won't use the book against Talia? What assurance can you give that I won't become a pawn in your twisted game?"

Gorgon's smile widened, revealing a veneer of false reassurance. "Rest assured, dear brother," he said with what seemed to be an air of sincerity, "Talia has fulfilled her purpose to me. Your powers will be yours to wield as you see fit. You can do whatever your heart desires to our little warrior princess."

Hunter's heart pounded in his chest as doubts waged war within him. The opportunity to regain his powers and seek vengeance against those who had wronged him was tempting, but the cost was high, which meant giving Gorgon that powerful book.

Hunter knew a choice had to be made. A choice that would unravel the intricate web they found themselves entangled in and determine the path they would tread upon — one that could lead to redemption or further descent into darkness.

A chill ran down his spine as he processed Gorgon's words. The depth of their rivalry and animosity had always been palpable, but now Gorgon's thirst for vengeance knew no bounds. The thought of using the Book of the Dead as a weapon against Talia sent shivers through him.

Pondering this treacherous alliance, Hunter knew accepting Gorgon's offer would come with dire consequences. Yet even though trapped in this dank prison cell with no hope in sight, the allure of reclaiming his powers and striking back at those who had wronged him swayed Hunter.

As the dim torchlight flickered in the distance, casting eerie shadows upon their faces, Hunter made his decision. He would venture into this dangerous pact with Gorgon, a pact that promised retribution and power beyond imagination but threatened to plunge him deeper into a realm of darkness and uncertainty.

Little did Hunter know that the outcome of this alliance would not only shape his own destiny but also determine the fate of the kingdom he once ruled, the bonds he held dear, and the very fabric of his being.

STORM SMOKE

BOOK TWO OF THE SUPERHUMAN SERIES PREVIEW

The sun flung its golden fingers over the hushed forest glade, seductively tracing the dense foliage and quivering water. Emperor Anu, hidden in the fertile undergrowth, let his hungry eyes feast on Viracocha as she swam in the pond beneath the waterfall. The tumbling water caressed her body, stroking her softly like a lover. Droplets clung to her bare skin like precious gems, catching the rays and setting off a seductive dance of light that left him breathless.

"Damn," he murmured, his voice choked with desire at the sight of her. His gaze slid greedily over the provocative dip of her neck and the inviting curve of her back—contouring lines that hinted at a sensuous playground below the water. She was blissfully oblivious to his heated observation as she swam the length of the pond.

His eyes traced down her body, pausing appreciatively at her rounded breasts that bounced gently with each stroke she took in the water. Her red hair floated around her like a seductive curtain, glinting under the sun's rays. He could almost feel the smoothness of her skin under his calloused hands, taste the fresh sweetness of her lips as he imagined pulling her close. His body responded enthusiastically to his imagination, heat pooling low in his belly.

He was not just observing Viracocha; he was worshipping her. He desired every inch of her—wanted to touch, taste, and possess everything he saw illuminated under that magical sunlight. His heart pounded relentlessly against his chest, echoing his need for this intoxicating woman unknowingly presenting herself to him in such an intensely erotic display.

As she neared the edge of the pond, the atmosphere changed subtly, hinting at an impending twist of fate. Unbeknownst to her, a sinister force lurked beneath the serene surface, waiting to ensnare her. Anu, his eyes narrowing with wicked satisfaction, watched as his plan unfolded before him.

With a flick of his wrist, an invisible snare wrapped tightly around her delicate foot, tugging her forcefully beneath the water's shimmering facade. Panic ignited in her eyes, and a desperate plea for help escaped her trembling lips, reverberating through the once tranquil glade.

His heart thrummed with exhilaration, but it was not fear that quickened his pulse. It was the intoxicating rush of power and control he felt as the orchestrator of her plight. A sinister smile crept across his lips, betraying his enjoyment of this twisted game he had devised.

Her arms flailed wildly in the water, each gasp for air growing more desperate as she fought against the invisible bonds that held her captive.

He moved closer to the struggling Viracocha, his steps measured and deliberate. His eyes gleamed with predatory anticipation and an unsettling hunger for dominion over her life. A whisper escaped his lips, almost lost amidst the murmurs of rustling leaves and trickling water.

"Your life is in my hands, Viracocha," he muttered to himself, relishing every syllable laced with dominance and control. This newfound hunger consumed him entirely. He reveled in knowing he alone possessed the key to her survival.

Desperation etched itself onto her face, her gasps for air growing more frantic. With her deep green eyes wide and pleading, she silently implored an unseen savior to rescue her from the clutches of his vile plot. Her struggles intensified, a testament to her unwavering will to survive against all odds.

He, consumed by his twisted desires, leaned closer, drawn in by the electrifying scene that unfolded before him. His voice carried on the wind, barely audible to her ears but weighted with an undeniable demand for submission.

"Help!" she managed to gasp between desperate breaths, her voice a fragile plea floating on the breeze. Her eyes mirrored terror and defiance as she fought against the invisible tether that bound her foot, determined not to succumb to his cruel intentions.

His demands lingered in the air like an evil promise. "Only if you come with me to my kingdom in the Afterlife," he declared, his voice weaving through the surrounding trees. Though barely discernible above the chaos of their struggle, his words bore an eerie resonance that struck fear into her heart.

As her dark emerald eyes filled with determination, he felt a flicker of uncertainty. He was not used to resistance, and her unwavering spirit caught him off guard. In that moment, he realized the complexity of their connection, deeper than mere desire or power. She was a force to be reckoned with, an unbreakable spirit that might challenge his own. With a flick of his wrist, he released the invisible tether binding her foot, watching as she surfaced with a gasp of relief.

And with that, he turned away from her, stepping toward a shimmering portal that had appeared in the clearing. The swirling vortex of colors beckoned him, leading to the realm known as the Far Viscera.

ABOUT THE AUTHOR

My whole life has been spent in Minnesota, never straying far from my childhood home. I'm the middle child and have always had a flair for storytelling and crafting imaginative worlds. Even as a child, instead of having my mom read me bedtime stories, I would tell my own. In middle school, I discovered my love for writing short stories and poems. Thanks to the encouragement of my high school English teacher, Mrs. Colby, I was able to take her creative writing class.

Aside from writing, I also enjoy winning at cards and darts against my best friends. In the summers, you can find me on a boat and in the winters, I love snowmobiling - that's just how we do things in the "Land of 10,000 Lakes." My dogs are like my children and they never fail to entertain me.

Writing has been a passion of mine since I can remember. After a successful 25-year career in accounting, I decided to take a leap of faith and pursue writing. For years, I kept this story inside, only sharing it with my loyal puppies.

But now, I want to share this world that I've created with everyone.

About the Author

Follow me on social media:

Tik Tok: @author.beebe.evans

Facebook: Facebook.com/Beebe.evans.author

Instagram: beebe.evans.author

Website: beebeevans.com

Sign up to become a Super Fan on my website and get access to exclusive content including complete character profiles, the prophecy, a free download for Word for the divine language, the events that I'll be attending, and first look announcements. It's free to join.

You'll also find a complete list of content warnings and a glossary of terms and places.

ACKNOWLEDGEMENTS

There are so many people in my life that I need to thank that made this book possible.

Jenna Jahns – My bestie author assistant and sister by choice, who has been around since this story was just a dream in high school and is my biggest cheerleader. Without her, this book would still be a notebook full of mindless scribbles.

Lori Whitwam – My editor, who allows me to use all the flowery words and cuts them out for readability.

Toni Rakestraw – My proofreader, who thinks that I throw a bag of punctuation at my manuscript and then fixes it for me.

Amanda Smith – My artist, who puts up with my pickiness on the cover designs and character art and always seems to amaze me with her talent.

Thank you to all my readers and sisters by choice that love this story as much I do.

Lastly, I would like to thank my dad, who always wants to be a character in my books, but he'll never read them. "Sorry, dad, I don't write historical nonfiction." He has always believed that I would be on the New York Times Best Seller list. Well, I hope he's right.